W9-BRR-293

Praise for the Remy Chandler Novels

Dancing on the Head of a Pin

"A fun read. The pace of the book is excellent . . . engaging, tightly written, and moves along at a rapid pace. You won't find a dull moment." —*Sacramento Book Review*

"Equal measures heartbreaking and honorable, Sniegoski has created a warm, genuine character struggling with his identity and destiny. . . . The fast pace, gratifying character development, and a sufficiently complex plot to hold your interest from start to finish make this one a winner." —Monsters and Critics

"Mr. Sniegoski nicely blends action, mystery, and fantasy into a well-paced story." —Darque Reviews

"With this book, Sniegoski tosses his cards on the table, revealing that he's working on a much larger scale than the average urban fantasy, and playing for a larger pot than the average noir detective tale. . . . The more Remy Chandler's world unfolds, the more I want to see." —The Green Man Review

"Back with all the trademark action, adventure, and angst of the previous novel, Remy's new challenge is a delight to experience. I cannot recommend this new series strongly enough. . . . In a publishing sea of cardboard cookie-cutter urban fantasy series, Sniegoski's Remy Chandler series is a bright shooting star." —CK²S Kwips and Kritiques

"What they are after and what it has to do with Lucifer's crypt in hell is the fun of this exciting tale, which leaves the series wide open for more sequels." —Henry L. Lazarus

"Thomas Sniegoski has certainly created an interesting world. . . . The author took some bold steps, both with his plotline as well as with character development." —BookSpot Central

continued . . .

A Kiss Before the Apocalypse

"The most inventive novel you'll buy this year ... a hard-boiled noir fantasy by turns funny, unsettling, and heartbreaking. This is the story Sniegoski was born to write, and a character I can't wait to see again."

—Christopher Golden, bestselling author of
The Lost Ones

"Sniegoski's choice to frame this high concept with a straight noir detective tale grounds the world for the reader and highlights the mystical elements."

—*Publishers Weekly*

"Decidedly different ... an outstanding entry to the urban noir genre ... sure to leave readers hoping for more." —Monsters and Critics

"Blurring the lines between good and evil, *A Kiss Before the Apocalypse* will keep readers riveted until the very end. This is an emotional journey that's sometimes filled with sadness, but once it begins, you won't want to walk away ... Fast-moving, well-written, and wonderfully enchanting, this is one that fantasy readers won't want to miss." —Darque Reviews

"Fans of urban fantasy with a new twist are likely to enjoy Sniegoski's latest venture into that realm between humanity and angels—this time with a more mature audience in mind." —SFRevu

"A fantasy crime noir tale of apocalyptic proportions! This book is at turns frightening, tender, heartrending, and full of twists and turns. The start of a great new series." —*News and Sentinel* (Parkersburg, WV)

"This reviewer prays there will be more novels starring Remy. . . . The audience will believe he is on earth for a reason as he does great things for humanity. This heart-wrenching, beautiful urban fantasy will grip readers with its potent emotional fervor." —Alternative Worlds

DANCING ON THE
HEAD OF A PIN

A REMY CHANDLER NOVEL

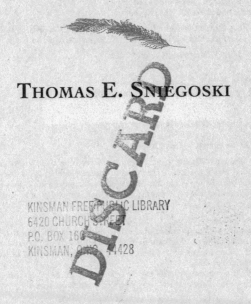

THOMAS E. SNIEGOSKI

KINSMAN FREE PUBLIC LIBRARY
6420 CHURCH STREET
P.O. BOX 166
KINSMAN, OHIO 44428

DISCARD

A ROC BOOK

ROC
Published by New American Library, a division of
Penguin Group (USA) Inc., 375 Hudson Street,
New York, New York 10014, USA
Penguin Group (Canada), 90 Eglinton Avenue East, Suite 700, Toronto,
Ontario M4P 2Y3, Canada (a division of Pearson Penguin Canada Inc.)
Penguin Books Ltd., 80 Strand, London WC2R 0RL, England
Penguin Ireland, 25 St. Stephen's Green, Dublin 2,
Ireland (a division of Penguin Books Ltd.)
Penguin Group (Australia), 250 Camberwell Road, Camberwell, Victoria 3124,
Australia (a division of Pearson Australia Group Pty. Ltd.)
Penguin Books India Pvt. Ltd., 11 Community Centre, Panchsheel Park,
New Delhi – 110 017, India
Penguin Group (NZ), 67 Apollo Drive, Rosedale, North Shore 0632,
New Zealand (a division of Pearson New Zealand Ltd.)
Penguin Books (South Africa) (Pty.) Ltd., 24 Sturdee Avenue,
Rosebank, Johannesburg 2196, South Africa

Penguin Books Ltd., Registered Offices:
80 Strand, London WC2R 0RL, England

Published by Roc, an imprint of New American Library, a division of Penguin
Group (USA) Inc. Previously published in a Roc trade paperback edition.

First Roc Mass Market Printing, April 2010
10   9   8   7   6   5   4   3   2   1

Copyright © Thomas E. Sniegoski, 2009
Excerpt from *Where Angels Fear to Tread* copyright © Thomas E. Sniegoski,
2010

 3 1088 1006 7354 8

Roc REGISTERED TRADEMARK — MARCA REGISTRADA

Printed in the United States of America

Without limiting the rights under copyright reserved above, no part of this pub-
lication may be reproduced, stored in or introduced into a retrieval system, or
transmitted, in any form, or by any means (electronic, mechanical, photocopying,
recording, or otherwise), without the prior written permission of both the copyright owner and the above publisher of this book.

PUBLISHER'S NOTE
This is a work of fiction. Names, characters, places, and incidents either are the
product of the author's imagination or are used fictitiously, and any resemblance
to actual persons, living or dead, business establishments, events, or locales is
entirely coincidental.
   The publisher does not have any control over and does not assume any responsibility for author or third-party Web sites or their content.

If you purchased this book without a cover you should be aware that this book is
stolen property. It was reported as "unsold and destroyed" to the publisher and
neither the author nor the publisher has received any payment for this "stripped
book."

The scanning, uploading, and distribution of this book via the Internet or via any
other means without the permission of the publisher is illegal and punishable by
law. Please purchase only authorized electronic editions, and do not participate
in or encourage electronic piracy of copyrighted materials. Your support of the
author's rights is appreciated.

For Liesa and James—

"... Let no force tear asunder ..."

ACKNOWLEDGMENTS

Love and thanks to LeeAnne & Mulder for helping me get through this one.

Many gratitudes also to Ginjer Buchanan, Cameron Dufty, Christopher Golden, Kenn Gold, Sheila Walker, Dave Kraus, Mike Mignola, Christine Mignola, Katie Mignola, Stephanie Lane, Joe Lansdale, Lisa Clancy, Pete Donaldson, Mom & Dad Sniegoski, Mom and Dad Fogg, David Carroll, Ken Curtis, Don Kramer, Greg Skopis, Kim & Abby, Jon & Flo, Pat & Bob, Timothy Cole and his band of Merrymen down at Cole's Comics in Lynn.

And for Steve Dias . . . get better soon, my friend.

Tom

CHAPTER ONE

It isn't easy being human.

And it was never more obvious to Remy Chandler than it was now, as he stared across the desk at the foul thing pretending to be a man.

He was bulky, wearing a loose-fitting leather jacket with only a wife beater beneath. Anyone who saw him on the street, picking up the newspaper and a few lottery tickets at the corner store, would think him to be one of *those* neighborhood types—y'know, just rough around the edges.

Rough around the edges didn't even begin to describe what this thing was.

"Is it all here?" he asked, his dry, raw voice echoing slightly in the cavernous warehouse. He snatched up a roll of dirty bills held together with a thick elastic band.

"Yeah," Remy said with a slight nod. "Just like you asked."

The thing posing as a man called himself Eddie, and as much as it pained Remy to admit it, they had once been the same, brothers of Heaven.

Angels.

But that was long ago, before the fall. What separated Remy from Eddie now was damnation. Remy had chosen to abandon the glories of Heaven; Eddie had been cast out for choosing to fight on the losing team.

For challenging the authority of the All-Powerful,

Eddie and all the others who had fought on the side of the Morningstar were banished to Hell until the Lord deemed that the first phase of their suffering was at an end. After a time in Hell they were brought to Earth to serve the remainder of their penance, earning forgiveness for their transgressions against the Almighty.

But His absolution was not easily given.

Remy wasn't sure what the Supreme Being was trying to say by forcing Heavenly creatures who once served His glory to live amongst the lowly beasts that caused the rift between the Son of the Morning and the Source of All Things to begin with. What he did know was that many of the fallen angels, those Denizens of the pits, chose not to lead a quiet life of contemplation, and instead continued their downward spiral into depravity.

They hadn't left Hell at all, really; they'd just brought a little piece of it with them.

Eddie sniffed the roll and smiled. "Smells about right," he said, and chuckled, shifting his bulk in the metal chair.

He reached down to the floor and lifted a white hard-foam cooler onto the desk before Remy. An undulating cloud of mist rose from the dry ice inside as he lifted the lid.

"They're all yours," Eddie said, reaching into the grayish fog and pulling out two eyeballs, delicately held between the thumb and index finger of each hand. "Here's a neat trick." He held the eyes before his own. "You can look through them—see a person as they truly are."

Remy had the urge to stop him, but what would be the use? Eddie would learn the truth sooner or later.

"Are you a good man or a bad man, my friend?" Eddie asked with a chuckle.

As if gazing through a pair of binoculars, he fixed the eyes upon Remy, and the response was immediate. Remy couldn't decide whether it was a look of fear or revulsion that appeared upon the fallen angel's face, not that it really mattered.

The twin orbs dropped from his fingers, falling back into the frothy mist of the cooler, and Eddie began to reach for something at his back.

Remy lunged up and over the desk, wrapping his right hand around the fallen angel's throat, driving him backward.

"Fucking Seraphim," Eddie gurgled as Remy slammed him against the wall, catching his wrist with his free hand before the fallen could use the dull black blade.

Remy could sense evil coming off the knife in waves. A blade like that in the right hands could do a lot of damage, but he doubted that Eddie was anything more than a common thug in the Denizen hierarchy, a parasite feeding off the sadness of the world.

So much for redemption, eh, Eddie?

"I'll take your eyes too," he hissed, froth spewing from his angry mouth.

"Is that any way for someone looking for God's forgiveness to talk?" Remy asked, allowing the holy fire of the Seraphim within himself a chance to flow through his body, igniting the hand that held Eddie's black blade at bay.

Remy's true nature clawed at its internal confines, yearning to be released, desperate for him to shed his mask of humanity. Since he had averted the Apocalypse just a few short months ago, this power he had worked so hard to suppress had become far too easy to set free. He fought the urge to let the power of Heaven burn away his human guise and assert its full potential.

He had to wonder if there would ever come a day when he was no longer strong enough to hold it back, when he would be too weak to be human anymore.

Eddie's scream and the sound of the knife blade clattering to the floor pulled Remy from his troubling thoughts. The stink of burning flesh wafted into his nostrils as he pulled back on the power, his angelic nature momentarily struggling as he exerted his full control.

Remy released the Denizen, and he fell to the floor

clutching at his injured hand. "What did you do to him?" he asked the former angel, glancing quickly to the cooler, struggling to control his anger.

Eddie cowered on the floor, holding his blackened appendage close, flecks of burned flesh raining down to litter the floor like blighted snow. The fallen slowly lifted his face, and Remy saw both pain and fear in his eyes.

Remy pointed at the cooler still resting on the desk. "Don't make me ask you again."

"He . . . he gave himself freely," Eddie stammered.

Remy was amazed. Though he was faced with the threat of further pain, the lies still flowed from this Denizen's mouth. It was typical of their kind, the time spent in Hell shaping them into things of deception.

His angelic nature surged forward, like a pit bull testing the strength of its chain. Remy reached down, grabbed Eddie by the front of his leather jacket, and yanked him to his feet.

"Where is he?"

Eddie's eyes shifted suddenly to the right, his fear becoming something else.

Anticipation?

And then Remy sensed that they were no longer alone. Still gripping the fallen angel by the front of his jacket, he spun him around, as two more Denizens emerged from the shadows of the warehouse, guns in hand. Eddie didn't even have time to protest before the bullets punched into his body.

Tossing his Denizen shield aside, Remy darted for the cover of some crates stacked in the corner of the large, open space. More bullets ricocheted off the concrete floor around him, while others burrowed deep into the wood of his cover.

The fury of his Seraphim nature roiled to be loosed, and he tried to ignore it. It would be so simple to set it free, to burn away the skin of humanity that he had worked so hard to maintain, leaving only the soldier of Heaven to deal with the foul betrayers of God's trust.

So easy not to be human anymore, to no longer feel the agony of his loss.

Madeline is dead.

It happened at the most peculiar times: taking a shower, grocery shopping, walking the dog, trying not to be shot. It was always there, eager to remind him just how much it hurt to lose the love of his life, making him relive the most painful experience of his existence.

Three more shots brought him back to reality, allowing him to forget the gnawing pain in his heart for now. He could hear them moving closer.

Where was his backup?

He looked around his hiding place for something to use as a weapon and found an old crowbar beneath an oil-stained tarp. Remy hefted the heavy piece of metal in his hand. It wasn't as deadly as a gun, but it would do in a pinch.

And this was most certainly that.

Holding the crowbar ready, he listened for the sounds of his attackers, but they had gone strangely silent. Carefully Remy peered out from behind the crates to see a lone figure standing in the center of the open room, two unmoving bodies at his feet.

"Where the hell have you been?" Remy asked Francis as he stepped out from his hiding place.

"Sorry," his friend replied, cleaning the blood from a fierce-looking blade with a white handkerchief. "I ran into a few of their buddies outside having a smoke. Always said that smoking was dangerous."

The bodies of the two fallen angels had already started to burn, their corporeal forms dissolving away to nothing as they ceased to exist. Their time on earth had been their last chance at redemption, and they had failed miserably.

"Learn anything?" Francis asked, sliding the knife into a concealed pocket on the inside of his gray suit jacket.

A pain-wracked moan filled the air, and Remy looked to see that Eddie was somehow still alive, although clearly not for long. He had propped himself against the corrugated metal wall, his breath coming in short, labored gasps. Plumes of smoke, like those from the head of an extinguished match, drifted from the bullet holes in the front of his dirty T-shirt.

"Won't be long now," Francis said, adjusting his black horn-rimmed glasses, the faint light of the warehouse glinting off the top of his bald head.

Remy knelt beside the Denizen, who seemed to be staring off into space, perhaps taking a good long look at the oblivion that awaited him.

"Did you hear that, Eddie?" Remy asked him. "It won't be long now."

Eddie turned his head slightly and looked into Remy's eyes.

"But there might still be a chance for you," Remy continued. "Do something right before it's over. Tell me where he is . . . the angel whose eyes you tried to sell me. . . . What did you do to him?"

"Fucking Seraphim," Eddie spat, then gasped as a spasm of pain wracked his body.

"Maybe we need the knife?" Francis suggested, pulling open his jacket to expose the hilt of the blade peeking from the top of the pocket.

"I don't think that'll be necessary," Remy said.

"If you say so." Francis shrugged.

"Can you feel it, Eddie?" Remy asked calmly. "That's oblivion barreling down the tracks to meet you. No more chances, pal. You're done, unless . . ."

The smoke from the bullet holes was thicker and carried with it the smell of rotting meat. Eddie tried weakly to staunch the flow with his good hand, but the effort was futile.

"I wanted . . . wanted to go home . . . to Heaven; I really did," Eddie began, his voice quavering. "It gets inside you . . . Hell does, makes it so you never forget." He shook his head quickly. "*I* never forgot. . . . How can you—something like that?"

Remy reached out, gripping the fallen angel's shoulder. The leather of his jacket was hot. "Where is he, Eddie?"

"He said he couldn't stand it anymore ... wanted to die. Wanted to pay for his sins."

The words ended in an awful scream as flames shot from the dying angel's wounds, expanding across his torso, up his chest, and down his legs. Remy managed to push himself away from the Denizen as, with a final burst of strength, he surged upward, flailing in the unnatural, hungry fire.

Remy caught Francis pulling a gun from another pocket. "No," he said, his eyes on the dying former creature of Heaven.

Eddie made it halfway across the warehouse before dropping to his knees. His body burned with a pulsing orange glow, the shape within the fire becoming less and less human. Then slowly he raised what remained of an arm, pointing to an area of darkness at the far end of the warehouse before succumbing to the final death, his body pitching forward, nothing more than orange embers burning upon the floor. And within moments those too were gone, leaving behind nothing to show that the fallen angel had ever existed.

"Stubborn prick," Francis growled. "You'd think that after nearly an eternity in Tartarus they'd be ready to leave this evil shit behind them."

The mention of Hell's prison sent an icicle of dread up and down Remy's spine. "You heard him," he said, approaching the spot where Eddie had fallen. "It gets inside you. It changes you, makes it so you can't do the right thing."

"But some do," Francis reminded him.

"Yeah, some do."

Remy continued toward the back of the warehouse and peered into the darkness. There were more crates and some scaffolding, but nothing of any significance that he could see.

"Wonder what they'd pay out there for my eyes," he heard Francis say.

Remy turned to see his friend holding the cooler. He had fished out one of the angel eyes and was looking at it. "Mine are as nice as this—maybe nicer."

"But you're not pure," Remy told him.

"Not right now, but I'm working on it," Francis said as he dropped the eye back into the fog created by the dry ice.

Francis had once been one of the Lord's most powerful Guardian angels, but even the greatest sometimes make mistakes. In the beginning, he had sided with Lucifer during the rebellion, but soon saw the error of his ways. He threw himself on the mercy of the Creator, begging his master's forgiveness. But the Lord does not forget slights easily and forgives them even less so. Still, He gave the former Guardian angel a special job—custodian of one of the many gateways between Hell and Earth.

Not the nicest of jobs, but better than a stint in Tartarus, and Francis made the best of it, even using some of the deadlier skills he'd learned from his time in the nether regions to become a highly paid assassin.

Yeah, he's working real hard on being pure.

"I think I found something," Remy called to his friend.

He wasn't sure exactly what, but he could feel the hair on his arms and at the back of his neck stand on end as he moved closer to a particular area. The shadows seemed thicker there, almost palpable.

"It's a doorway," Francis said, coming up beside him and sticking his hand inside the thick, inky blackness. "There's another room beyond it."

"Must be where my two friends back there came from," Remy said. He too stuck a hand into the shadows. The darkness was cold and damp, like the bleakest November night.

"Angel magick," Francis observed. "Ain't it something?"

Angel magick had been created by the Watchers, the first of the angelic hosts to be banished to Earth. Even though fallen angels were stronger and more durable than the average human, they were nothing compared to a full-fledged angel. Denizens used the magick as well as weapons chiseled from the black stone walls of Tartarus and smuggled out by parolees to protect their illegal dealings from angels and humans alike.

Use of either was considered a sin against God, but that didn't stop the Denizens.

"I think Eddie answered my question as he died," Remy said.

"Wouldn't be the first Denizen to see the light as their own was being permanently extinguished. So are we going in?"

Remy didn't answer. Instead, he took a deep breath and stepped forward, immersing himself completely in the fluid darkness.

Though brief, the journey through the darkness made Remy think of every bad thing he had ever done, the ebony wetness seeping in through his pores, drawing out the poison, reminding him of how devastated—*lost*—he'd felt since the passing of his wife.

"Well, that was certainly pleasant," Francis said, brushing traces of clinging dark matter from the sleeves of his suit jacket. He adjusted his glasses, a nervous habit, and looked about at their surroundings.

Remy tried to shake off the hungry sadness, but there was little else to occupy his thoughts these days.

Madeline is dead.

"You all right?" Francis was looking at him, the feeling behind the question emphasized by the intensity of his gaze.

"Yeah," Remy lied, as he stepped away from the thick patch of shadow. "Where do you think we are?"

Francis shrugged. "Not far from where we started," he said.

They were in a corridor that turned sharply to the right in front of them. To keep his thoughts at bay, Remy began to walk.

"Let's see what we've got down here."

He studied the walls as he went. The entire structure appeared to be made from shadow—from the darkness itself. An eerie inner light, a sort of bioluminescence, dimly illuminated their way from behind the black walls.

The hallway led to a larger room, empty but for a single table, upon which lay the body of an angel. A small cart, its surface littered with bloodstained surgical instruments, was positioned nearby.

Remy could only stare.

Francis had been the first to hear the rumor, a whispering among the unnatural community that the Denizens had acquired a full-fledged angel, and that its most holy body, every inch of it—a thing of great power—was for sale. He'd asked Remy to help him investigate, and the more they poked around—the more rocks and rotted logs they flipped—the more they realized that the disturbing rumor was indeed true.

And here it was, manifested in its true form, feathered wings splayed out beneath its naked, broken body. The angel's flesh had been cut, strips of its skin peeled away to reveal the pink musculature beneath. Most of its hair had been shaved down to the scalp. Its face was a gory mask, two empty black sockets where its eyes had been. The chest had been cut open and the rib cage exposed—an angel's heart was worth an absolute fortune.

Slowly Remy approached, fighting back a wave of revulsion. He did not recognize the angel, or the host from which it had come.

"Do you know him?" he asked Francis, unable to take his eyes from the disturbing vision before him—like some perverted version of dissection for a high school biology class, a creature of Heaven instead of a fetal pig.

Francis remained strangely quiet as he approached the surgical cart and picked up a plastic container. With a finger he flipped off the lid and reached inside. He pulled out what appeared to be a bloody piece of cloth, but what Remy quickly realized was a large section of flesh flayed from the angel's body.

"He was a Nomad," Francis said, holding the skin in the open palm of one hand, tracing the black tattoo in its center with a finger.

Remy leaned in closer to look and saw that Francis was correct. There was no mistaking the mark worn by the sect of warrior angels that had abandoned their violent ways after the Great War, departing Heaven, disillusioned, very much like himself. In the most archaic version of angelic script, the mark meant "waiting between Heaven and Hell." What the Nomads were waiting for was the real question.

"How could he have ended up like this?" Remy asked, more than disturbed by the sight of something once so magnificent, now so horribly ugly.

"You actually have to ask that?" Francis questioned. "The war screwed a lot of us up. It isn't easy to forget what some of us did back then."

Remy had known it was a stupid question as soon as it had left his lips. He knew he wasn't the only one to turn his back on Heaven. It was just so very rare that he encountered any other expatriates—they tended to keep to themselves.

"He didn't deserve this," Remy said as he reached out to place a hand on the angel's shoulder. The flesh was cold beneath his fingertips, like the feel of a marble altar.

With a wet, sucking gasp, the angel rose to a sitting position, his wings flapping spastically as he took hold of Remy's shoulders in a trembling grip. Remy stared in awe, unable to believe that something so horribly mangled could still be alive.

"The sins live on," the angel gasped, the stink of rot

exuding from his lacerated flesh. "They think it done . . . the war, but they deceive themselves, and the deceivers live on, the black secret of their purpose clutched to their breast."

The angel's head lolled upon his shoulders, his body wracked with spasms of excruciating pain.

"I could bear the deceit no longer. . . . My secret sin consumes me. . . ."

The final words left the angel's mouth in a gurgling wheeze, and he began to convulse. Flapping wildly, his damaged wings lifted him from the table but were not strong enough to support him. His damaged body crashed into the smaller table, spilling the bloody instruments. He lay atop the tools that had been used to dissect him, trembling and gasping for air.

"I've seen enough," Francis said coldly. He dropped the angel's flesh and removed a pistol from the holster beneath his arm. "Don't have any idea what he's talking about, secret sin and all, but nothing deserves to suffer like this."

Remy blocked his companion's way.

"What are you doing?" Francis asked, brandishing the weapon.

"I think we can do this another way."

The angel was crying tears of blood, streaks of crimson draining from the blackness of his barren eye sockets.

"We think ourselves so smart . . . so clever, but it will be our ruin, and the ruin of all that we hold dear," the injured creature of Heaven whispered as it writhed in pain upon the floor. "We should be punished. . . . Oh, yes, we deserve so much more than this."

"What's he talking about?" Francis asked. He still had the gun in his hand.

"I don't know, and I don't think we'd get a straight answer if we asked." Remy couldn't wrap his brain around what he was seeing. This pathetic creature appeared to be here by choice. He was not bound or restrained in any way. He was going to let the Denizens have him—cut him up and sell his parts to the highest bidder.

"He's in a lot of pain."

"Then let me stop it," Francis insisted.

Remy knew that the sight of the dying angel was getting to his friend—they were not used to seeing beings of such power in a state like this.

"Let me put him down. It'll be quick and relatively painless . . . less painful than what he's going through now anyway."

Remy shook his head. "It is ugly, but after going through all this"—he gestured about the room, at the operating table, the bloody surgical instruments strewn upon the floor—"he deserves better than that."

The angel had curled himself into a tight ball, his body trembling so severely that it practically blurred the sight of him.

Francis sighed. "What are you going to do?"

"I'm going to help him end it himself," Remy explained. "I'm going to convince him to let go of his guilt . . . his pain, and return to the Source."

How many times since Madeline's passing had he thought of doing that very same thing? To abandon it all, to will himself and all that defined him into nothingness. To return to the energies that shaped the universe and all it entails.

"What makes you think he's going to listen?" Francis asked.

"I don't know if he will, but I have to try." Remy stared at the pathetic sight shaking upon the floor. "I can't imagine that whatever he's done, he hasn't at this point paid for it a hundred times over."

Francis slid the lethal weapon back inside its holster. "So what now?"

"Make sure the building is empty," Remy told him as he knelt beside the tormented angel. "Things could get a little destructive if he abandons this form."

The former Guardian nodded, turning to head back

the way they'd come. "Are you going to be all right with this?" he asked from the doorway.

"I'll be fine," Remy replied, gently pulling the angel into his arms, attempting to stifle the bone-breaking spasms that wracked the Heavenly creature's body. "We're just going to have a little talk."

Francis remained in the doorway, unmoving.

"Go on," Remy urged. "I want to get this over with. He's suffered enough."

"I'll see you outside," Francis said over his shoulder as he turned into the hallway of shadow.

Remy leaned forward, his mouth at the angel's ear, and spoke in the language of the Messenger—the language of God's winged creations.

"Are you ready, brother?" he whispered. "Are you ready to let go of the wreckage that is this material form?"

The angel turned his face toward Remy, and he could not help but stare into the sucking black of the empty sockets.

"I deserve no such thing," the angel rasped, clutching the front of Remy's jacket with a bloodstained hand. *"We're no better . . . than those cast down into the inferno."*

"Let go of your sin, brother," Remy soothed. "Return to the Source and know the forgiveness of—"

The angel suddenly pushed him roughly away. *"I would never dream of tainting the purity of the Source,"* he cried, rising to his knees.

Remy tried to stop him, but the angel moved with surprising swiftness, his hand finding what appeared to be the sharpest of the knives and gripping it tightly.

"No!" Remy reached out to stop the action, but he was swatted aside by one of the angel's flailing wings.

"I deserve no less," the angel spat, and plunged the blade into his heart. He withdrew the knife and repeated the horrific action again, and then again, before falling to his side, legs thrashing as if he were trying to run, as the life left his body.

Remy was stunned. By taking his own life, the angel had damned himself, trapping the life force within the body, to slowly dwindle away as the corpse decayed.

He couldn't bear to see the body of the holy being left to the devices of scavengers. Reaching deep within himself—into the resources of his own suppressed divinity—he laid his hands upon the angel's waxen brow and carefully called upon the power within.

The fiery essence of the Seraphim ignited his hand and spread onto the dead Nomad's body. The fires of Heaven were voracious, consuming the flesh, muscles, bones, and feathers.

Hand still burning with an unearthly orange radiance, Remy pulled the fire back into himself, struggling to stifle the urge to burn away his own human guise and let his angelic identity roam free. And slowly the power was returned to that deep, dark place inside.

A place where it waited for him to abandon the charade that he had begun since leaving the golden plains of Heaven.

Remy rose to his feet, backing toward the exit, watching, waiting for the sign that he was expecting.

The body of the angel lay upon the ground, consumed in holy fire. Its grinning skull peered out at him from within the marigold flame, before collapsing in upon itself with a loud crack like a gunshot. At that point the fire grew larger, burning brighter—hotter—igniting the floor before spreading to the walls of the chamber, burning away even the shadows.

Satisfied that there would be nothing left for the scavengers to salvage, Remy left the room, the spread of divine flame burning hungrily at his back.

CHAPTER TWO

The fire burned hotter than any earthly flame. The entire warehouse, every inch of brick, steel, mortar, and glass, was engulfed in a matter of minutes.

Remy was lucky to get out with his skin intact.

But would it really have been so bad—to let the scourging flames eat away the fragile human form he had constructed for himself, to abandon this charade and return from whence he came? A tiny piece of him screamed its approval, but the remainder of the man was not yet ready to say good-bye to the world that had been his home for so long, even with all its imperfections.

"Did you get everybody out?" Remy asked Francis as they stood on the corner of Summer Street watching the building burn.

The Boston Fire Department arrived with a wail of sirens, the firemen leaping from their vehicles to battle the raging conflagration. But before they could even mobilize their hoses, the warehouse collapsed in upon itself with a mournful roar.

"There was nobody alive inside," Francis said, taking a pack of Tic Tacs from his pocket and shaking some into his mouth. "Though I did tell a few rats that they might want to find other accommodations." He shook a few mints into his mouth. "Thanks for helping me out with this one," he continued after a moment.

"No problem," Remy answered. "It was the least I

could do. The idea of one of us in the hands of the Denizens is not—"

"One of *you*," Francis interrupted. "It's been a long time since I had my wings."

The disturbing imagery of the tortured angel filled Remy's thoughts as he watched the fire burn. "What could have brought him to that?" he asked aloud.

Francis' face was illuminated by the light of the roaring fire; twin images of the inferno reflected on the surface of his eyeglasses. "I can think of a few things," he said. "Things you would give anything to make right."

Remy didn't press him. Francis was still making penance, and would be doing so for a good long time.

"He was a Nomad," Francis said, glancing at his palm where he'd held the angel's flesh. He wiped the hand on the side of his pants. "Can't remember the last time I've seen one of them."

"They're around," Remy answered, still watching as the intensity of the flames began to die down. "Don't come out in the open often, too busy contemplating their place in the grand scheme of things, or something like that."

Francis grunted in understanding.

"I should probably try to contact Suroth," Remy said reluctantly. It wasn't something he was looking forward to. He didn't care for anything that reminded him of what he'd left behind.

He felt something being forced into his hand and looked down. "What's this?" he asked, holding the same roll of money he had used to pay Eddie for the angel's eyes.

"Retrieved it before getting out of the building," Francis explained. "It belongs to you now, for services rendered."

"Forget it," Remy said.

Francis jumped back, arms spread. "No arguments. You've taken time away from your own business to help me. You've earned it."

As much as Remy hated to admit it, his friend was right. He had been delinquent from the agency for quite some time. Since Madeline's death he'd barely worked at all, finding it hard to generate interest in just about anything. The money would come in handy to pay some bills.

"Thanks," Remy said, putting the roll inside the pocket of his jacket.

"No, thank you."

Clouds of white steam billowed up into the night air as the firemen were finally able to turn their hoses on the smoldering wreckage of the warehouse.

"Want to go for a drink?" Francis asked.

It would have been nice to go someplace else, to delay the inevitable, but Remy had somebody waiting for him back at the house.

"Marlowe probably needs to go to the bathroom," he said, feeling warm pangs of affection for the black Labrador retriever fill him.

"How's he doing?" Francis asked. "You know, with the whole Madeline thing?"

"He still asks about her from time to time," Remy said. "But I think it's just in a dog's nature to accept the inevitable and move on."

"And you?"

Remy looked at his friend, not sure what to say, his silence conveying more meaning than mere words could express.

Remy read the yellow Post-it note pressed to the window of the entrance to his Pinckney Street home. Homicide detective Steven Mulvehill had stopped by. He couldn't remember the last time he'd seen his friend.

He pulled the note down, crinkling it up and shoving it into his pocket. He dug for his keys, letting himself into the foyer, and smiled faintly at the sound of an excited dog barking on the other side of the door.

"Just a sec, buddy," he said as he put the key in the lock and opened the door.

The black Labrador surged out into the hall, his toe-nails clicking like castanets on the tile floor as he danced around Remy.

"Hello to you too," Remy said, bending down to accept the fervent attentions from Marlowe's eager tongue.

"Miss you," the dog said.

"And I missed you," Remy told him. "C'mon, let's go inside."

"Yes, inside. Yes," the animal agreed.

"Did Ashley take you for a walk?" Remy asked as he took off his jacket and hung it in the hall closet.

"Yes. Walk, yes. Ashley. Like Ashley."

"She is something, isn't she?" Remy didn't know what he'd do without Marlowe's teenaged sitter, and dreaded to think of the fix he'd be in when she went off to college.

He stood in the hallway, feeling like a stranger in the home that he had lived in for more than thirty years.

It was when he was standing still that the problems arose.

"Do you want an apple?" he quickly asked the dog.

"Yes! Apple," Marlowe barked. *"Want apple."*

"I knew that was a stupid question." Remy moved toward the kitchen with the excited Labrador by his side. "And I think I'll have some coffee."

He had to do something, anything, or his thoughts would begin to wander. He would hear things, see things: echoes of the past. And he couldn't stop them.

He saw her standing there, his beautiful Madeline. Her back was to him as she stood before the stove in her white terry-cloth robe. She was making a cup of tea, and by the way she was holding herself he could tell that something was wrong.

The conversation had gone something like . . .

"Are you okay?"

"I'm fine, just a little sore today."

"Are you telling me the truth?"

She had slowly turned around, holding on to the stove for support, and her eyes had filled with tears.

"No."

Marlowe whined and the past momentarily fled.

Remy was standing in front of the kitchen counter, apple in hand. The dog was staring intently, a puddle of drool on the floor beneath his mouth.

"I'm sorry, pal," Remy said, reaching for a knife. He was cutting the apple into strips when the memories returned unbidden.

Again they were standing in the kitchen. She had her heavier jacket on, looking small and fragile within its folds. There was a suitcase at her feet, and she was looking around.

"What are you doing?" he asked, coming to stand beside her. Remy took her in his arms and gently kissed the side of her head.

"I'm committing it to memory," she said. "I don't want to ever forget what it looked like."

"Don't be silly; you'll be back before you know it," he told her, squeezing her close.

The disease had progressed faster than they had expected, the amount of care she now required more than he could provide.

"They'll get you on the straight and narrow, and you'll be home before you know it."

He'd known it was a lie, and so had she. But she hadn't let on, allowing him his fantasy.

"The straight and narrow can't come fast enough," she said, leaning in to kiss the side of his neck.

He returned to the present, watching his dog gulp down the cut-up slices of apple he had placed inside the animal's bowl. A chill danced up and down his neck, and he raised a hand to his throat. He could still feel her kiss, the last they'd shared in their home.

The dog was done with his snack in record time, and returned to wipe his slobber on Remy's leg. "That's a good boy," Remy told him, thumping the animal's side like a drum.

"Good apple," Marlowe said, then belched loudly.

And suddenly Remy heard the ghostly sound of her laughter drifting throughout the lonely house; a million tiny little things would send them into fits of hysteria—Marlowe's burps being one of Madeline's personal favorites.

So many memories, triggered like the fall of dominoes inside his brain. It was if he were caught inside some elaborate trap, his every action springing a recollection that left him emotionally mutilated.

Does it ever get easier? He was certain that it must, but didn't know how much more he could take. He'd always imagined himself made of sterner stuff.

He made a pot of coffee, even though his desire for the hot beverage seemed to have waned dramatically of late.

Mug in hand, he gestured to Marlowe, lying attentively in the center of the kitchen floor. "Want to come sit with me?" he asked, not waiting for a response as he headed into the dark living room.

He set the steaming cup down on a side table and sat in his chair. He did not put any lights on, preferring the darkness.

Marlowe padded into the room, jumped up onto the sofa, and plopped down with a heavy sigh, snout between his paws.

Remy thought about watching television, or trying to read a few chapters in the book he'd started a few nights ago, but television after all these years bored him to tears, and he couldn't even remember the title of the book. Sleep was out of the question. Since Madeline's death, a night's sleep had become something of a rarity, and because he really didn't need it, his bed—the bed that he and his wife had shared—remained empty.

So he did what he'd been doing just about every night

since Madeline's death. He sat in the dark, listening to the quiet snoring of his dog, and allowed the memories to wash over him.

Remy was at the office early the next morning. It had been at least two weeks since he'd last been there.

Since narrowly averting the Apocalypse, the world had become a much darker place. He had hoped that humanity, overjoyed by the fact that they had been given a second chance to embrace life, would have tried to make things better, but in fact they didn't even seem to notice. He was sure that on some level they were aware that something was up, that something had come pretty close to screwing up a lot more than a golf date, or that sixth trip to Disney. But the end of the world didn't happen, and life continued just as it had before.

But whether they noticed or not, the world had become a little bit darker. The approaching end of the world had churned things up—like the bottom of a deep, dark lake, the slimy silt, mud, and sediments stirred by a powerful storm above.

Things not of this world, which had chosen—*in some instances it had been chosen for them*—to make the Earth their home, had become aroused by the closeness of the cataclysm, and were greatly disappointed when it had not occurred.

Leave it to Remy to spoil a potentially good time.

He stood in the lobby of the Beacon Street building that housed his agency, trying to get the accumulated mail out of his box. Swearing beneath his breath, he tugged on the wedged-in catalogues, flyers, and bills, trying not to damage them too badly as he extracted them.

He stuffed the stack beneath his arm and climbed the stairs to his second-floor office, thinking about the angel he and Francis had found last night, and his final words cursing himself and some mysterious others for committing an unforgivable sin.

What that sin was exactly Remy had no idea, and

it ate at him, or, more precisely, it gave him something other than his troubles to think about. He would need to ask the Nomad leader when he saw him. The sudden reminder of the meeting dropped around his shoulders like a weighted scarf. *Maybe I'll just forget it,* Remy thought. *The Nomads will learn of their comrade's death sooner or later.*

The air inside the office was stale and unmoving. Throwing the mail down upon the desktop, he went to the window and opened it to release the stagnant smell. Out of the corner of his eye he saw the once-lovely fern given to him by an appreciative client, now withered and brown. He picked up the pot and studied the plant's remains, searching for any sign of green, hoping for an indication that the plant could be saved, but there was none.

Remy sighed as he dumped the plant in the wastebasket. He was painfully aware that the once-thriving plant had died because of his neglect, a neglect that could very easily be affecting not only his office plants, but his business, as well as what remained of his personal life.

It was decided just like that. No more bullshit. He would go and see the Nomads. First he'd straighten out the office, return phone calls and e-mails; then he'd try to find Suroth and his flock.

But it was just so damn hard to care about anything anymore.

Madeline had been the primary reason why he lived as a human—she was his anchor to humanity—and with her gone . . .

His thoughts again started to wander, and he saw her the day he'd revealed his true self to her. It was early morning, as the sun came up over the Atlantic Ocean on Nahant Beach. They had been out dancing, and there wasn't a soul around. He remembered the expression on her face when he said that he had something he wanted to show her.

Remy smiled sadly with the memory, certain that

what he had revealed had never even entered her realm of possibility. How often did the guy you were dating reveal that he was an angel of the host Seraphim? *Not often,* he imagined. He hated these thoughts of the past, but at the same time embraced them like a long-lost friend.

Or lover.

The sudden banging on his office door removed him from the moment, and his anger surged. He could actually feel his true nature writhe in preparation, as if it expected to be unleashed.

Not good. Not good at all.

"Yeah," Remy said as the door swung open and one of the subjects of his recent neglect ambled in, bags in hand.

"Look who decided to come to work today," the gruff homicide detective said as he placed the two bags he was carrying on the corner of Remy's desk and returned to the door to close it. "I'm not interrupting anything, am I?"

There would be time for the memories later, whether Remy wanted them or not.

"No, it's good. Sorry I missed you last night."

Mulvehill started to rummage through one of the bags. "Had a bottle of Glenlivet with our names on it, but since you weren't around, I had to cross yours off," he said, removing a large coffee and placing it in front of Remy. "I felt really bad, but I didn't want it to spoil."

He removed one for himself and smiled. He lifted the plastic lid and took a sip from the scalding liquid. "Your loss, I guess."

"My loss," Remy repeated as he removed the cover from his own coffee.

His friend looked as he always did, tousled black hair, five-o'clock shadow, clothes wrinkled as if he'd just rolled out of bed, and with Steven, that very well could have been the case. He lived the job, not really having much else.

Mulvehill removed his light spring jacket and hung it on the coat rack by the door. "So where were you last night? Working a case?"

He pulled out the seat in front of Remy's desk and sat down, but before he relaxed, he reached for the other bag.

The dying angel appeared within Remy's brain, the empty eye sockets like twin whirlpools trying to suck him down, further into despair.

"Yeah, pretty much wrapped it up last night."

"Cheese Danish?" Mulvehill offered, pastry in hand. "I got an apple one in here too."

"No, thanks," Remy said. "The coffee is all I want."

Mulvehill shook his head in mock disgust. "And you wonder why I'm not as svelte as I used to be." He took an enormous bite from the pastry, crumbs raining down onto the front of his shirt and pants. He then wrinkled the top of the waxed-paper bag closed, and placed it on the floor beside his chair.

"I'll save the other one for later," he told his friend, retrieving his coffee cup from the desk. "Playing catch-up?" he asked, motioning with the Danish toward the pile of mail.

"Yeah," Remy answered, flipping through some of it. "Amazing how quick it piles up."

The cop nodded, slowly chewing. There was an uneasy silence starting to develop, something completely unfamiliar to their friendship, and Remy had an idea as to where the conversation would be going next.

"How are you doing?" Mulvehill finally asked.

Remy nodded, slowly turning the paper cup on his desktop. "I'm doing all right," he said, trying to sound convincing.

"Yah think?" Mulvehill responded, shoving the last of the Danish into his mouth, and brushing the crumbs from the front of his shirt onto the floor.

"Yeah, I think," Remy answered, unable to hide the beginning of annoyance in his tone.

"Haven't seen you in weeks. Every time I stop by the office or your house you're not there. I just wouldn't have a clue if you were doing good or not," Mulvehill explained, leaning back in the chair and crossing his legs.

"I've been trying to keep busy," Remy said.

He could feel the detective's eyes scrutinizing him, searching for signs that things were not okay at all. Remy doubted that he would need to look all that closely.

"Why don't you cut the shit and tell me the truth."

Remy glared at his friend, the power of Heaven writhing at his core. It wanted to be free—it wanted to destroy what offended it.

"Do you want to hear that I'm miserable?" he asked. "That when she died a large piece of myself died with her? Is that what you want to hear?"

"I want to hear the truth," Mulvehill responded. "Call it a side effect of my job. Since Maddie passed you're not the same; there's something not right."

Remy brought the cup of coffee up toward his mouth. "It's to be expected," he said, taking a long drink. It was hot, burning hot. It felt good to feel something other than sadness.

"With most folks, yeah, but with you it's different. You're not the same person anymore, and that's really sad."

Remy set his cup down. "Who am I, then?" he asked, directing the question as much to himself as to his friend. "Maybe when she died Remy Chandler died with her, and this is the new guy who got left behind."

Everything grew very quiet, the emotion suddenly so thick that it was almost difficult to breathe.

"Any chance of the old guy coming back?"

"Why, does he owe you money?" Remy joked, trying to lighten the mood.

The scruffy man shook his head. "Nah," he said. "Just pure selfishness on my part. I'm not ready to say good-bye to him yet."

"I hear he's been going through some pretty rough shit," Remy said as he picked up his cup, looking inside at what remained of the contents. He finished what was left and grimaced at the bitter end.

"Thought I heard something to that effect," Mulvehill said, moving to the edge of his chair to retrieve the empty bag from the floor. He put his own empty coffee cup inside it. "I hope he swings around again sometime soon so I can tell him that he's not alone in this, that he has people who give a shit about how he's feeling, and what he's going through."

Remy wheeled his chair closer to the barrel where he'd recently disposed of his plant. "I'm sure he's aware of that already, but it doesn't hurt to tell him again." He threw away his coffee cup.

"Yeah," Mulvehill said, rising from his seat. "He's kind of thick like that."

The detective retrieved the bag containing the apple pastry and crinkled the top tighter. "Sure you don't want this?" he asked.

Remy shook his head. "I'm good."

Mulvehill accepted this, walking across the office to the coatrack for his jacket.

"So if you should see him," he began.

Remy looked up from an electric bill he'd retrieved from the pile, at first confused.

"Our mutual friend, the one we were just discussing?" Mulvehill clarified. "If you should see him, pass on that I wish him only the best."

He adjusted the collar on the jacket and, satisfied that he was presentable, opened the door to leave.

"And that I really miss her too," he added as he left, closing the door behind him.

CHAPTER THREE

Remy stood before his wife's grave, as he'd done so many times since she'd left him.

He had managed to make it through all the mail and even returned a few phone calls before deciding not to push his luck. He'd stopped at home to pick up Marlowe, then headed for the cemetery.

A thin, snaking vine clung to the face of the marble grave marker, the delicate purple flowers that grew from the vine embellishing her name.

MADELINE CHANDLER: BELOVED.

It always stunned him how beautiful it was, no matter the season; there were always flowers of various colors and sizes growing on and around the grave, a gift of gratitude from Israfil, the Angel of Death, for Remy's assistance in keeping the world from ending.

"Hey there, beautiful," Remy said, kneeling upon the thick green grass. He reached out, letting his fingers brush the engraving of her name.

He knew that she wasn't there with him, for when she had passed from life, her essence—her soul—had joined with countless others, as had been done since creation, to become part of the very fabric of the universe.

To become part of the Source.

He of all people knew how it worked, but he liked having a place that he could come to—to think, to chat with her as if she were still with him.

From out of the corner of his eye he saw Marlowe zip past, obviously on the hunt.

"Are you going to come over and say hi?" Remy called to the animal that was darting between the head-stones, snout pressed to the ground.

"No," the dog answered. *"Finding rabbits."*

Remy turned his attention back to his wife's grave.

"Things have been kind of crazy," he said, picking away some of the dead, dry leaves that hung uselessly from the veinwork of vines that covered the front of the marker. "You know, lots of the weird stuff."

Whenever he was involved in a case outside the walls of normalcy, Madeline had always referred to it as *that weird stuff.* When your husband was a disenfranchised angel from Heaven, working as a private investigator, the weird stuff just had a tendency to find you. She never liked it, saying that it gave her the creeps, but over time had learned to tolerate it.

"Yeah, yeah, I know; you hate that crap." He laughed softly, hearing the sound of her complaining as if she were there with him. "But it keeps me busy . . . keeps me distracted."

He read her name on the stone over and over again.

"I'm surprised that you didn't run from me scream-ing that morning when I showed you," he said.

When I showed you what I was.

Nahant, Massachusetts, 1950

"What are you doing?" Madeline Dexter asked him, a smile creeping around the corners of her seductive mouth. The warm wind whipped off the water as she picked some stray strands of her tousled hair from her mouth, her beautiful brown eyes riveted to him.

They had been out all night dancing at the Wonder-land Ballroom, just one of the hundreds of joyous times they'd shared since she had first come to work as his office manager.

There was something about this woman, something that demanded that she know the truth.

"I have something to show you," he said to her.

He let her hand go and stepped back. His eyes quickly scanned the beach around them, wanting to be certain that they were indeed alone. The sun had just come up, and there wasn't another soul to be found. At that moment, as far as he was concerned, they were the only two people upon the planet, like Adam and Eve.

He hoped things worked out for him and Madeline better than they did for those two.

Madeline moved her shoes from one hand to the other. "What is this, Remy?" she asked, with a nervous giggle. "What're you going to do, some sort of magic trick?"

Remy smiled at her warmly. After what he had left behind in Paradise, he had never believed he could trust something so completely. She made him want to belong. For the first time in more than a millennium, he truly felt a part of humanity, not just some impostor going through the motions.

She made him feel human, and he couldn't bear to hide the truth about himself any longer.

"A magic trick," he repeated, and laughed.

He tried to recall the last time he had shed his human guise. It was before he'd come to Massachusetts, and maybe even before Massachusetts had been established, for that matter. It had been a long time, and he did not relish the act.

But it had to be if their relationship was to continue down this path.

"You've often talked about how honest I am, how I can't lie to save my life."

She stared at him intensely. She was starting to look worried, maybe thinking that he was going to reveal that he already had a girlfriend, or perhaps even worse, that he was married.

If only it was that simple.

"But I have been lying, Maddie," he told her, "lying about what I am."

She stepped toward him, concern on her face. "You don't have to do this," Madeline said. "Whatever it is you've been hiding ... it's all right, Remy; we can work it out."

Madeline was afraid, and if he were to be perfectly honest, so was he.

Remy didn't want to lose her, and by revealing the truth, he knew that he very well might. But he couldn't lie anymore, especially to her.

"Don't ruin this," she begged.

Gently he pushed her back, the fear intensifying in her eyes.

"I have to do it," he said.

"No, you don't," Madeline commanded as she stamped her bare foot in the sand. "Don't do this to me. ... Don't take away what we have. ... Please."

He couldn't torture her anymore. Remy reached down within himself, deep into the bottomless darkness where he had hidden his true self, and called to the power of Heaven.

He wished he could say that it was happy to see him, that this was about to be a pleasurable experience, but then he really would have been lying. It hated his human guise and eagerly attacked it, burning away his clothes and the tender flesh to reveal the truth beneath.

Tears streamed down Madeline's face as her pale, delicate flesh was illuminated in the glow of his divinity.

But she did not run; she did not scream in terror.

The essence of the Seraphim exerted its full power, exploding from his body in a flash of brilliance. Remy tossed his head back and yelled to the Heavens as two great feathered wings emerged from his back, their gentle beating tossing sparks of fire to smolder in the sand.

Exhausted, Remy—now in the guise of Remiel of the Heavenly host Seraphim—dropped to his knees on the beach.

"I couldn't hide this from you any longer," he said, his odd-sounding voice making her flinch. "I had to tell you—show you the truth."

Slowly, Madeline dropped to her knees. "I always knew there was something different about you," she whispered. There was no fear in her tone, no disbelief, just a breathless wonder. "Something special."

She reached out, touching his bare, luminescent flesh. "You're real," she said with a laugh, the tips of her fingers causing his skin to tingle pleasurably.

"I am," Remy answered, taking her hand in his. "More real now, since you've come into my life, than I've been in . . . in a very long time."

"So you're an angel?" she asked, a smile beaming from ear to ear, tears filling her eyes.

"Of the host Seraphim." Remy nodded, softly rubbing his thumb across the top of the hand he held.

"Why are you here?"

"I've been searching for something," he began to explain. "Searching for something that was lost to me in Heaven—something I wasn't sure I would ever find again."

"This something," Madeline asked, "have you found it?"

Remiel looked deeply into the woman's teary eyes, the object of his quest glimmering there, just within reach.

"I believe I have," he told her.

Madeline moved in closer and threw her arms about his neck. He responded in kind, pulling her tightly against him as his wings of Heavenly fire enfolded them both in a loving embrace.

A cold nose nuzzling his ear returned him to the present.

"Hey," the dog spoke.

"Thanks," Remy said, throwing his arm around the animal's thick neck. "Catch any rabbits?"

"Smell them," Marlowe stated. *"No find."*

"Maybe next time," Remy consoled the Labrador, planting a kiss on the top of his blocky head. "What do you say? Want to go home?"

"Eat?" the dog asked, looking up at him as he stood.

Remy pulled the sleeve up on his jacket to look at his watch. "Yeah, soon. By the time we drive home it'll be time."

Marlowe darted toward the path, excited by the prospect of food.

"Don't go too far ahead," Remy called after the running dog, just as his cell phone started to ring.

The angel reached into his pocket and removed the slim phone, flipping it open to see who was calling. He didn't recognize the number but decided to take the call anyway.

"Yes," Remy said, the phone placed to his ear. Marlowe was sniffing the base of a tree alongside the path; then he lifted his leg, but to little effect. His tank was empty.

"Mr. Chandler?" asked a dry, raspy voice.

"Speaking. How can I help you?"

"Mr. Chandler, my name is Alfred Karnighan, and I'm very interested in retaining your services."

"I'm sorry, Mr. Karnighan, but my caseload is currently pretty full and—"

"People have spoken very highly of your skills," the older-sounding man interrupted. "I'd be willing to pay your fees and expenses with an additional twenty-five percent added on if you would consider my situation."

A part of Remy still wanted to refuse, but he then remembered the stack of bills sitting in the middle of his desk, and his conversation with Mulvehill about the old Remy coming back sometime soon.

"Can you give me an idea of what you'd like me to do for you, Mr. Karnighan?"

"Of course, Mr. Chandler," the man answered. "Some belongings of mine have been stolen—very valuable and important belongings. And I would like you to find the person or persons responsible and have my property returned to me."

Remy reached his car, parked outside the cemetery, where Marlowe was waiting patiently to be let into the backseat.

"Have you talked to the police about this matter?" Remy asked, opening the door to allow the dog inside.

"I have, but their performance . . . has been less than satisfactory."

Remy climbed into the driver's seat and closed the door.

"Mr. Chandler?"

"Yes, Mr. Karnighan. Why don't we meet Wednesday morning, around ten? How does that sound?"

"Like the answer to my prayers, Mr. Chandler."

Remy had heard that the Nomads had taken up residence somewhere on Tremont Street. They seemed to be drawn to high places, and he figured a recently completed, and so far unoccupied, office building might be the kind of place that they would take a liking to.

The closer he got to the glass-and-steel skyscraper, the better he knew that his assumptions had been correct. He didn't have to focus all that hard to sense them; a gathering of angels this large caused a weird kind of ringing in his ears, his inhuman nature roused to attentiveness.

He'd gotten up early and had treated Marlowe to a walk in the Common, generally wasting as much time as he could. But he had to get this over with, and the quicker he got it done, the better off he'd be.

There had been rumors that he'd been the one to inspire the Nomads, that his actions in leaving Heaven after the war had motivated those of like mind to band together. He didn't like to think of his actions as inspirational to anyone. They were his decisions, and his alone.

Willing himself unseen, he entered the lobby. A real

estate agent was showing the building to a group of potential renters, his voice droning on about how the building was state-of-the-art and so on and so forth, as he ushered them toward the elevators. Remy joined the group. They went as far as the twelth floor, the doors opening onto a spacious area just ripe for some sort of commerce, and cubicles of happy worker bees.

Remy hit the button for the top floor, the closing doors cutting off the sales pitch of the real estate agent, and leaving him with the hum of the elevator's ascent. He liked the sound the elevator made much more than the eager voice of the agent. They must have been sort of desperate, for as far as Remy knew, this building had been empty since its completion more than a year ago.

He wondered if the building's rather unusual squatters had anything to do with that. It was possible; though invisible to most, their presense could often still be sensed. Not a comfortable feeling, he imagined, often blamed on bad energy flow, or feng shui, if you like.

The doors opened and Remy stepped out onto the twenty-fifth floor. It was a nice space, huge floor-to-ceiling windows looking out onto a gorgeous view of the city.

Strolling across the open space, he found the door that accessed the stairwell to the roof. The strange sensation in his ears had intensified, the sound now something more akin to a song—a chant—and the Seraphim that he kept locked up inside him grew frantic with excitement at the idea of mingling with others of its kind.

At the top of the stairs Remy reached for the handle, but the door swung open on its own. They must have known he was coming—certainly if he could sense them, they could him.

Remy stepped out onto the roof. At first he saw nothing more than the building's heating and cooling units, and the stunning city view beyond the roof, but altering the composition of his eyes, allowed him to see so much more.

And there they were, the Nomads standing upon the rooftop, gazing out beyond the city below, the eerie song they sang wafting about them. Their dark robes seemed to be crafted from a night sky, a dusky bluish black that twinkled with pinpricks of starlight. They wore hoods that hid their features. There were eleven of them, and Remy wondered where the others might be. In his mind, he pictured skyscrapers around the world, Nomad angels standing atop them, frozen in eerie contemplation, singing their strange song.

"There is genocide in Darfur," one of them stated suddenly, his voice like the rumble of thunder at a distance. The angel turned its hooded head to stare at Remy, and he recognized Suroth.

Suroth's eyes were distant, still seeing the atrocities perpetrated by supposedly civilized cultures in the western Sudan. Tears of sorrow streamed down his face, the manifestation of the sadness he witnessed.

Remy remained silent, allowing the angel's eyes to focus upon him.

"Hello, brother," Suroth stated, a hint of a smile teasing the corners of his mouth. "I sensed that someone of an angelic persuasion was visiting us, and I'm pleasantly surprised to see that it is you."

"Hello, Suroth." Remy bowed his head slightly.

"It has been too long," the Nomad leader stated, moving toward Remy, away from the others, who continued to stand in quiet observation.

Suroth was huge. Even covered in robes, the Nomad leader couldn't hide what he had once been, an Archangel commander in service to God. But he had abandoned his weapons of war, shed his armor, and replaced them with the robes of the wandering Nomadic order.

An order in search of answers to the questions birthed by the savagery of war.

"It's horrible," Remy said, looking out over the world. "Horrible what they do to one another."

Suroth's large hands disappeared within the sleeves

of his robe. "It has gone on since the beginning, and will continue until they are no more."

"I like to think that eventually they'll learn."

"As we learned?" Suroth asked. "Beings that once stood within the radiance of our Lord and Creator?"

Remy remained silent. There was truth to the angel's words. The Great War had shown how far from perfection they actually were.

"To what do I owe this visit?" Suroth then asked. "Have you come at last to join us, brother Remiel?" the Nomad leader continued, using Remy's formal name. "Adding your mysteries to our own, awaiting a day when we will have our solution, and a new beginning will dawn."

"It would be nice," Remy said, returning his focus to the rooftop and the powerful angelic being towering before him. "No, I'm afraid I've come with some bad news."

Suroth tilted his head inquisitively. "Bad news, brother?"

Remy nodded. "One of your own has died," he said. "We found him in a Denizen hiding place. He'd given himself to them."

The Nomad leader said nothing, his eyes again going frosty as he searched the world.

"He was called Amael," Suroth stated. "I feared something like this."

"I spoke with him before he ended his life," Remy explained. "He said that he deserved what was happening to him."

"Amael never truly adjusted to our Nomadic ways," the leader of the order said. "The pull of Heaven was great upon him, but the guilt over what he had done in God's name . . . he felt that it robbed him of his place there, that there was no way he could ever return."

Remy recalled the look of torment on the angel's face. "He said that he bore a secret sin; that was why he had to suffer."

Suroth leaned his head back, his features lost within the shadow of his hood. "We all have our secrets, Remiel."

Remy glanced toward the building's edge, and found that the others had all turned and were staring. He could feel the intensity of their eyes upon him.

"For some, the weight becomes too much to bear."

It was silent on the rooftop, and Remy began to wonder if they had gone back to observing the world again, when Suroth spoke.

"His material form?"

"Destroyed," Remy said. "I couldn't leave it for the scavengers."

"We owe you a great thanks, Remiel," the leader said, and all bowed in unison.

"No problem," Remy told them. "I thought you should know."

He glanced at his watch. He'd had pretty much all he could take of the mysterious Nomads, and besides, he was supposed to meet Francis for lunch.

"Your time with us is at an end?" Suroth asked.

Remy put his hands into his coat pockets. "Other responsibilities," he stated. He backed up toward the door. "I'm sorry for your loss," he said, immediately feeling like an idiot.

"Are you certain that you must leave?" Suroth asked. The other hooded Nomads had come to stand around him. "Our number is deficient by one," he stated, holding up a long finger. "Do you not seek the same answers as we?" the Nomad asked. "Join with us, brother, and we shall find the solutions together."

"Join with us, brother," the other Nomads repeated in unison, their hands reaching out, beckoning to him.

"I'm sorry," he told them. "The answers I need I'll find on my own."

Suroth's hands disappeared inside his robes again.

"Know that there will always be a place for you," the leader said.

The others had already left him, returning to the building's edge, looking out beyond the city, singing their strange song, searching for the answers to the questions of their existence.

Francis was sitting outside at a table in the far corner of the little Piazza café on Newbury Street.

Remy was about to call out to his friend when he realized that the former Guardian angel had hidden himself from the lunch crowd that was taking full advantage of the first springlike day. Remy did the same, anyone who had taken notice thinking that he had been nothing more than a trick of sunlight and shadow on their eyes.

"Why are you sitting here invisible?" he asked, joining his friend.

Francis craned his neck to see around him. "I don't want to be obvious."

"Obvious about what?" Remy asked, turning to follow Francis' gaze.

He could see a waitress taking an order from a table of two women, multiple shopping bags at their feet. "The two women?" he asked.

Francis shook his head. "The waitress."

"The waitress?" Remy turned in his seat again.

She was cute—tiny—no taller than five-two, shoulder-length dark hair, athletic build. She danced on the line of beautiful but clearly didn't take herself too seriously, a nice quality to have.

"Very nice," Remy said as he turned back to Francis. "Now, why are you sitting here, invisible, watching a waitress?"

Francis shrugged, his eyes behind dark-framed glasses following the woman as she walked across the patio and into the restaurant.

"Y'know, that's a good question," he said. "One that I've been trying to put my finger on for the last few weeks."

"You've been watching her for a few weeks?"

Francis nodded. "Think it has something to do with the whole Guardian angel thing. In the old days she would've had a legion of us fighting over the right, but now she's got nothing."

The waitress returned with a tray of drinks for the ladies: a Corona for one and some kind of fancy cocktail for the other.

"Her name's Linda Somerset: age thirty-five, was married, but now divorced, takes night classes in childhood development at Northeastern, lives in Brighton."

Remy looked back at his friend. "What, no astrological sign? No dress size?"

"She's a Leo, and her dress size is—"

"Enough," Remy said, holding up his hand. "It's very nice that you've found a hobby in stalking this poor woman."

"Not stalking," Francis said indignantly. "I'm looking out for her well-being."

Linda left the waiter's station to check on one of her other tables.

"Why don't you just introduce yourself?" Remy asked. "Talk to her."

"I couldn't do that," Francis said bluntly. "That's not how it works."

"How what works? You're not a Guardian anymore, so why are you acting like one?"

"Old habits die hard, I guess," Francis said.

"I guess," Remy agreed. He crossed his legs, watching the crowds pass on the busy Boston street.

"I went and saw the Nomads this morning," he told his friend.

"You found them?" the Guardian asked, surprised.

"Yeah, I'd picked up some information a while back that they were on Tremont Street."

"Let me guess," Francis said. "Someplace high?"

"Yeah, office building."

"They give me the creeps," Francis commented, pushing his glasses farther up onto his nose.

"Why's that?" Remy asked, curious.

"I just don't understand them," he started to explain. "They were Heaven's elite, but they gave it all up, and now they wander between the earthly plane and Hell. They say they're looking for answers, but I can't even figure out the fucking questions."

A woman with a yellow Labrador puppy jogged by, and Remy remembered when Marlowe was that small. It seemed like only yesterday.

"It all happened so fast," Remy said. "One moment we couldn't imagine being more happy, one with the Creator and all, and the next thing, we're killing one another." He paused, the weight of it all bearing down on him. "I think they just want to understand how something so amazing could turn so horribly wrong."

A hostess tried to seat an older couple where Remy and Francis were sitting, but the woman insisted on another table. Big surprise.

"What was the name of that guy you asked me about?" Francis asked, changing the topic.

"Alfred Karnighan," Remy said, happy to oblige.

"Karnighan," Francis repeated. "I think I had some dealings with him a few years back at a private auction. He's a collector. Both of us had our eyes on an especially sweet medieval battle-axe, if I'm not mistaken. What's up with him?"

"Got a phone call from him yesterday," Remy explained. "Says he wants to hire me. I don't know the specifics yet, but it involves stolen property. I'm meeting with him tomorrow morning."

Francis nodded his approval.

"So that's it? He's a collector. Anything more you can tell me?"

"Nothing more to say, really," Francis said with a shrug. "The guy deals in rare antiquities, with a special appreciation for weapons. You can see how we would've crossed paths."

Remy could, ancient weaponry one of the only things

the former Guardian angel actually seemed to take enjoyment from. That and *Jeopardy*; the fallen angel loved *Jeopardy*.

"The guy's got bucks," Francis stated. "If I were you, I'd charge him double." And then he was out of his seat.

"What's up?" Remy asked.

"Looking after my charge."

Francis moved past him to a table where a less-than-pleasant man was giving Linda a hard time. Evidently the bartender had decided to cut him off and he was taking it out on his waitress.

Bad idea.

It was when the guy, his face flushed from too much alcohol and anger, picked up his empty glass and shattered it on the tabletop that the invisible Francis made his move, sinking his fingers into the soft, fleshy area around the man's thick neck.

Remy winced in sympathetic pain as the drunken man suddenly leaned violently forward with a scream, his face bouncing off the table. The shrieking continued as he lurched to his feet, tipping over his chair as he tried to pick bloody pieces of glass from his face. Linda, along with some of the other Piazza waitstaff, had retreated to the safety of the restaurant doorway. The manager and what appeared to be the bartender were now dealing with the injured man. In the distance, a police siren wailed.

Realizing that he was likely in trouble, the big man grabbed a cloth napkin from a nearby table and wiped at his mess of a face. Tossing the stained white cloth to the ground, he tried to force his way past the café employees.

Francis stuck out his foot, and the fleeing man tripped, his drunken bulk plowing into a recently vacated table, still covered with dirty lunch dishes. The crash was tremendous, the man falling to the ground, the table and all its contents landing atop him.

At least he had the good sense not to get up again.

Francis returned to their table as the police pulled up. Remy shook his head, trying to hide his smile of amusement.

"It's an absolute sin when a man can't hold his liquor," Francis said, watching as two officers picked the bleeding man up from the patio floor, and escorted him to the waiting cruiser.

"Good thing he wasn't driving."

CHAPTER FOUR

Remy had been to this place before.

The air was rich with the smell of the sea, aroused by the passing storm, the moist sand cool between his toes. He was on a beach at the Cape—in Wellfleet. This was where the Apocalypse had been thwarted, where he had joined with the Angel of Death to realign the balance of nature—of life and death.

Where he had refused God's request to return to Heaven.

He sensed their approach, as he'd done that cataclysmic day when the world almost came to an end, and turned to face them.

Thrones.

They were God's messengers, bringing His word to those deemed worthy enough to listen.

"The Creator asks for your return to the City of Light—for the honor to sit at His right hand," they had said that day, in voices that sounded like the planet's largest orchestra tuning their instruments at once.

And Remy had told them no.

Now here he was before them again, their pulsing radiance like three miniature suns, though the surface of the sun, he was pretty sure, was not covered in multiple sets of scrutinizing eyes.

The Thrones silently stared at him, their resplendent forms rolling in the air before him.

"Greetings, emissaries of Heaven." Remy finally spoke to them in the language of his ilk.

The Thrones remained silent.

"To what do I owe this latest visitation?"

And suddenly his mind was filled with the sound of their voices, his face contorting in pain as the cacophony assailed his senses.

"We were called, and we have answered."

Remy was startled. "You are mistaken. I did not summon you."

"No, you *did not,"* the Thrones replied.

He was about to question them further when he felt his Seraphim nature stirring, beginning its ascent from the dark recesses of his being. Finally he understood who had summoned the Thrones and why. With all his might he tried to push it back down, to quell the powerful and destructive nature. What he was ... what he was capable of scared Remy, and he would do all he could to keep that part of himself locked away. In the past he had been strong enough.

But now it seemed impossible.

Remy began to scream, his human guise turning to so much ash as the Seraphim exerted control.

As Remiel exerted control.

"Why have you summoned us, Seraphim?" the Thrones asked the armored angel now kneeling before them.

"I want to go home," Remiel said, lifting his gaze to them, bathing in the light of their resplendence.

"I wish to return to Heaven."

Remy awoke with the sound of the Seraphim's request echoing in his ears.

It was still dark outside, and he lay atop the comforter. This was his first night back in the bed that he had shared with his wife, and he could not yet bear the thought of lying beneath the covers.

Marlowe stared at him from the foot of the bed, his

animal eyes glinting red in a flash of headlights as a lone car drove up Pinckney Street.

"It's all right," Remy tried to reassure the dog, as he pushed himself up into a sitting position. He studied his hands to make sure that the human flesh was still present, and not the pale, luminous skin of the Seraphim. "Just a dream, is all."

He threw his legs over the side, somewhat surprised that he had actually managed to put himself in a semirestful state. It had been a while, though he could have done without the dream.

Or should it be called a nightmare?

Marlowe hauled up his bulk, stumbled across the mattress, and plopped down beside him. *"Okay?"* he asked, flipping Remy's hand, demanding to be petted.

"Yeah, I'm fine."

Remy sat for a while in the early-morning darkness, scratching behind the dog's ears, thinking about his dream.

Is it possible? he wondered. On some subconscious level did he really wish to return to Heaven? He'd certainly thought about it from time to time, when things weren't going well. He'd thought about it mostly since Madeline had died.

But is that what he really wanted? Had he really played at being human long enough?

"Hungry," Marlowe grumbled, leaning his head against Remy's leg as he was rubbed behind the ear. *"And have to pee."*

"Let's get you fixed up, then." Remy stood, grateful for the distraction, as the dog jumped from the bed and ran down the stairs to the first floor.

The air outside was crisp, the tail end of winter not wanting to surrender to the inevitable spring. Marlowe ran to the far end of the small yard, and then bounded back inside to eat.

It was the same routine every morning, almost mechanical in the performance of the tasks: fresh water down, a cup of food in the bowl, a pot of coffee to brew.

Remy hit the switch on the coffeemaker and leaned against the counter, watching the animal scoff down his breakfast. *It's like he hasn't eaten in a week,* he thought—and then wondered how many thousands of times he'd thought that very same thing as he leaned against the kitchen counter in the early morning.

Over the centuries, when he had met with others of his kind who visited the world of man, they often talked about the monotony of it all, the tedium of humanity's day-to-day existence.

He'd never seen it that way. He'd found a unique excitement in the simple act of living amongst them—*as* one of them. And that excitement had only become all the more enthralling when Madeline had become a part of his life.

But now she's gone.

"Out?" Marlowe asked, standing by the door again.

"Sure," Remy answered, his thoughts continuing down a troubling path.

Marlowe finished his business and settled down with a carrot, as Remy poured himself a cup of coffee. He was just about to climb the stairs to his bedroom when he heard Marlowe speak.

"Heaven?" the Labrador asked.

Remy stopped and turned toward the animal that stood staring from the kitchen doorway. "What's that, pal?"

"Go to Heaven?"

Remy set his coffee mug down on the steps and went to the dog. He often forgot how closely he and the animal had become linked during the years they'd shared each other's company. What Remy experienced in his dream state, was oftentimes shared by the dog.

"I'm not going anywhere," he explained as he squatted down in front of his friend, massaging him behind the ears. "That was just a crazy dream."

The dog grunted softly with pleasure as Remy continued to rub.

"Marlowe go?" the Labrador then asked.

Remy sighed, finishing up by thumping the dog's side with the flat of his hand. "I told you, I'm not going anywhere."

He returned to the stairs and picked up his coffee. As he began to climb, he glanced over his shoulder to see Marlowe watching him with serious, dark eyes.

Eyes that didn't know whether to believe him or not.

A lumber-truck rollover on Route 128 had traffic backed up all the way into the city, but despite the delay, Remy still found himself on Route 2 to Lexington by ten past nine.

He didn't listen to the radio, preferring the noise inside his head to morning deejays, Top 40 pop tunes, the news, and the weather.

Remy had a lot to think about.

On the one hand was his concentrated effort to return his life to some semblance of normalcy. Madeline was gone, and that sucking void could never be filled, but he had to try something. He had to find the special things in the human life he'd built for himself, and grab hold to prevent them from being drawn into the black hole as well. He had to continue to live, even though his wife had not.

It was what human beings did every day.

But then there was an alternative, the flip side that he did not really care to entertain, hoping that it was just a passing thing—a part of his prolonged grief. The idea that he could return to Heaven.

He thought of what it had been like there before the war, and wondered if there was even an inkling of a chance that it could be that way again. Remy already knew the answer.

The Seraphim inside stirred with the thought.

Nearing his exit, Remy pushed the troubling thoughts aside, switching his focus to the job at hand. He picked up the printout from Mapquest and gave the directions a quick perusal.

He threw his blinker on, getting over into the right-hand lane so that he would be ready for the next exit.

Not all that familiar with Lexington's layout, he'd used one of the online services and printed out directions and a map to Karnighan's home. He'd been in the town only once, the last time being more than ten years ago, when he and Madeline had been out shopping for antiques—well, Madeline, really—and they'd gone to one of the stores in the downtown area of the historic location.

Lexington was probably best known for its history, being home to many historical buildings, parks, and monuments dating from colonial and revolutionary times. Driving a ways, he glanced out the driver's window to a triangular patch of green that he understood to be the Lexington Battle Green, which, according to the history books, was considered the birthplace of American liberty. On that spot more than two hundred years ago, the first shots of the American Revolution were fired. Remy tried to recall where he was at that time but couldn't really remember—somewhere in the Middle East maybe.

He was looking for Florian Drive and found it without any difficulty, steering down the paved driveway that led to an open metal gate. As he drove through the gateway, he noticed a wobbling plastic sign stuck in a patch of grass to the right of the driveway advertising Heavenly House Painters; a cartoon angel with white robes and a yellow halo brandishing a paintbrush hovered with feathery wings below the company logo.

Normally he would've been amused by something like this, but of late nothing really seemed to penetrate the fog of gloom that surrounded him.

The driveway ended in a spacious cul-de-sac, a fountain, not yet turned on for the season, in its center. The house was big, expensive-looking, and with some scaffolding still in place around the side, it appeared to be having some work done to it. With the Heavenly House Painters sign out front, it all made sense.

He got out of the car, pocketing his keys, and walked toward the front door. He'd just about reached the front steps when he heard the heavy, excited sound of panting, and toenails clicking upon concrete. From the corner of his eye he saw the three large dogs tearing around the side of the house, heading straight for him, low rumbling growls escaping from deep in the rottweilers' broad chests.

They didn't appear to be in the least bit happy to see a stranger on their doorstep, so Remy figured some introductions were in order.

"Stop," he commanded, in their canine tongue.

The obvious pack leader came to a sudden halt, the two others stopping as well.

"Intruder," the leader barked. *"Intruder. Intruder."*

"Intruder. Intruder. Intruder," the other two barked in agreement. *"Stop, intruder. Stop!"*

"I'm not an intruder," Remy explained to the animals. "I'm here to see your master."

The leader stopped his vocalization and started to sniff the air toward Remy. *"Invited?"* he asked tentatively.

The others sniffed as well.

"Yes. Your master and I have some business to discuss."

"Business?"

The leader padded closer, smelling the ground around his feet. *"Smell dog,"* he said, moving closer to his pants leg.

"Yes, I have a dog. His name is Marlowe. What is your name?"

"Luthor," said the leader. *"Name Luthor."*

"That is a very strong name, Luthor," Remy praised the animal. "And might I say what a good job you and your pack are doing protecting the master's house."

The nubby tails on all three of the rottweilers started to wag.

"I Daisy," said one of the others.

"I Spike," said the last.

Remy extended his hand for Luthor and his pack to sniff. "My name is Remy."

Luthor placed its large head beneath Remy's hand, hungry for affection. Remy sensed a sudden change in the animal's powerful demeanor.

"Not good. Bad. Useless."

The dog's body began to shiver with nervousness. The other two members of the pack had crowded around him as well, starving for the same affection that their leader was receiving.

"I don't think that's true," Remy told them. "I think you're all very good dogs."

"No. Bad dogs. No good."

They pushed one another out of the way, each of them wanting to be petted and praised. He had an idea where their self-esteem problem was coming from, especially since he had been summoned here to help with the investigation of a theft.

He was doing his best to give the guard dogs the attention they were craving when the front door to the house suddenly opened.

The dogs' heads all turned to look at the man standing in the doorway.

"Mr. Karnighan?" Remy asked. "Hi, I'm Remy Chandler."

The man was very old, leaning upon a cane carved from dark cherrywood that reminded Remy for some reason or another of solidified blood.

"It appears they like you, Mr. Chandler," the old man sneered, his voice hinting of a strength now passed. He slowly lifted his cane and pointed it at the dogs.

Remy noticed them flinch.

"It seems that they like everyone, which is why I am currently in need of your services."

The old man's expression softened as he tore his gaze away from the animals.

"I'm Alfred Karnighan," he said, hobbling farther

outside the door, his hand extended. Remy met the man partway, shaking hands with him.

"If I can tear you away from your new friends, why don't you come inside so that we can discuss business," Karnighan said with a hint of sarcasm.

He made a brief clucking sound and motioned with his hand toward the animals. Heads hung low, the dogs trotted off, as Karnighan returned his attention to him, now gesturing with the cane for Remy to go inside.

The inside of the home was like a museum.

Remy walked slowly alongside the elderly man, taking in objects of art tastefully displayed around him as they progressed through the house.

"You have some very nice things," Remy said as they passed a beautiful piece that he recognized as being by Monet, not a foot away from a glass case that displayed a porcelain vase that could have quite easily been from some ancient Chinese dynasty.

"Thank you, Mr. Chandler, but I consider these items merely knickknacks in comparison to what has been taken from me."

"These are some very expensive knickknacks, sir," Remy commented.

The room that they passed through next was in disarray, the floor covered with thick drop cloths. The smell of fresh paint hung heavy in the air.

"Please excuse the mess," Karnighan apologized. "I'm having some renovation work done. Since I'm not traveling as much as I used to, I've decided to make my home more pleasing to the eye."

Reflexively, Remy took the old man's arm, helping him to navigate the cloth-covered floor.

"Thank you, that's all I need—to fall and break my hip." The old man looked at him, a strange mixture of anger and sadness evident upon his ancient features. "Don't get old, Mr. Chandler. It's not a pretty thing."

Remy smiled politely, his thoughts suddenly distracted by similar statements made by his wife in her waning years of health.

They continued on into a hallway of rich, dark oak.

"We'll take the elevator down to the storage vaults."

Karnighan opened a door to reveal a closet-sized elevator. "After you, Mr. Chandler," he said, ushering Remy inside.

Remy obliged, cramming himself into the corner.

"What made me purchase this home some years ago was the sprawling wine cellar, but not having a taste for the grape, I converted it into an elaborate storage place for my most valuable pieces." He closed the door, using an old-fashioned hand control to make the elevator descend.

"Here we are," he said, bringing the conveyance to a graceful stop.

Karnighan opened the door and stepped out into a lobby of sorts. It too was decorated in dark wood, framed paintings of considerable value hanging on the walls. Directly to the right of the elevator exit, there was a large safe door that seemed totally out of place with the stylings of the room.

"You've piqued my curiosity," Remy said, eyeing the heavy steel door.

"I wish you could have seen them," the old man said as he slid back a panel in the wall to reveal a hidden keypad. Karnighan punched in a code.

Remy could hear the door-lock mechanisms start to hum, whirring and clicking into place. Then came the sound of a bolt sliding back and the vault door slowly, silently began to open.

"This way, Mr. Chandler," Karnighan invited, passing across the threshold. "I can't tell you how sad it makes me to come into this room now, knowing that my most prized possessions have been taken."

Remy joined the man inside the room. It was much larger than he would have guessed. Display cases of varying sizes filled with weaponry of all kinds lined the walls. There were guns of every conceivable size and shape from as far back as their invention. There even appeared to be an area designated solely for hand grenades. And there were weapons from older times as well: swords, spears, knives, and axes, as well as maces, helmets, and suits of armor.

"Wow," Remy said as his eyes danced around the room from one of the cases to the next, objects of bloodshed from the dawn of man to the present on display here, a history of violence.

"Do you think?" Karnighan asked, leaning on his cane. "Over the years I've lost my objectivity." He looked around the room, trying to see it as Remy did.

"All I can think of is what's missing," the collector said with a sad shake of his head.

"And what is missing, Mr. Karnighan?" Remy asked.

The old man made his way toward an empty waist-high case, the lights within still lit, as if displaying nothingness.

"Weapons," Karnighan said, his voice much softer as he looked down into the case, as if hoping he'd been mistaken, that his beloved possessions were still there. "Some of them were just that, but there were others . . . so much more."

Remy could hear the emotion in the old man's voice—it was almost as if he were talking about missing loved ones.

Not too long after, Remy and Karnighan sat in a study upstairs finalizing their business over coffee.

"So you'll have the documents sent over to my office?" Remy asked as he brought the delicate china cup down from his mouth to the saucer he held before him. The coffee was good, some of the best he'd had in a while.

Karnighan had just taken a drink of the scalding liquid, waiting to swallow before answering.

"Yes, of course. I've kept detailed records of all my

acquisitions over the years," he said, carefully placing the cup and saucer on a table beside his chair. "My records are currently in a bit of disarray because of the renovations, but I'm sure I'll be able to gather them up by this afternoon and have them couriered over to you."

The old man winced as he crossed his ancient legs.

"So I guess it's safe to say that you'll take the case?" he asked with a cautious smile.

Remy nodded. "Of course. It'll be two hundred and fifty dollars a day plus expenses, if that's agreeable?"

The old man reached into the breast pocket of his shirt and removed a check. He unfolded the piece of paper and looked at it before handing it to Remy.

"I took the liberty of writing this up before you arrived."

Remy stood to take it from him. "That's very generous," he said, glancing at the amount.

"An advance, plus a bonus for your anticipated hard work. There is more where that came from, Mr. Chandler. It may seem pathetic to you, but I've come to realize that without these items my life seems suddenly meaningless."

Remy listened to the man as he refolded the check and placed it inside his own shirt pocket. "I'll do everything I can," he told the old man. "There are no guarantees, but I won't stop working on the case until all possible leads have been exhausted."

"Very good, sir. I believe we understand each other perfectly."

Karnighan struggled as he attempted to stand.

"No need to get up," Remy told him. He approached the collector and again extended his hand. "I'll see myself out."

Remy bid the man good-bye, leaving him to finish his coffee, when a question that he had been meaning to ask Karnighan again rose to the surface.

"Oh, yeah," he said, stopping momentarily in the

doorway of the study. "I was wondering, Mr. Karnighan, where was it that you heard about my agency?"

The old man smiled, china cup in one hand, saucer beneath it in the other. "I really don't remember, Mr. Chandler," he said, taking a careful sip of his beverage. "But whoever it was, spoke very highly of your abilities."

It wasn't quite the answer he was looking for, but it would do.

He left the house and started toward his car, spying the guard dogs watching him from an open area that ran alongside the house. He wondered how Karnighan kept them from running away, or from getting into trouble with neighbors, when he noticed the thick collars around their necks. An electric fence, he guessed. A brief electrical shock would be transmitted through the collars if they wandered too far from the property.

Then he had an idea and wandered back over to the animals.

"Luthor, I've got a question for you," he said to the pack leader.

The dog came over to him, again looking for some attention, with which Remy obliged him. How could he refuse?

"When your master's things were stolen, do you remember seeing anything or maybe hearing something out of the ordinary?"

"No," the dog said, eyes closed with pleasure as Remy rubbed behind his ears. *"That's why bad dogs. Useless. Master say useless."*

Daisy and Spike tried to muscle in on Luthor's attentions, the pack leader turning his square head to growl at them. The pair whimpered sadly as they backed up.

"That's not true; you're very good dogs," he assured them. "Your master is just upset that somebody was able to get inside and take his things without you knowing. Are you sure you didn't notice anything?"

The dog pressed his cold, wet snout to Remy's hand.

"*Yes,*" the dog said in between snuffles. "*Strange smell.*"

Daisy and Spike were now sniffing Remy's pants, and he reached down to give them each a scratch before Luthor noticed.

"What kind of strange smell? Can you describe it to me?"

The rottweiler looked up, his dark brown eyes deep and soulful like Marlowe's.

"*Like you,*" the dog said, a spark of realization in his eyes. "*Smell like you.*"

CHAPTER FIVE

Karnighan had done as he'd promised, delivering the paperwork by courier by the time Remy had left the office that afternoon.

It hadn't been such a bad day, catching up on phone messages and sorting out bills. Remy had left his office with a sense of accomplishment, more connected to his work than he'd felt in quite some time.

But it didn't end there; he'd returned home, got Marlowe fed and walked, made himself a quick bite to eat, and put a fresh pot of coffee on. In the old days, Madeline used to call this *getting the bug*. It happened when a case slowly began to worm its way into Remy's life, when there was something that he couldn't quite put his finger on that made it so he couldn't—or didn't want to, really—think of anything else.

He believed the Karnighan case was going to go something like that.

The man certainly had been telling the truth when he said that he'd kept detailed records. There were pages and pages of notes, and even photographs of the stolen weapons, some beautifully crafted, others crude and primitive in their execution. The notes were painstakingly detailed, describing the origins of each piece, the name of the craftsman, and in some cases, who had owned the particular dagger, sword, or spear over the span of centuries.

Remy found himself lost in the pages and time periods, remembering snippets of his own past when weapons such as these were carried with as much ease as a designer purse or an iPod.

He wasn't sure how much time had passed as he flipped through the extensive records. It was a low-throated *woof* that interrupted his deep concentration. Noticing the stuffed monkey on the floor by his desk chair first, Remy angled himself around to see Marlowe waiting at attention, tail wagging eagerly.

"Is this your monkey?" Remy asked, leaning over to snatch up the brown-furred primate from the floor. He held it out toward the dog, giving it a bit of a wiggle. Marlowe flinched, stomping his paws down on the hardwood floor.

"Yes, monkey. Yes."

"Want me to throw it?" Remy asked. He knew that was exactly what the dog wanted, but he thought he'd play with the Labrador's head a bit.

He made a move as if the throw it, the dog taking off, waiting for the stuffed animal to fall, but it never did.

"Hey!" Marlowe said, turning around to check him out.

Remy still held the monkey and gave it another shake.

"Tricked ya," he said.

"No trick ya," Marlowe grumbled, coming back to stand before him. He tried to pull the monkey from his hand. Remy let him get a grip before he started to pull. The Labrador growled in play, enjoying a good tug-of-war as much as retrieving things.

This went on a bit, the animal pulling with all his might, his growls getting louder and more excited as he tried to yank the stuffed animal from Remy's hands.

With the help of the stuffed monkey, Remy drew the Labrador closer, leaning his own face in toward the growling animal. "This is a blast, but I've got to get back to work," he told his best friend.

Marlowe released the toy, jumping back, ready to fetch.

"No, play," he said, his tail wagging furiously. Now that he had gotten a taste, he didn't want to stop.

"Maybe later," Remy said, throwing the monkey into the corner of the room. Marlowe leapt across the floor, his nails clicking and clacking on the hardwood as he went in pursuit of his prey.

Remy turned back to the notes, surprised to see that he had actually made two separate piles.

"More play now!" Marlowe demanded, attempting to shove the stuffed animal beneath the arm of the chair and into his lap. *"Monkey! Crazy monkey! Throw! Pull!"*

"What did I say?" Remy grabbed the monkey from the dog and tossed it over his shoulder, never taking his eyes from the two stacks. The dog took off again after the toy as Remy began to examine the piles. One contained most of the information on the weapons, but the other he had no recollection of ever seeing, never mind making a separate stack.

He sensed that Marlowe had returned and ignored him, pulling the smaller stack that he had made over for a closer look. It contained the information on four specific weapons. He removed the photos, lining them up in front of him on the desk—Japanese katana, a medieval battle-axe, an intricately etched Colt 45, and the beautiful simplicity of twin daggers.

What was it about these particular weapons that seemed to so interest him?

Marlowe sighed, dropping his seventy pounds to the floor beside Remy's chair with the stuffed monkey, depressed that he'd been rejected.

"Sorry, buddy," Remy apologized. "But I've got to figure this out."

He picked up the photograph of the Japanese sword, staring at it before carefully reading the notes that accompanied the fearsome blade. According to the information, the katana was created in the year 1565 by master sword maker Asamiya.

"I know that name," Remy muttered, leaning back in his chair. Marlowe lifted his head, thinking that maybe it was time to play again. "Where do I know that name?"

It wasn't long before he remembered.

Remy wasn't sure how many years ago it was, but he was certain that it was no more than three or four. Francis had returned from one of his out-of-state assignments with something that he couldn't wait to show to his friend. The special something had been a Japanese sword crafted by Asamiya, supposedly the greatest Japanese sword maker who had ever lived.

He looked at the photo of the sword a bit longer before stacking it with the other information and placing everything back inside the envelope in which it had been delivered. What he had to do, then, was obvious. If anybody could give him some insight on these weapons, it was Francis.

He pushed his chair back and stood up, reaching over to turn off his desk lamp.

Marlowe was already standing, limp monkey dangling from his mouth, the anticipation of more playtime twinkling in his dark brown eyes. But what Remy was about to ask the animal was even better than playtime.

"Do you want to go for a ride?"

The response was as he expected.

A ride in the car trumped chasing a stuffed monkey, hands down.

It wasn't common knowledge, but there was an entrance to Hell on Newbury Street.

It had been there for nearly forever, even before there was a Newbury Street, when the Back Bay was underwater. And Remy was sure that the fissure had existed even long before that. There was no specific reason why it was there, no violent series of events so horrible that it had ripped the very fabric of reality. Nothing so dramatic. It was just that all over the planet there were places where the barriers between this world and the worlds beyond it were quite a bit thinner, and doorways between these planes of existence had been established.

As luck would have it, Remy had found a parking space at a meter that still had close to an hour left on it. He didn't figure he'd be that long, but he popped a few quarters into the meter anyway. One never could tell when a legion of meter maids would descend, dispensing their forty-dollar greetings. The seventy-five cents was much more palatable.

"I'm a good dog," Marlowe said to him as they stood beside the car, Remy sliding the chain collar attached to the leash around the animal's neck.

"I know you are, but you still have to wear the leash when you're in the city," Remy explained.

"Good dog, won't run away."

"I know you won't run away, but some people are afraid of good dogs and don't appreciate you trying to say hello." Remy placed the file folder of his latest case beneath his arm.

"Say hello," the dog said, wagging his tail at a man in a very expensive suit who walked by talking on a cell phone.

"I doubt that man would like slobber on his suit. C'mon." Remy gave the leash a slight tug and the two of them headed down Newbury. "Let's go see what Francis is doing."

"Say hello, Francis?" Marlowe asked, looking up at Remy as they navigated the somewhat busy sidewalk.

"You can say hello all you want to him. Francis likes slobber."

The former Guardian angel's brownstone had been built in 1882. Francis had actually supervised its construction himself and had lived there ever since, acting as doorman and parole officer between the prison realm of Hell and Earth.

It was his job to guard this passage, allowing only those fallen who had served their time in the pit to pass. Some really did try to live good lives, hoping that someday they would be allowed to return to Heaven, while others seemed to be permanently altered by their time in the pit, gravitating toward a life of crime as a Denizen.

Marlowe stopped at the tree in front of the brownstone, before angel and dog started up the steps. Remy pulled open the heavy wooden door, allowing the dog into the entryway first. He was about to push the buzzer to let Francis know that he had arrived, when the door into the building opened from the inside.

A man was backing out of the door, holding a box in both hands, a long duffel bag slung over his shoulder. He turned to leave the building and nearly fell over Marlowe, whose tail was wagging so hard it made his whole body shake.

The man gasped, throwing himself back against the door, so frightened that he nearly dropped the large cardboard box.

Remy reached over, grabbing hold of Marlowe's collar and pulling him away. "Sorry about that," he apologized, forcing the dog to stand at his side as he reached to hold open the door to the brownstone. "He thinks everyone is his friend."

"Say hi!" Marlowe barked happily.

The man glared at them, eyes filled with both fear and anger. The look was one Remy had seen before, of someone who had once known the glory of Heaven but had been subjected to the tortures of Hell.

Which way will you go? Remy thought, as the man quickly left the building without a word. *Will you seek the forgiveness of God, or the company of those tainted by the netherworld?*

"Not nice," Marlowe said.

"No, he wasn't," Remy answered as the two entered the lobby.

Francis lived in the building's expansive basement, and that's where Remy headed, opening another door to the left of the lobby. Marlowe excitedly passed through first, his nails clicking on the wooden stairs as he descended.

"Careful," Remy called after him.

"See Francis," the dog woofed. *"Get cheese."*

Isn't it just like a Labrador, Remy thought, holding on to the banister as he walked down the steps. *Only excited to see you if there's a promise of food somewhere in the equation.*

Marlowe had already disappeared through a doorway at the end of the stairway, and Remy expected to hear Francis respond to the dog's appearance, but he heard nothing.

Remy entered the apartment. The place was simple in its furnishings, an old leather couch by the wall, a recliner not too far from the ancient furnace that squatted like a monster in the center of the living room area. Gray metal heating ducts snaked from its squat body across the ceiling, exiting up to the multiple residences above. A blocky armoire across from the recliner hid the big-screen TV. A framed movie poster from *The Wild Bunch* hid a door to a closet where Remy knew his friend kept a large majority of the weapons he used during his freelance work.

The coffee table was covered with Sudoku books and sundry other puzzle magazines. Most angels loved puzzles, but Remy couldn't stand the things. His wife had been the puzzle person in their household. He felt that sad feeling in the pit of his belly again, remembering how she'd spend what seemed like hours at the grocery store magazine racks searching for just the right puzzle magazine.

Marlowe barked from one of the back hallways.

"Did you find Francis?" Remy asked as he maneuvered around the coffee table.

The Labrador stood before another door, his body rigid, tail wagging. This door was weathered, the paint peeling as if it had been exposed to the constant changes of New England weather.

"*In there,*" Marlowe said, body rigid, head bent to sniff at the crack at the bottom of the door.

"You might want to get away from there," Remy suggested.

The door began to tremble in its frame, shaking so hard, so violently, that pieces of peeling paint started to flake to the floor. Remy reached out to grab Marlowe's collar, pulling him back, the door suddenly opened, giving them both a glimpse of the infernal realm.

From what Remy could see, it hadn't changed a bit.

If Heaven was a place of awesome beauty and wonder, then Hell was its polar opposite.

Marlowe yelped in fear as a warm wind tinged with the scent of hopelessness wafted from the realm beyond the open door.

"Go," Remy told the frightened animal, who had lost control of his bladder, leaving a puddle of urine on the wood floor in front of the door.

Marlowe ran off as Remy stared out across a bridge made from the bodies of the most unrepentant of the fallen angels. Their moans and cries for mercy made the hair on the back of his neck stand on end, and the Seraphim nature crave to be unleashed so that it could end the suffering of its brethren.

He would have preferred to turn his back on the sights before him, but the realm of Hell demanded to be looked upon, to be feared and respected.

Geysers of molten lava exploded up from the blighted land far below, the intense glow from the liquid rock illuminating the nightmarish landscape. It was said that there lived bands of fallen angels, those who chose not to complete their penance upon the Earth, preferring to live out the remainder of their contrition upon the wastelands of Hell.

Remy couldn't imagine how they survived.

Turning his attention from the fearsome landscape to what loomed at the end of the bridge, he had to wonder, which was actually worse: the wilds of Hell . . .

Or Tartarus?

The prison glistened before him, and though surrounded by the scorched, molten landscape, it remained frigidly cold. Tartarus grew up from the barrens of the nether regions, so cold in its growth that not even the fires of Hell could melt it. It was wide at its base, rising to a jagged, gradual point like a pyramid of ice crafted by a long-extinct polar civilization.

Remy's head was suddenly filled with a quote from a poem by Robert Frost, *"Some say the world will end in fire, some say in ice."*

It wasn't the end of the world—Remy had already been close enough to see what that would look like— but as a sight to steal away any sense of hope, it ran a close second.

The screams and moans from the bridge made of the fallen grew suddenly louder, their bodies writhing in horrible discomfort, causing the fleshy structure to undulate.

And Remy then saw the reason for the fallens' distress, an orange light, like the pulsing of a star, had appeared from behind the wall of ice at the front of the frozen prison. The light grew brighter, and brighter still, an opening—an exit—melting in the face of Tartarus.

Remy stumbled back a bit, bumping into the wall behind him as two Sentries emerged. They were fearsome creations, angels whose sole purpose it was to watch over the magnitude of Tartarus' prisoners, none more deadly than Lucifer Morningstar.

He could not see their faces, for their entire bodies were adorned with ornate armor forged from the stuff of Heaven, making them impervious to the malignancy of this damnable place. Their wings were armored as well, each and every feather coated in the same Heavenly metal that dressed their bodies.

Remy could feel their eyes on him, assessing whether or not he was a threat to them. They must have deemed him harmless because they turned back toward the cavernous opening, standing on either side as two more figures emerged from within the chilling blackness.

Francis escorted a naked man from the icy prison, holding on to his scrawny arm as they passed under the gaze of the Sentries, whose helmeted heads slowly turned to watch them as they passed.

Francis appeared as he often did, unfazed and perhaps even a little bit bored by the whole thing. He was wearing his gray suit, with a coral-colored dress shirt and red-and-black-striped tie. Remy wasn't entirely sure that the colors matched, but for some reason, it worked for the former Guardian.

The naked angel looked a wreck, his emaciated body caked with the filth of confinement in Tartarus. His eyes bulged from his skull, obviously in a state of shock. They walked across the bridge of misbegotten flesh, the screams and moans of those whose bodies they walked upon agitated all the more by the fallen's passing. They knew that he was leaving and were jealous of him.

Just before reaching the doorway to the earthly plane, the Sentries turned and walked back into the ice prison. At their passing, the frozen wall began to re-form, and soon there was no trace that a door had ever been there at all.

"Hey," Francis said with a friendly nod as he caught sight of Remy in the doorway.

Remy gave a wave.

The former Guardian was about to step over the threshold with his charge when he came to a sudden stop.

"Who the hell pissed on my floor?"

*   *   *

The parolee from Hell sat in the chair, wrapped in a towel, and shivered. Remy wasn't sure if it was from cold or from having the residue of Tartarus scoured from his lean frame by Francis.

Francis handed him a steaming cup of coffee. "Here, drink this. It'll warm up your guts."

He took it, his eyes filled with emotion. It was probably the first act of kindness he had been shown in God only knew how long.

Remy watched the fallen bring the mug slowly to his mouth, a look of euphoria spreading across his haggard features as he took the hot liquid into his system. In Tartarus, they were denied any physical sensation at all, except for pain.

The toaster popped, and Francis took two slices of bread from the machine and slathered them with butter.

"You're going to give the guy a heart attack," Remy said as his friend brought the plate over to the towel-draped figure. With a shaking hand he set his coffee down and took the offered plate. With a ravenous glee, he began to devour the toasted bread.

"He needs some meat on his bones," Francis said.

Marlowe's wagging tail thumped the floor as he covetously watched the man eat.

"Where mine?" he asked.

"You're not getting anything; you pissed on my floor," Francis said to him.

Marlowe lowered his head, ears flat in shame. *"Scared,"* the dog whined sadly. *"Marlowe scared."*

Remy reached down and patted the big dog's side. "That's all right, buddy. We cleaned it up. It's all good."

Before the toast was completely devoured, Francis reached down to the man's plate, grabbing one of the pieces and tearing away a section of crust.

"As long as you're sorry," he said, tossing it to the dog.

Marlowe snapped it out of the air, swallowing the

bread with a minimum of chewing. *"Very sorry,"* the Labrador said. *"Pee outside only."*

"Yeah, well, you be sure and remember that next time."

"You're such a hard-ass," Remy said, petting his dog's head.

"Damn straight," Francis agreed. "Got to keep up my reputation."

He turned his attention back to the man sitting wrapped in a towel, eating toast and drinking coffee.

"How are you doing?" Francis asked him. "Do you know where you are?"

The fallen looked around the room. He seemed to be in shock, which would be perfectly understandable, considering where he'd just come from. He opened his mouth to speak, but could only manage a dry croak. Remy gestured for him to drink some more of the coffee.

He did and once again attempted to answer Francis' question.

"Limbus," he managed.

The earthly plane was looked upon by the fallen angels as a kind of Limbo—or Limbus, as they called it—a sort of waiting period they would have to endure before it was determined whether or not they would be allowed to return to God.

"Bingo," Francis said, gripping his shoulder. "So you probably know what's up for you now, but in case you don't, I'll be brief. This is the next phase of your penance for crimes against the Lord God Almighty."

Francis left the man's side, going to a wooden cabinet in the corner of the kitchen area. He opened the door and removed folded clothing, a towel, and some toiletries.

All the parolees from Tartarus were given the same things.

He handed the stack to the man, who tentatively took it.

"Although not as torturous as the time spent in Hell's prison, your stay here on the world of God's man will provide you with many challenges."

The man seemed distracted, running his hands over the smoothness of the clothing, reveling in the pleasant sensation, nearly overwhelmed by something other than sheer agony and suffering.

"What's your name?" Francis asked, snapping his fingers in front of the man's face to distract him.

"Silas," he said after some thought.

"You will live here in this building, Silas, until you become acclimated to this city, and to the world," Francis explained.

"I . . . I will live here?" Silas stammered.

"Exactly. You will live here with others of your ilk—others who have begun the next phase in their rehabilitation."

"How . . . how long must I . . . ," the fallen began.

Francis reached down to grab the man beneath the arm, pulling him up from his seat. "Haven't a clue," he explained. "When the Big Man decides that you paid enough for your betrayal of His holy trust, I guess He'll allow you to return to Heaven . . . but then again, maybe He won't. God's funny like that; you never know what He's going to do."

Still holding his arm, Francis guided the fallen toward the door. "My suggestion is to live a good life, keep your nose clean, and you never know what good might come of it. You're on the second floor, first door on your right—number 213; I left it open. Go up, get settled, and if you have any questions, don't be afraid to come find me."

Silas started up the stairs, looking as though he really wasn't quite sure what was happening. It would take him some time to get used to his new, less agonizing setting, but it would happen eventually, Remy thought as he watched the man go.

"I didn't think he'd ever leave," Francis said, closing the door behind him, heading into the kitchen on a course to the coffee machine.

"What do you think?" Remy asked. Marlowe was lying on his side, sound asleep, looking as though he'd been shot. "Think he'll stay clean, or will he be seduced by the dark side?"

"I hate it when you make *Star Wars* references," Francis sneered, taking a sip from his own cup of coffee.

"Would you prefer *Trek*? You're so old-fashioned that way."

Remy joined his friend in the kitchen. Marlowe suddenly sat up, probably afraid he would miss some food.

"Where?" the dog asked groggily.

"Just getting some coffee, pal," he told the animal. "Go back to sleep. Don't worry. I'll wake you up if something good is going on."

He found a mug in the drainer by the sink and poured himself a cup.

"So what do you think? Will Silas return to Paradise?" Remy leaned against the counter, sipping from his cup.

Francis shrugged on his way into the living room. "Not my job," he said. "I'm just supposed to get them here, and then that whole free will business that the Big Guy is so famous for kicks in. Personally I don't think it lives up to the hype."

He groaned as he slowly lowered himself into a beat-up old recliner. "If it wasn't for free will, none of us would be in this situation."

Marlowe had moved closer to the Guardian, dropping down on the area rug beside his chair.

Remy pushed himself away from the kitchen counter and took a seat on the couch. "What's that supposed to mean?"

"No free will, no Lucifer deciding that he wanted to be the boss, no war in Heaven, and I just keep moving along doing what I was created to do." He had some more of his drink.

"And what about me? If the war never happened, I'd never have left Heaven, come to Earth, loved Madeline . . ."

"Exactly," Francis interrupted. "There'd have been a whole lot less pain for the both of us."

There was a tiny part of Remy that agreed with the fallen Guardian, a tiny part that wanted to be stronger, but he refused to allow it to grow. Even with all the pain he'd suffered these past few months, he wouldn't have given up what he'd experienced with his wife. She had helped to define him, shaping him into the man he was today.

Yes, *the man*.

The Seraphim inside came awake in the darkness, far stronger than it had been in centuries. It knew that the power that had once suppressed it was gone, that a chance existed that it might one day regain control, and that knowledge made it content.

Patient to wait.

"Did you just stop by to cheer me up, or did you want something?" Francis suddenly asked, interrupting the uncomfortable silence that now filled the former Guardian's dwelling.

Remy motioned to the file he'd left on the corner of the coffee table.

"What's this?" Francis asked, snatching it up. "Case you're working on?"

The angel started to flip through the pages. "Nice," he said, nodding at the weaponry. "This is the Karnighan business, right?"

Remy watched him carefully, looking for a specific reaction.

"Hey there, good-lookin'," Francis suddenly said, eyes fixated on a specific item.

"Let me guess," Remy said. "It's either a medieval

battle-axe, a Japanese katana, two daggers, or an old Colt 45."

"It's the Colt," Francis said, holding up the picture. "But now you've made me curious about the other three." He searched the stack, finding them.

"What do you think?" Remy asked.

Francis adjusted his dark-framed glasses. "They're all gorgeous, real collectors' pieces, but these particular items are fucking golden."

"I don't know shit about this stuff, and those same items gave me a similar reaction. Why do you think that?"

He shrugged. "Maybe some of my exquisite taste in tools of death and destruction has finally started to rub off on you," Francis said, continuing to ogle the pictures.

"So you've got nothing for me?"

"Nothing other than these things giving me a hard-on," Francis said. "What I wouldn't give to have just one of these in my collection."

He picked one of the pictures from the stack and stared at it. Remy could see that it was the Japanese sword.

"Thought you'd like that one," he said.

Francis looked up from the picture. "There's a legend that says that just before he died, Asamiya forged his masterpiece, a sword that would make its wielder invincible in battle."

Remy leaned forward on the couch. "Do you think that's it?"

"That would be so fucking cool," Francis said, coveting the ancient weapon. "There're stories like that about all kinds of weapons," he explained. "Supposedly every weapons smith has made a piece so perfectly that it stands far above any of its predecessors. Together these weapons were called the Pitiless."

"Pitiless?" Remy asked, not quite getting the reasoning behind the name.

"Supposedly these particular weapons were favored by Death and blessed with its power; no enemy could escape their intent."

"Special," Remy said.

Francis smiled, slowly nodding in agreement.

"And if they existed, worth a fucking mint."

CHAPTER SIX

Remy wanted to call Karnighan right there and then but realized that it was a bit too late for business.

In the morning for certain.

Leaving Francis' brownstone, he'd driven home, his head buzzing with questions. Was it possible? Had Karnighan somehow managed to find these priceless, legendary weapons? And since he'd failed to mention what these weapons actually were, was there anything else that he'd neglected to share?

Questions, with a heaping portion of questions on top of those.

There wasn't a parking space to be found anywhere on the Hill, forcing him to park down on Cambridge Street. He locked up the vehicle, and he and Marlowe walked up the rather steep incline of Irving Street, turning right onto Myrtle.

Remy didn't mind the walk and certainly neither did Marlowe. It was a pleasant spring night, and the exercise would do them both good.

Trudging up the street, Marlowe slightly ahead, gently tugging on the leash, Remy reviewed what Francis had shared with him about the weapons ... about the Pitiless. The former Guardian had known about the Japanese katana crafted by Asamiya, but had heard only whispers about the other weapons that made up the deadly arsenal. Supposedly the weapons had found their way into the hands of individuals throughout the centuries, and had been responsible for some of the largest body counts ever to be chronicled. Their notoriety grew with the spilling of each new drop of blood.

And because of that, their value became immeasurable.

At the corner of Myrtle and Anderson streets, Marlowe stopped to sniff at the left-turn-only sign, running his dripping nose up and down the metal before lifting his leg and splashing it with urine.

"Anybody you know?" Remy asked him casually.

"Doone," the dog grumbled, sniffing again to make sure his scent was the strongest. Doone was a Weimaraner who lived farther up Pinckney Street, and who had attacked Marlowe when he was just a puppy. The two had been sworn enemies ever since.

"He's got some nerve peeing on your signpost," Remy said.

"Yes," Marlowe agreed. *"My signpost. Not Doone. Mine."*

"Exactly," Remy chuckled as they headed for the house.

Marlowe stood in front of the door to the brownstone, tail wagging, as Remy fished in his pocket for his keys. He opened the door and held it for Marlowe, and that was when he sensed them.

He quickly closed the door on Marlowe and was turning as they came up from behind him. One put his arm around Remy's throat, and yanked him backward away from the door. Marlowe started barking furiously on the other side, obviously sensing danger.

He wasn't sure how many of them there were, taking a guess at three. One of them hit him in the stomach hard, and he tried to pitch forward but was held fast by the one behind him. The wind exploded from his lungs as he was hit again, the image of a balloon losing all its air as it sailed around a room filling his head.

Sometimes you think of the damnedest things when

you're getting the shit kicked out of you, he thought, feeling himself released and falling to his knees upon the street, gasping and gagging.

He was surprised that he hadn't sensed these Denizens creeping up behind him sooner, but clearly he had to show them what a mistake they had made in attacking him outside his home.

The Seraphim waited patiently just below the surface, as if it had somehow known that its fury would be called upon. Dropping the mental barriers just a crack Remy allowed a small portion of the power to emerge, feeling the fire of Heaven flow through his body to ignite his hands.

"I wouldn't do that if I were you," one of his attackers warned.

Remy ignored him, preparing to satisfy the Seraphim's hunger for battle. He looked up—and noticed one of the Denizens standing at his door.

The fallen angel was pointing a gun through the glass into the foyer of his home, where Marlowe still barked wildly.

Remy's hands crackled and sparked.

"You just might make Balam nervous," the Denizen continued from behind Remy, "and who knows what terrible things might happen then."

The one called Balam tapped the glass in the door with the barrel of his gun, making Marlowe bark all the louder. The look on his face told Remy he was hoping he would be able to fire the weapon.

Fearing for the dog's safety, Remy pulled back on his angelic essence. Though it fought him, he managed to force it again behind the mental barriers where it could do no harm.

"Good idea," the spokesperson for the group commented as the fiery glow from his hands began to dim.

Remy slowly rose to his feet, eyeing the gathering standing around him. There were actually four of them, three around him and Balam at the door.

"You've got my attention," Remy stated.

"Good," the leader answered with the hint of a smile. "That's a very sweet-looking dog you have, and I'd hate to have anything—"

"Cut the menacing bullshit and get to the point," Remy interrupted. "I get it; you'll hurt my dog if I don't behave. Fine. What the fuck do you want?"

The Denizen leader started to laugh, and seeing that it was okay, so did the others. "If we didn't need you, I'd do something about that smart mouth," he said.

"Lucky for me," Remy answered.

"Yeah, it is," the leader agreed.

They glared at each other, Remy searching the fallen angel's dead features for something familiar. Had he known this angel once? Had he once called him brother before the fall? Remy couldn't tell. The time spent in Hell changed them outside, as well as in.

"My employer is very interested in your current job," the fallen said. "So interested, in fact, that he wants to know all about your progress." The angel removed a business card from inside his coat. "No skimping on the details. Do you understand . . . Remy?"

They moved toward him as their backs suddenly became illuminated in the glare of approaching headlights. The fallen leader let the card drop from his hand as he passed.

"Nice," Remy said.

"I'll be looking forward to hearing from you," the leader said over his shoulder.

Remy squatted down to pick up the card, giving it a quick read before stuffing it into his coat pocket.

Old Scratch Contracting.

Cute, Remy thought, watching as the four men climbed into the black BMW truck and pulled out of the parking spot in front of his house.

How'd they manage such a good space? he ruminated, remembering where he'd have to walk tomorrow to retrieve his car.

The vehicle whose headlights had prompted the party to end pulled into the spot, the window coming down to reveal a familiar face.

"This was meant to be," Steven Mulvehill said as he put the car in park. He turned the engine off and climbed out of the vehicle with a paper bag held lovingly in his arms. "While at the liquor store I said to myself, if I was meant to share this bottle of fifteen-year-old Scotch, there'll be a spot for me in front of the lucky individual's humble abode."

He partially pulled the bottle of alcohol from the bag to give Remy an enticing peak at the contents. "And as luck would have it, you were the first house on my list."

Remy smiled in spite of what had just transpired there on the street. It was good to see his friend, and a drink was just what he could use about then.

Marlowe continued to bark as if insane from inside the hallway, capturing the homicide detective's attention.

"What's the matter with him?"

Remy shrugged, retrieving his keys again and heading to the door.

"I think he smells something bad in the air."

"So who were they again?"

Mulvehill poured himself some more Scotch as he waited for Remy to answer.

"I thought you didn't like to know about the weird shit," Remy said, swirling the ice around in his glass as he reclined farther in the patio chair on the rooftop deck of his building.

Mulvehill dropped a handful of ice from the full bucket into his finger of alcohol. "Normally I don't, but I'm fascinated by the concept of anybody smacking you around."

Remy set his glass down on the patio table and reached inside his pocket to remove the business card.

"They were Denizens," he said in explanation. "Fallen angels."

Mulvehill returned to his seat across from his friend, sipping on his ice-filled drink as he sat down.

"And these are the guys that used to be in . . . y'know."

He motioned with one of his hands, pointing to the ground, not wanting to say the word.

"Hell," Remy finished for him. He found it interesting that the legends and stories of the prison realm had made it so that humanity was terrified of the place as well, even though their kind would never see it. Hell was only for those who had fallen from their servitude to *Him*.

"Right. They used to be in Hell, but now they're here and they like to beat you up."

Remy was taking a drink and laughed. "That's right," he said, wiping a dribble of Scotch from his chin. "They just love to kick my angel ass."

Marlowe, who was resting by his chair, suddenly sat up at attention.

"No kick ass. Marlowe will bite them," the Labrador said with what he intended to be a menacing growl.

Remy reached down and stroked the dog's soft black fur. "Of course you would have. You're the bravest animal I know."

"Yes, Marlowe very brave," the animal agreed.

"What's he going on about?" Mulvehill wanted to know.

"He just wants to reassure me that he would have protected me from the bad guys that smacked me around."

The homicide detective nodded. "Now, why were they threatening to shoot your dog again?"

Marlowe lay back down on his side with a heavy sigh, closing his eyes and almost immediately drifting off to sleep.

Remy shrugged, the ice in his tumbler tinkling like the bells of Christmas.

"Do you have run-ins with these fallen guys . . . these Denizens . . . often?"

"They have a tendency to run in darker circles than I usually like to travel in, but lately I've found myself entering those places more often." Remy had some more to drink.

"They're not very nice," he continued. "Like most organized crime families, really. They gather in groups, as if looking to find what they'd once had with their angelic hosts in Heaven, only there's very little interest in serving God now."

Mulvehill shook his head as he shifted in his seat, uncomfortable with the complex world of the supernatural. "And you wonder why I drink so much?" he said, finishing the Scotch in his glass.

"No, not really. You're just a drunk."

They both had a good laugh. It had been quite some time since Remy had laughed—since he'd *really* laughed. It felt good, and for the briefest of moments, he had the most unusual idea that he wouldn't be sad forever, that eventually he would be able to think about something other than how much he missed his wife.

Wouldn't that be something, he thought, knowing that it was likely very far away, but still having a sense that it was there, somewhere beyond the horizon.

"So we've established that they're bad guys and they like to do bad things as a way of flipping the bird at God," Mulvehill said, grabbing the bottle of booze and pouring himself another. "Now do you have any idea what you did to piss these bad guys off?"

Remy shrugged again, attempting to form some kind of image from what little information he had. It was becoming more likely that Karnighan's missing property could very well be the legendary Pitiless, and that they could have been stolen by persons of an angelic persuasion.

Smelled like you, the voice of the rottweiler Luthor echoed in his head.

He could only begin to wonder what the Denizens' involvement in this would be.

"I think their Satan has an interest in the new case I'm working on," Remy said as he tipped his glass toward his mouth, letting what remained of the ice fall into his mouth.

Mulvehill almost choked.

"Their Satan? Are you saying that their boss is the fucking Devil?"

Remy chuckled. "It's not what you think," he explained. "Satan is a title . . . a designation, like *capo* or *don* in the Mafia."

"Almost gave me a heart attack," Mulvehill said. "So their leader—their Satan, if you will—has an interest in your case?"

"It appears so," Remy answered. "But at this point what that interest is I haven't a clue. I suppose I should probably find out."

Remy went for the bottle again, offering it first to Mulvehill.

"No, thanks," the homicide cop said, placing the flat of his hand over his glass. "I think the drunk's had about enough."

"Suit yourself," Remy said, splashing a bit more of the golden liquid into his glass.

Mulvehill rose from his seat and stretched. "Probably should think about getting home. For some reason it's always harder for me to get my ass out of bed after a night of visiting with you. Wonder what that's all about."

Remy swished what he'd just poured around in his mouth before swallowing.

"Haven't got a clue," he said. "Maybe you could come by tomorrow night and we can discuss the possibilities as we finish this off?" He held out the half-empty bottle of Scotch.

"That's a good idea," Mulvehill said, slowly making his way toward the stairs that would take him down into Remy's home.

Marlowe stood, gave himself a good shake and followed the homicide detective to the doorway.

"Steven," Remy called out to his friend. He held the bottle in the crook of one arm, the two empty tumblers in his other hand.

Mulvehill turned, giving Marlowe's black tail a playful swat as the dog passed. "What's up?"

"Do me a favor?" Remy asked, coming to join him.

"If I can."

"Keep your ears open," he asked. "If you hear anything from your friends in Burglary about weapons—antique guns, knives, or swords—give me a call."

"Antique weapons," Mulvehill said, his eyes searching Remy's for more.

"Yeah, if you hear anything, think of me first, all right?"

The Boston homicide detective put an arm around his shoulder as they headed for the stairs.

"With the weird shit, you're never far from my thoughts."

It was like he had traveled back in time.

Except for the ringing of his cell phone.

Madeline had brought him back to her apartment, the two of them soaking wet after being caught in a sudden summer downpour. She'd commented on them looking like a couple of drowned rats before pulling him closer, kissing him hard on the mouth.

She'd said something about the two of them getting out of their wet things before they caught their death of cold. And then she'd laughed, one of the most arousing sounds he'd ever heard in his long lifetime, and started to remove their clothes.

The sound of his phone was distracting, tugging at him, pulling him from this special place in time.

It was the first time they'd made love, not even making it to her bed. They'd dropped down upon the living room floor, feeding each other's passions their only intent.

He'd been with other humans before, more out of a

perverse curiosity than anything else. If he was going to be one of them, he needed to experience everything, sampling all their wants and desires. Sexual dalliance was inevitable.

But nothing had compared to this.

She had awakened something within him, something that had become still over the centuries, deathly quiet since he'd left Heaven. She made him want to be part of something larger; she awakened his need to connect.

The feel of her body against his, the awkwardness of their attempts to satisfy a passion that grew in intensity over the passing seconds.

He had felt it. Actually felt it.

Connecting in the instant their bodies grew together, the rhythm of their furious lovemaking like the heartbeat of some giant, long-extinct animal.

No. Like the heartbeat of the world.

Remy knew what it was like to be *them*. He wasn't just pretending anymore.

He knew what it was to be human.

The phone wouldn't stop, soon drowning out the sounds of their lovemaking, and suddenly he wasn't there anymore.

The harsh reality of the present had found him once more, as it always seemed to.

Lying in the darkness, he felt his wife's touch upon his body, phantom caresses growing softer, and softer still, until all he had left was their memory.

Marlowe stirred at the foot of the bed, lifting his large head as if to ask Remy if he would ever answer that damnable piece of technology.

Remy's hand moved like lightning, and he was tempted to throw the trilling device at the wall, but what good would come of that? He'd only have to buy a new one.

"Yes," he said after flipping open the cell. He saw on the face of the phone that it was a little after four in the morning, and had a suspicion about who would be calling him at this hour.

"Did I wake you?" Francis asked. Remy could hear the sound of a television blaring in the background. It sounded like a game show, probably *The Price Is Right*. Francis had a thing for Bob Barker, thought he was the coolest MC that had ever graced a game-show stage.

"No, I was just lying here in the dark waiting for your call."

"You need a good hobby. Collecting Hummels would suit you, I bet. Have you ever thought about collecting Hummels?"

"What do you want, Francis?"

Marlowe lifted himself up from where he lay, walked up to the top of the bed and plopped down again. It was like somebody dropping a seventy-pound bag of laundry beside him.

"Got somebody I think you should talk to," the fallen Guardian said. The sound of a television announcer wailed, "Come on down," as an enthusiastic crowd clapped, cheered, and whistled in the background.

"About Hummels?" Remy asked.

"Almost as good," Francis answered without missing a beat. "I got somebody who knows a thing or two about missing property, and would be willing to talk to you."

Remy reached over and began to scratch beneath Marlowe's neck. The big dog reacted immediately, rolling onto his back. The Labrador preferred belly rubs.

"I guess it would be too early to talk to him now."

"Your powers of observation are fucking amazing," Francis said through a mouthful of something that could have been potato chips. "Have you ever thought about being a detective?"

"The thought's crossed my mind. Would I make a lot of money and meet fabulously interesting people?"

Francis laughed. "Can't really say about the money, but interesting people you'll meet by the wheelbarrow full. In fact, I've got one that wants to meet you at lunchtime."

"Awesome," Remy said without an ounce of excitement.

"And, oh, yeah, you're bringing the lunch."

CHAPTER SEVEN

Francis was waiting for him in the parking lot of the Lock & Key Self-Storage building located off of the Expressway in Southie. You could see the building from the highway, an inflated padlock and chain draped around the front of the boxy structure.

Remy pulled his car alongside his friend's Range Rover. Francis stood at the front of his vehicle smoking a cigar and staring up into the sky at a flock of geese flying in a V formation to parts unknown.

"Remembering what it felt like?" Remy asked as he slammed his car door closed. Though the gift hadn't been lost to him, as it had to Francis, he seldom flew anymore. It gave the Seraphim nature too much strength.

Francis looked away from the birds, taking a final puff of the foul-smelling stogie before dropping it to the ground and crushing it beneath his foot.

"What what was like?" he asked coming around his car, pretending that he hadn't noticed the birds.

"To fly," Remy said, instinctively looking up into the sky as a plane flew overhead on its descent to Logan.

"Can't remember that far back," Francis said. Remy noticed a twitch at the corner of the Guardian's eye that told him he was lying. "Can't miss what you don't remember."

There was a moment of uncomfortable silence before Francis started up again.

"Did you remember lunch?" he asked, looking at Remy's empty hands.

Remy moved around to the passenger-side door of his car. "Stopped off at Primos before I got on the road," he said. "Two large: one with extra cheese, the other pepperoni." He opened the door and carefully removed the two stacked pizza boxes.

"That should do it," Francis said. He started across the parking lot toward the front entrance of the self-storage building.

Remy followed, pizzas in hand. He'd seen this building from the road for years, never imagining that it contained anything more than promised.

"So he has a storage bin here or something?" he asked.

"Rents at least one of the floors," Francis said as he ambled up a handicapped-accessible ramp to the front door. "Has places all over the city, I guess. Mason's the guy to come to when you need something that nobody else has."

Standing in front of the door, Francis pulled out his cell and dialed a number. "We're here," he said into the phone, listening for a second before hanging up.

"They'll be right down," he said, closing the phone and slipping it back inside his coat pocket.

"Been here before?" Remy asked, inhaling the enticing aroma of baked cheese and pepperoni. He hadn't thought he was hungry, but his mouth started to water.

"No," Francis answered with a head shake. "Been to his space in Lynn and another smaller one in Chelsea."

"The man's got lots of stuff," Remy said, noticing two figures approaching the door from the inside.

A big guy with thick black hair, dressed in a navy blue Windbreaker, pushed open the door for Francis to enter, his eyes darting around, looking for anything that might've seemed out of place.

"You bring lunch?" he asked, his South Boston accent thick.

"That was his job," Francis said, hooking a finger over his shoulder at Remy.

Remy lifted the boxes to show the man as he followed his friend.

"Where'd you get those?" he asked as Remy came into the building.

"Place called Primos on Myrtle Street."

"Fucking garbage," the man muttered beneath his breath, pushing past them to lumber toward the elevator at the back.

The second man stood back, silently watching with icy blue eyes. He was thin, clothes likely the smallest adult size that could be bought hanging loosely off his skeletal frame. His skin was sickly pale, and his blond hair was dry, like straw. Remy noticed the multicolored aura around his head out of the corner of his eye, immediately recognizing him for what he was.

The man smiled simply, following Southie, who was holding the elevator doors open for them.

"Any fuckin' day now," the big man complained with a roll of his eyes and shake of his head.

They all crammed inside, the pizzas filling the cab with their intoxicating aroma as they rode silently up to the sixth floor.

The doors slowly parted, Southie stomping out first to go about his business, the other stopping just outside to wait for Remy and Francis.

The elevator had opened on what looked to be office space, the surrounding walls having multiple sets of metal sliding doors. Southie had ended up inside one of the open units, and appeared to be counting up cartons of cigarettes, which he pulled from inside large boxes stacked along the inside wall of the unit.

"Those all fell off the backs of trucks," Francis said, leaning over to speak in Remy's ear.

Other unit doors were open as well, the spaces containing everything from patio furniture and stereo components to plasma televisions. Some of the units remained closed, but that didn't prevent Remy from picking up some strange vibes from whatever was contained inside.

"What's inside them?" Remy asked Francis, gesturing with his chin toward the closed units.

"That's the shit that didn't fall out of the backs of trucks," Francis said, taking Remy's elbow and leading him away from the elevator and into the main area.

In the far corner there was a makeshift desk made from a door and some cinder blocks, its surface covered with computer monitors, modems, and hard drives. Remy could hear a methodical clicking sound as someone typed on a keyboard behind the multiple computer screens.

"Give me just a sec," said a voice, the words slightly slurred.

The thin man seemed to drift into the room, and Remy was again distracted by the multicolored halo that pulsed around his head.

The man was an Offspring, the child of a Denizen and a mortal. It was frowned upon by the higher powers, but it didn't stop it from occasionally happening.

He remembered how sad Madeline had been when she realized they would never have children together. He'd tried his best to explain it, that there was usually something wrong with the babies—that they could even be dangerous. His wife had understood, but it did little to take away the hurt of what their love was denied.

Offspring were often mentally handicapped, but prone to exhibit paranormal talents associated with those of an angelic nature.

The man turned to look at Remy, that same simple smile again forming on his face. *"Do you know the tongue of the Messengers?"* he deftly asked, speaking in a language fashioned before the inception of humanity.

Remy was taken aback by the fluent use of the angelspeak, remaining silent until another sound filled the room, the whining sound of a motor, followed by a voice he'd heard briefly only minutes ago.

"Neal is such a show-off," the obese figure confined to the electric wheelchair said as he carefully maneuvered around the computer table and rolled toward them. His words were slightly distorted, and Remy could see the reason. He held a long stick in his mouth, likely what the man used to punch the keys of his computer keyboard. The stick dropped from his mouth into his lap, and a tiny monkey balanced on his shoulder obediently dropped down to snatch up the tool. It then leapt down to the floor, scampering off to place the stick on a small tray with a brush, handheld mirror, toothbrush, and toothpaste, before returning to its master's shoulder.

"How's it rolling, Mason?" Francis asked with a wiggle of his eyebrows.

"Blow me, Francis," the man said with disgust. "I don't even want to talk to you; it's your friend that I like." Mason brought his wheelchair closer, staring at Remy with round, watery eyes. "Magnificent."

Remy had heard stories about Mason Aronoff, born with spinal muscular atrophy, a neuromuscular disease that caused the degeneration of the motor neurons in the spinal cord, which relay signals from the brain to the muscle cells. When these neurons fail to function, the muscles deteriorate, leaving the afflicted nearly paralyzed. The man had been this way since childhood and had attempted to take his own life on more than one occasion to escape his suffering. These near-death experiences—these multiple glimpses of an afterlife—had somehow served to give the handicapped man a special kind of sight.

Mason could see things in the world that no one else could; he could see the unearthly beings that walked hidden amongst them. The handicapped man could see beneath the masks.

And he could see Remy for what he actually was.

"Why on earth would you want to look the way you do now," Mason said in a whisper, "when you actually look like *that*."

Remy could feel his Seraphim nature stir, eager to emerge to greet the man, but he wouldn't be having any of that.

It was silent in the storage facility except for the sound of Southie, muttering from one of the bins, as he continued to unload cartons of cigarettes.

"Do you know how hard it is to buy shirts with a sixty-foot wingspan?" Remy asked, finally breaking the silence with a joke. He then held up the pizza boxes.

"Anybody interested in lunch?"

They'd opened the boxes of pizza and laid them on the end of the computer table.

Remy had just finished a slice and was considering another as he stood watching the man in the electric wheelchair and his simian helper.

The capuchin monkey stood up on the man's expansive lap, holding the slice of pepperoni pizza up to Mason's slack, but hungry, mouth. It was a fascinating process to watch. The monkey would give the man a bite, set the piece of pizza down, use a napkin to wipe the grease off the man's mouth, and then begin again.

"She's something, isn't she, Remy? I can call you Remy, can't I?" Mason asked, noticing that he was staring.

"Sure," he answered, startled that he'd been caught in his observation.

"Her name is Julia, and I don't know what I'd do without her," he said as the monkey softly chattered to itself, licking some of the pizza grease from its little digits.

"Without her you'd have to depend on Ichabod here, or Mr. Sunshine, to feed you your lunch," Francis commented, referring to the Offspring, Neal, and Southie, who had gone to separate corners to eat their pizza slices.

"I wouldn't trust them to wipe their own asses," the crippled man commented nastily. "If it wasn't for the fact that they occasionally have their moments, I'd have monkeys doing all their jobs."

Julia threw her tiny arms around Mason's face and licked his forehead. The man started to giggle, his flabby body undulating in the electric wheelchair like a plate of Jell-O whacked with a stick.

"You're such a naughty girl," he said between laughter as the monkey chirped and squeaked.

Remy didn't have the heart to tell the man that based on what the capuchin was saying, it was only enjoying the saltiness of his skin.

"It looks like you two might want to be alone, so why don't we take care of business so you can get on communing with nature, or whatever the fuck you'll be doing as soon as we leave."

Francis snatched up one of the napkins on the table and wiped his hands fussily.

The monkey stopped licking Mason's face and glared at Francis. It squeaked something—*the monkey equivalent of fuck you*—and climbed up onto its owner's shoulder, a scowl upon its furry features.

Neal started laughing, likely understanding what the monkey had just said. Remy didn't have to guess about at least one of the angelic talents this Offspring had inherited from its fallen sire.

"Francis says you might have some information for me," Remy interjected before things got any nastier between the disabled man and the former Guardian.

"Antique weaponry, Remy?" the man asked, a crooked smile upon his doughy features.

"That's what I was told was stolen."

Mason's flaccid hand manipulated the controls of his wheelchair, moving him closer to Remy. "Francis said these weapons could well be the legendary Pitiless."

"It's a possibility," Remy said, turning to glare at Francis.

"So shoot me." The Guardian threw up his hands. "I'm excited."

Mason closed his eyes, a twisted smile spreading across his doughy features. "I'd pay a small fortune just to look at them," he said, a trickle of saliva beginning to dribble from one of the corners of his mouth. "But I've heard nothing, Remy," Mason said.

Julia had returned to the man's shoulder and was now grooming his hair, in search of something to snack upon.

"And if they're as valuable as you say, I doubt you'd tell me if you did."

Mason's smile broadened, the drool flowing like a river. "It depends on whether or not the person who retained your services was offering a comparable reward, and to be perfectly honest, Remy, I'm not too sure I'd really care to have these priceless objects in my possession. They have a bit of a history. A nasty history."

"They're like the ultimate weapons," Francis said, taking a congealed piece of greasy cheese pizza from the box and bringing it up to his mouth. "What would you expect?"

Moving his chair in the Guardian's direction, Mason responded. "Lore states that death is the end result of anybody who possesses the accursed weaponry," he explained. "It is said that they were not meant for human hands, but for Death itself."

Francis waved the claim away. "Death doesn't need a fucking sword or a pistol. He just has to look at you to get the results he wants."

The capuchin eyed Remy from her perch upon Mason's shoulder, bored with grooming his stringy hair. Tensing her legs, Julia leapt.

"Then who . . . or what were they made for?" Remy asked, catching the flying monkey, allowing her to climb up onto his shoulder.

Mason looked panicked, staring at his simian helper, who seemed perfectly at home on this stranger's shoulder. "That is the mystery," he said, making noises with his mouth, attempting to call the monkey back to him.

Julia squeaked *no* in her primitive tongue.

"Some writings say that they were weapons meant

for gods," Mason continued. "And for any other to possess them was to seal their fate."

Remy whispered to Julia, asking the monkey to return to her master, and the creature begrudgingly complied.

"There's my girl," Mason cooed, more at ease now that she had returned to him.

"So can I count on you to give me a call if you should come across anything that might be of interest?" Remy asked. He reached into his shirt pocket and removed a business card.

Julia squealed with excitement as Remy placed the card in her tiny hand. Holding it on either end, she proceeded to nibble its corner.

"I'll be more than happy to keep you in mind, Remy," Mason said, amused by his monkey's antics. "Things of a . . . How shall I put this? Things of an eclectic nature have a strange habit of finding their way into my possession."

The sudden noise was practically deafening in the small space, and they all turned toward one of the storage units.

Southie looked sheepishly in their direction, dropping to his knees to pick up the contents of the unit that had spilled out when its door had been opened.

Bones—thousands of bleached remains from every conceivable part of the human anatomy—lay upon the storage-facility floor.

Things of an eclectic nature. Mason's last statement echoed in Remy's ears.

It certainly did seem to be the case.

"All things considered, that went well," Francis said as they walked to their cars.

"Let's just see if he does as he says," Remy commented, fishing his keys from his pocket. "If these weapons turn out to be what we think they might be, they'll be worth an awful lot of money to someone looking to amass some serious power."

Francis pointed his remote at the Range Rover, starting the vehicle with the push of a button.

"And if they're actually as dangerous as legend says, things like the Pitiless in the wrong hands could be very bad news," the Guardian said, the look on his face showing that he was weighing the consequences. "Things are already tense between the various Denizen hosts. If one of the Satans got their hands on these weapons, there'd be freakin' war."

Remy sighed. "Great, another war. Just what we need."

The two angels stood silently in the parking lot, at a loss for words.

"Where to now?" Remy asked his friend.

"I was thinking of heading over to Newbury Street."

"Have you introduced yourself yet?"

Francis shook his head. "It's not like that," he explained, reaching to open his car door. "I couldn't do what you did." The fallen angel paused. "Not sure how I would've survived what you've been through."

Surviving, Remy thought. Was that what he was doing now?

He thought of the Throne representative, and its request for him to return to Paradise, but quickly pushed it away. He didn't want to think of such things.

"One does what one has to," Remy answered, not wanting to talk about it anymore.

He too went to his car, opening the door. "I'd tell you to say hi for me, but there's really no sense in that, is there?"

"It's the thought that counts," Francis answered, climbing up into the Range Rover.

In the rearview, Remy watched Francis leave the lot, two quick toots from his horn, and then he was gone.

It was an odd sensation, and it surprised him, but he was actually a bit jealous over what Francis had, a level of intimacy suddenly absent from his own life.

"Look at what you've done to me," Remy muttered beneath his breath, imagining he was speaking with his departed wife. "It's a sad day when I'm jealous of Francis for anything."

He turned the car's engine over and reached into his pocket for his phone.

It was time to make the call.

Dialing the number, he waited through quite a few rings before the phone was picked up.

"Mr. Karnighan," he said, putting the car in drive and leaving the parking lot. "This is Remy Chandler. I'm on my way over. I believe there are some things we need to discuss."

CHAPTER EIGHT

Remy was just about to get onto Route 128, heading north, when he got the call. It was Steven Mulvehill, and he was speaking in careful whispers.

"You might want to come over to Huntington Ave," he said, his voice barely audible over the sounds of traffic leaking into the car.

"What's up?" Remy asked, nearing the exit that he would need to take if he was going to continue on to Lexington.

"Let's just say something that has Remy Chandler written all over it, and leave it at that."

Remy didn't take the exit, instead reversing to head back in the direction he had come. He hadn't been too far from the address Steven had given him, and it wouldn't take him long to get there.

Something's come up that has Remy Chandler written all over it. Nice, he thought.

Traffic was relatively light for that time of day, and he was able to get to Huntington Ave in almost record time. Even being nearby didn't gurantee anything in Boston traffic; this just happened to be one of the good days. Who knew, maybe it was a sign of good things to come.

Yeah, right.

He had no trouble finding the right building—the police cars, ambulance and coroner's van a dead giveaway. Slowly, he drove by the run-down tenement building.

Finding a parking spot proved to be more difficult than the entire ride, but he finally managed, leaving his car on the next street over, and hoofing it to the building in question.

The police had put up yellow crime scene tape around the entrance, keeping the gawkers at a safe distance. Remy stood across the street with the growing crowd, searching for a familiar face.

Eventually Steven Mulvehill came through the door of the building with his partner, Rich Healey. They were talking, Mulvehill removing a pack of cigarettes from his suit coat pocket and putting one in his mouth. Healey nodded, going back inside as Mulvehill walked down the steps to the street, butt dangling from the corner of his mouth while he scanned the crowds of curious onlookers.

Their eyes locked as they found each other, the detective motioning for Remy to follow. He moved through the rubberneckers, watching Mulvehill doing the same on the other side.

Remy crossed the street, navigating traffic that had slowed to a crawl to take a peek at the scene. The detective was standing out in front of McVee's Liquors puffing on his cigarette.

"Not sure how McVee's is for old Scotches, but maybe we can find a vintage bottle of Mad Dog."

"Don't tempt me," Mulvehill said, sucking on the end of the cigarette as if it were life support. "After what I just left, being three sheets to the wind would suit me just fine."

"What's going on?" Remy asked.

Mulvehill dropped what remained of his cigarette, rubbing it out as he exhaled a foul-smelling cloud of smoke. "Follow me," he said as he started back toward the building. "Oh, and do that thing you do," he said, turning slightly and waving his hand in the air. "You know, so you can't be seen and shit."

It would raise a whole lot of questions for Mulvehill

KINSMAN FREE PUBLIC LIBRARY

if Remy were to be spotted at the scene of an active investigation. Remy's being invisible would make it easier for everyone and would give him the chance to really look around.

Remy followed close to his friend as he maneuvered through the crowds outside the crime scene tape. A beat cop lifted the tape so that Mulvehill could get under; Remy had to practically jump onto his back so that he could make it under with him.

"Do you mind?" Mulvehill spoke softly from the corner of his mouth. "You weigh a freakin' ton; I thought angels were supposed to be as light as a feather."

"It's all that Scotch you've been making me drink," Remy whispered from behind. "Because of you I'll probably have my wings revoked."

"Go screw," Mulvehill said.

"Excuse me, sir?" a uniform asked as he pulled open the door for the detective.

"Nothing," Mulvehill said quickly, entering the rundown lobby. "Talking to myself, is all."

The lobby was empty and for the moment strangely silent, as if something unnatural had stolen away the sound.

"Are you ready for this?" Mulvehill asked, starting up the creaking wooden staircase. The stairs were covered with what had once been a flowered print runner, the pattern now practically invisible from years of stains and the treads of countless feet.

Remy was thinking of cracking wise, maybe something along the lines of *I was born ready*. But it just didn't seem like the time for that.

There was something in the air of the apartment building, and as they climbed the steps, getting closer, it became stronger, more oppressive.

Something unnatural.

They reached the top of the stairs and proceeded down the hallway. There appeared to be two apartments on this level, the one that they were looking for obviously being at the end of the hall, with police detectives, uniforms, and two guys who belonged to the meat wagon out front, standing in front of the open door chatting amongst themselves. The guys from the medical examiner's had placed their stretcher across the doorway as they laughed it up with two of the uniformed police officers.

They noticed Mulvehill coming down the hallway and immediately changed their demeanor, standing taller and attempting to exude an air of professionalism.

"We'll be removing the deceased shortly, sir," one of the drivers said. "The photographers just left, and Detective Healey is finishing up. As soon as he's done, we'll—"

Healey appeared in the doorway, sliding the stretcher out of his way. "All right, boys; it's all yours," he said.

He then noticed Mulvehill standing there and shook his head, a look of unease upon his face.

"I don't know what to say," he said, removing a pair of rubber gloves from his hands.

"Do you think I could take another look before you pack 'im up?" Mulvehill asked, turning to the drivers.

They looked at each other and shrugged.

"Sure, take your time," one of them said.

Mulvehill moved the stretcher out of the way so that they could both pass through with little difficulty.

"I've got no idea what could have caused that kind of damage," Healey said, again shaking his head. "Maybe if we look together we can—"

"Go grab a smoke," Mulvehill told his partner. "You've done your part; let me take it from here."

"You sure?" Healey asked, already moving, eager to leave the building.

Remy maneuvered around both men, starting down the hallway inside the apartment, checking out the rooms on either side, pretty sure that he'd know the scene of the crime when he came across it.

"I'm sure. And if you hit the store, pick me up a

coffee," Mulvehill told the younger man. "I shouldn't be long here, wait for me outside. We'll head over to Brigham to see what we can get out of the girlfriend."

"Got it," Healey said, on his way toward the stairs.

Remy was standing in a doorway looking into a filthy kitchen as Mulvehill came up from behind.

"What's this about a girlfriend?" Remy asked.

"We're guessing that she walked in on what you're about to see," the detective said, continuing down the hallway. "It's down here."

Remy followed, noticing a strange, smoky aroma wafting in the air the closer they got to the room at the end of the hall.

"What do you make of that?" the homicide cop said, motioning with his hand for Remy to look into the room.

The first thing he noticed was the gaping hole in the wall, seconded by the body of a man, probably in his mid- to late thirties, lying on his back on the floor of the room. His stomach and chest had been exposed—set afire and extinguished. The man's body still smoldered, explaining the drifting stink of roast pork in the air.

"I don't know what to say," Remy said, unable to take his eyes from the corpse. Though the stomach and rib cage appeared blackened, the rest of the man's remains were untouched.

Remy moved closer and squatted beside the body. The frozen expression on the victim's face was horrible, as if he couldn't believe what was happening to him.

"Who is he?" Remy asked.

"Douglas Bender," Mulvehill said from the doorway. "A familiar face to Burglary. They got a hysterical call from the girlfriend before we did. I guess she and some of the guys had bonded over their love for poor misunderstood Dougie."

Remy's eyes moved over the body and to the area around it. There were deep gouges in the hardwood floor surrounding the murdered man's corpse. He was immediately reminded of something he himself had seen before, marks very similar to this left in the hard-wood floors of his own home by Marlowe's nails, only these appeared much deeper.

"Where is she now, the girlfriend?" He looked away from the corpse to his friend.

"She's at the hospital, in shock. Whatever she walked in on practically pushed her over the edge."

"Did she tell anyone anything? Anything that could explain this?" the angel asked, standing, eyeing the extensive damage to the room. It was as if somebody had driven a truck through it.

The detective shook his head. "We found her in the entryway pretty banged up. She'd fallen down the stairs and just kept screaming and crying." Mulvehill shook his head. "It was pretty bad, and of course I thought of you immediately."

"Thanks." Remy looked around the room. There were boxes stacked everywhere, some of the contents having spilled out onto the floor in the apparent struggle. The boxes were filled with an odd assortment of things: video-games systems, a toaster oven, stereo receiver and speakers, an iPod or two.

Something caught Remy's eye and he moved toward it. The box was jammed into a corner, an old VCR having tipped off of it, pulling open the flaps of the box.

"I was wondering how long it would take you to notice," Mulvehill said. "When I found them I figured I should call you."

Remy pulled back one of the cardboard lids and looked down into the box. Though they were wrapped in pieces of bubble wrap, and even some newspaper, there was no mistaking the antique nature of the items within. He reached inside.

"You might not want to touch those without gloves," Mulvehill warned, reaching into his pocket for an extra pair.

"No worry. There won't be fingerprints if I don't want

there to be," the angel said, carefully removing one of the tightly wrapped objects.

"Fucking show-off," the police detective growled.

Remy unwrapped the bundle, seeing that it contained an antique dagger, vaguely recalling that he had seen a photo of this knife in Karnighan's paperwork.

But not one of the supposed Pitiless.

"Did you happen to find anything else of interest?" Remy asked, rewrapping the blade and placing it back inside the box. He looked about the room again, his eyes constantly drawn to the condition of the dead body there.

What did this to you?

The detective shook his head. "Poked around some, but that's pretty much all that I could find in regard to what you were asking about. I gather that isn't all of it?"

"No," Remy said, looking into the box again to be sure. "There were a few other pieces of more considerable value," he explained.

"The guy on the third floor said that Dougie and the missus had somebody crashing with them for the last few weeks. We're working on a name. Maybe he'll know where the other stuff is."

If that was all they had, it would have to do, Remy thought, standing up from the box. He was thinking that maybe he would go over to Brigham and Women's to speak with the victim's girlfriend when his eyes were again drawn to the deep gouges in the wooden floor. Some of the planks had actually been splintered, partially pulled up to reveal the old floor beneath.

Remy poked the jagged furrows in the wood floor with the toe of his shoe.

"We should think about getting out of here," Mulvehill said from the doorway. "I'm sure they want to get Dougie here over to the morgue before . . ."

It was as if Remy had stepped on a live wire, his entire body going rigid as violent images flooded into his head. Scene after scene of brutal acts, two delicate knife blades slicing through the air to cut short the lives of multiple victims. It was almost more than he could stand. Remy was blind to the world, seeing only one murder flowing into another.

From somewhere in the distance he heard his friend's voice, filled with concern.

Sound became muffled, distant, and he found himself falling, dropping to his knees upon the floor. The images grew stronger, faster, more pronounced and more savage. Men, women, and children; the blades; whoever wielded them undiscerning in who was felled by their razor-sharp bite.

A cascade of savagery almost suffocating in its relentless onslaught continued, and multiple voices could now be heard, voices that did not wish to speak to him, but to his other side.

Voices that spoke to the Seraphim, urging it to come forward.

Here, they hissed inside his head as he watched the image of a woman's throat being cut so deeply that it practically severed her head.

The visions halted momentarily, and Remy found himself staring at a section of flooring. It wasn't obvious, but on closer examination he saw where the floor had been cut to create a hiding place beneath.

Compelled by the voices inside his head, Remy clawed at the floor, his fingernails digging into the edges of the boards.

He saw the dead man—Dougie—wrapping something in a towel, hiding something away. The next images were like a head-on collision: multiple flashes filled with muffled screams, frozen moments of death and destruction.

"What the fuck is going on?" he heard Mulvehill ask from what seemed like miles away, but he couldn't tell him. He couldn't speak.

Something had come through the wall, something

large and bestial. It had first attacked Dougie before turning its attention to the room.

Searching.

The board came loose from the floor, and Remy tossed it over his shoulder before plunging his hands inside the darkness of the hidey-hole.

The memory of a woman's scream exploded in Remy's mind; the scream had driven whatever it was—the beast—away. It hadn't found what it was looking for.

But Remy had.

His hands emerged from beneath the floor holding something wrapped in an old, black-checked dish towel, the same something that he'd seen Dougie holding in the flash of the past. Remy dropped the wrapped object to the floor, pulling apart the cheap cloth to reveal what was hidden within.

Brother and sister daggers.

Two of the Pitiless.

Holding the daggers was even worse.

The images became more clear, more focused and precise, accompanied by the sounds of the death and misery that the brother and sister had caused.

The knives were stuck to his hands, and although repelled, he never wanted to let them go. The Seraphim was aroused, enticed by the song of the blades. Remy could feel his flesh grow warm, the masquerade of humanity that he wore ready to be sloughed off and cast aside.

"No!"

He used all the strength that he had remaining to open both hands, causing the daggers to drop to the floor.

Perfectly balanced, they spun around, their razor-sharp tips digging into the hardwood. They protruded there, vibrating with malice, urging the angel to again take them up.

"What the fuck is going on?" Mulvehill asked again

as Remy stumbled backward, away from the weapons' siren call. He leaned on his friend for support.

"There's something very wrong about those knives," he gasped, forcing the angelic essence back down.

"Did I just see your skin start to smoke?" Mulvehill asked, a hint of panic in the man's voice. Again the unseen world that scared him so was peeking around the corner, waving to him.

"Yeah, but I'm all right now," Remy said, eyes searching the room. In the corner there was a stack of cheap sweatshirts with various Boston colleges' insignias decorating the fronts. He darted over to the stack, snatching up one of the heavy pullovers. Using the sweatshirt as a buffer, he carefully pulled the two blades from the floor, wrapping them tightly in the heavy fabric.

"I need to take these," he said, doing all he could to ignore the whispering from the blades that he could still hear inside his head. Even through the layers of cloth, he could hear them—feel them.

Mulvehill just stared.

"You can have the others," Remy stated. "But I need to take these. This is much bigger than a case of stolen property."

"Detective?" a voice called from the apartment's doorway. It was one of the drivers from the medical examiner's office. "Is everything all right?"

Mulvehill looked briefly from the doorway of the room back to his friend. "Take them," he said. "Something tells me they're not something we should have lying around in Evidence anyway."

Remy bit the inside of his cheek, fighting the images of murder and death that tried to fill his mind.

"You're right," the angel said, resisting the urge to throw the daggers away.

Mulvehill stepped into the doorway so that he could be seen by the man at the entrance to the apartment. "I'm just wrapping things up," he said. "I'll be right out."

The detective gave a casual wave and returned to Remy.

"Thank you," Remy said.

"Are you going to be all right with those?" the detective asked. "You look a little green around the gills."

"I'll be fine," Remy said, "but the sooner I get rid of them, the happier I'll be."

He followed the homicide detective through the building, out the front entrance, and down onto the street. The crowds had diminished slightly, many of the gawkers probably tired of waiting for something horrible to see, satisfied to go home and watch it on the evening news instead.

"I'll let you know what I find out," Remy whispered in his friend's ear as he headed in the direction of his car.

Mulvehill was lighting up a cigarette. "Watch your ass," he muttered, cigarette clamped between his lips. Some of the remaining crowd gave the man talking to himself a sideways glance before turning their attention back to the apartment building.

The diehards will be getting their payoff soon, Remy thought, cutting across to the side street where he'd parked his vehicle. *Dougie's bagged body will soon be coming out on a stretcher, a prize for their endurance.*

The Pitiless daggers beneath his arm screamed to be noticed, but he managed to close his mind to the disturbing imagery they tried to force upon him.

Remy got to his car and tossed the wrapped blades down onto the passenger seat. His thoughts raced with what he would need to do next.

He slipped the key in the ignition, deciding that he would continue on to Karnighan's. The old man had to know more than he was letting on. The engine turned over, and he thought that it might be wise to give Ashley a call to go over and feed and walk Marlowe. Who knew how long the business in Lexington would take, and he didn't want his four-legged friend back home to suffer.

He was thinking that Francis might need a call as well when the black SUV seemed to appear out of nowhere, cutting him off as he pulled out of the parking space, blocking his exit.

He'd been around long enough to know that nothing good was about to happen.

The truck's doors opened and four familiar faces emerged.

This shit never gets any easier, Remy thought, almost sure that he could hear his angelic nature chuckling to itself as the four Denizens who had attacked him at home surrounded his car.

He didn't have Marlowe to worry about this time, and that was good.

"You told me to call when I had something," Remy said as he slowly got out of the car, his attention focused on the spokesman from their last meeting. "I don't have anything yet, but you never know, I might be coming into some information shortly."

"My employer says that you're taking too long," the spokesman said.

There was a barely perceptible nod, and one of the Denizens was coming at him, his hand inside his coat pocket.

Remy didn't have time to wait to see what it was. He met the fallen angel halfway, moving as quickly as he could, slamming his fist into his attacker's face.

The Denizen stumbled back, nose spurting blood, a short knife with a blade seemingly made from a polished black stone clattering to the ground.

Remy was glad he hadn't waited; that particular blade, made from the walls of Tartarus, could have done some serious damage to him.

He knew the name of only one of them, Balam—the one that had pointed a gun at his dog—and decided that he would deal with that one next. The memory of what he had done caused a terrific anger to flare within

Remy, and he let the Seraphim inside have a brief taste
of freedom.

Balam hadn't pulled his gun, and Remy figured they
probably wanted him alive, but this particular Denizen
was large and powerful, moving far more quickly and
gracefully than Remy expected. He threw a punch that
Remy attempted to avoid, but he moved a tad too slow,
and the man's knuckles grazed the side of his face. It
hurt like hell, and for a moment he saw an explosion of
stars.

Balam took immediate advantage, gripping him by
the back of the coat and pulling Remy toward him. The
arc of his fist was a blur as the hit connected with Remy's
stomach, doubling him over with a painful explosion of
air from his lungs.

Again with the stomach.

But it had brought him close enough.

Close enough to strike.

Remy allowed Heaven's power a moment's freedom,
the fires of the divine collecting at the tips of his fingers.
He thrust his hand at Balam's stomach, the burning fingers connecting with the satiny material of the dress shirt
he wore, burning through, and into the flesh beneath.

And the fire did not stop there.

Balam screamed as his body began to ignite, the fires
of Heaven fueled by his wickedness. He immediately
dropped to the ground and began to roll.

"Oh, for fuck's sake," the spokesman moaned, rolling
his eyes.

There was movement to his left, and Remy whirled,
the man who had tried to stab him earlier was charging.
Where's the knife? His thoughts raced as he grappled
with the fallen, trying to keep his hands in view. They
tumbled to the ground, each of them trying to get the
better of the other.

The remaining attacker must have ducked around
Remy's car, coming at him from a blind spot.

Remy wasn't even aware that he'd been stabbed—in

the shoulder—until he felt his entire right side begin to grow numb.

Fists were raining down from above him as he attempted to get up, but one of his legs had become useless, tingling and trembling.

"That's enough," he heard the spokesman say, and the two Denizen thugs stepped back.

The leader stood over him, a hate-filled flicker of fire burning in the center of his eyes. "If my employer didn't think you were valuable to him, I'd have you cut to ribbons and sold to anybody who wanted a piece."

Remy's shoulder throbbed with the steady beat of his heart. "Why don't we cut the bullshit and you just tell me what's going on," he grunted as he struggled to stand.

"I will kill him," a dry hiss of a voice rasped. His buddy Balam tried to get at him but was held back by two of the others. His body still smoldered, the Heavenly fire having badly burned his face and chest as it spread. He had his gun out and was waving it around.

Remy was almost on his feet when the spokesman came forward and, with a kick, knocked him back down to the ground.

"We've been watching you, waiting for a chance to talk to you without your Guardian angel friend being around."

They were afraid of Francis, and he couldn't blame them. He'd had a scary reputation even before he fell from God's grace.

"We think you've found some things out," the spokesman said. "Things that my employer would be very anxious to hear about."

"You first," Remy said, lying on his back, finding it very difficult to keep the world from spinning. "First tell me why your boss is looking for the Pitiless, and I'll fill you in on what I know. Who knows, maybe between the two of us this whole mess will start to make some sense."

The spokesman came toward him then, the fire of his hate burning even brighter in the center of his coal black eyes, but then a sudden voice interrupted his murderous intent.

"Hey, Arioc," one of the Denizens called.

Arioc, the name echoed inside Remy's skull.

"You might want to see these," one of the fallen angels said.

Remy managed to pull himself into a sitting position. They were at his car, the passenger door open. The Denizen was handing his superior the bundled sweatshirt with the daggers at its center.

"No!" Remy barked, and again attempted to climb to his feet. This time he was successful, lurching toward his vehicle.

"What have we here?" Arioc asked, hefting the item handed to him. "Do we have something more here than dirty laundry? By your reaction, I would have to say that's a big yes."

They all laughed. The Denizen who'd searched his car, and had been the one to stab him, again came at him from behind, pushing Remy roughly up against his car.

Face pressed to the cold metal of the hood, he managed to twist his head enough to see what was happening. The Denizens were all standing around their leader as he unwrapped the sweatshirt.

Remy could feel himself beginning to fade, finding it harder and harder to remain conscious as the poison from the Hell blade's bite continued to course through his system. He was forced to drop the barriers again, allowing the power of Heaven to course through his frame, burning away the toxins that if allowed to spread would kill him.

He was able to stand now, a sudden vitality making his muscles hum with divine power.

Arioc had exposed the blades, eyes wide in wonder as he looked upon them. He reached within the cloth, removing one of the daggers and holding it up. The blade glinted seductively in the glow of a streetlight that had just come on. By the twinkle in his beady eyes, Remy could tell that the murderous images conjured by the weapon were now filling the Denizen's mind. The fallen angel smiled, reveling in their intensity. He held the dagger aloft, pointing it into the sky, toward Heaven.

"Oh, isn't this the sweetest thing," Arioc said, as all eyes were glued to the seductiveness of the single Pitiless.

Remy was at a loss as to what he should do. He was considering the insanity of trying to get the blades back and making a run for it when things went from bad to worse.

It didn't even register at first, his brain attempting to process what it had seen, and then attempting to delete the information as a side effect of having the shit knocked out of him again.

The wind had kicked up; at least he believed it to be the wind. There was a sudden rush of air—a roar—and something far more substantive was moving amongst the Denizens.

Arioc's head was suddenly gone from his body, the crimson arterial spray shooting up into the air like a fountain. The others barely had the opportunity to take their eyes from the Pitiless blade still being held aloft before they too were taken down.

Balam was next to go, his burned and blackened facial features registering danger well before the others.

Remy started to yell as Arioc's headless corpse finally collapsed to the ground, the stump of his neck still pumping blood out onto the street. He pushed off from the car, his warrior's nature urging him into battle. Closer now, he could just about make out the blurred shape of the thing that moved amongst them. It was large, about the size of a jungle cat.

The thing from the vision he'd experienced back at the apartment. The thing that had killed Dougie.

Balam was attempting to get a bead on the blurred

shape with his gun when his hand was abruptly no longer attached to his wrist. Remy watched the hand, still holding the weapon, sail through the air, bouncing off the side of the SUV and clattering to the ground.

It had all happened so fast that the fallen angel didn't seem to know that he was now weaponless, pointing the bloody stump at the shape that circled him, preparing for its next strike. Balam's stomach was torn open next, the burned flesh sounding like the crackling of autumn leaves as the former angel was savagely disemboweled.

Whatever it was that attacked them was nearly invisible to the human eye, it moved so quickly. Fueled by the Seraphim's lust for battle, Remy advanced toward the bloody scene. Another of the Denizens had gone down, while the other looked on, stunned, his face spattered with the blood of his companions.

Remy squinted, altering the composition of his eyes to look upon the world not as a human, but as an angel, and at last he was able to see what exactly they—*he*—was up against.

It had the shape of a large dog, but its body resembled that of something that had had its skin pulled away to reveal raw sinew and musculature. Its pointed head seemed to be made entirely of exposed bone, its yellow eyes like two LEDs illuminated from within the deep black caverns of the eye sockets.

It was perched on the back of the third Denizen, who thrashed beneath the thing's weight. The dog thing eyed Remy before lowering its head to bite into the back of its prey's neck, and with a savage shake, it broke it. The beast was drooling, and Remy noticed that everywhere the saliva touched, it sizzled and burned. The unpleasant image of Dougie's burned open belly filled his head, and he suddenly understood.

The monster looked back to Remy, distracted from the remaining blood-spattered Denizen, who stood frozen in place, his eyes riveted to the terror that had laid waste to them.

The thing's body was rigid except for the slight movement of its yellow eyes. Remy stared back at the beast, attempting to draw it closer to him, away from the other man.

The surviving Denizen began to back away, but his movement caught the attention of the animal. It turned with a shrieking hiss, as its red-veined muscles tensed to pounce on the escaping prey.

The nature of the Seraphim exerted control, and Remy found himself bounding at the animal as it prepared to strike. Remy snatched up the Pitiless dagger that Arioc had dropped from a cooling puddle of blood, and then found the other still nestled snugly within the confines of the sweatshirt lying in the street.

In his hands, the daggers began to sing an aria to the glory of the violence to come.

This is what they had been created for.

The beast sprang, catching the remaining Denizen with little effort, and was about to maul him savagely when Remy launched himself through the air, twin daggers poised to strike.

The animal looked away from its prey, mouth open in a roar of savagery, a roar drowned out by the cry of a warrior.

A warrior of Heaven.

CHAPTER NINE

The beast was in motion, turning from its fallen prey to attack Remy. With a powerful thrust, he plunged one of the Pitiless daggers into the bloodred flesh of its muscular hide as it descended. It tossed its skull-like head back in a bellow of pain and he slid the second blade into the soft tissue below its jaw.

The animal panicked, its powerful form recoiling from the attack. The beast was not accustomed to its prey biting back, and Remy managed to jump backward, taking the bloodstained blades with him as he avoided the monster's slashing black claws.

The Seraphim rejoiced in its freedom, Remy barely maintaining enough control to prevent its power from fully manifesting. He battled not only the wild monstrosity crouched and growling before him, but the fury of the angel within.

It begged to be released, demanded to be fully free, but Remy ignored the commands, desperate to hold on to his humanity. Yes, it had become wounded over the last few months with the death of his one true love, but it was not yet dead, and he had no intention of allowing it to be eclipsed by the ancient power fighting to emerge.

Distracted momentarily by his inner struggle, Remy reacted too slowly as the monster pounced again. He managed to get only one of the daggers up as the full weight of his bestial attacker fell upon him. He pushed up on the dagger as he was driven back to the ground by the behemoth's full weight, the animal's tough, leathery hide resisting the piercing point of the Pitiless blade.

He hit the ground with tremendous force, his head striking the ground with equal intensity, and his world exploded into a reality of flashing colors and overwhelming nausea.

Fighting to remain conscious, he looked up into the eyes of the behemoth, laser points of yellow like the final moments of a dying star as it burned its last in the thick velvet tapestry of the night sky.

Its breath stank of blood and something else.

Brimstone.

And he then knew where the creature had originated, but he did not have the slightest clue as to how it had come to hunt upon the streets of Boston.

It was a question that nagged at him as the weight of the beast crushed him against the unyielding street, the darkness exploding inside his head, making it difficult to focus, making it difficult for him to remain conscious.

He watched through a spreading black haze as the beast drew back its bony face, its jaws opening wide before its jagged bite descended toward his throat.

Explosions of thunder crashed in the heavens as a curtain of darkness fell, sparing him the moment of his unpleasant demise.

The Pitiless blades chattered.

Even deep beneath the crushing waves of unconsciousness he could still see the moments of their existence. Death after death; he thought he would drown in the blood spilled by their being.

Eventually the visions of death ran thin, and he was shown the sight of their conception and birth, materials mined from the earth, nothing but raw matter to be melted down to liquid and poured into molds to be crafted into the objects of death they would become.

But the special knives wanted him to see more, wanted

him to know all their secrets. They took him deeper into their memories, showing him what they were before they had fallen from the sky to the world of man.

What they were before they were dropped from Heaven.

Heaven?

The darkness was suddenly ablaze with a vision of one of the Lord's chosen—the angel Azazel, weapons master of the angel hosts, working his artistry within the hallowed confines of his workshop within Heaven's armory. Rows upon rows of beautiful armament lay waiting for the day that they would be called upon in battle.

Remy knew—*sensed*—that this was a time before the war, before the fall.

Azazel's wings fanned the flames of a fire that burned hotter than the center of a sun. The armorer worked the stuff of Heaven, manipulating the divine material, shaping it into a thing of the utmost beauty, as well as a tool of devastation.

Remy could now see what it was that the angel armorer worked upon, what he toiled so diligently to produce.

One had already been birthed, lying there patiently, waiting for its sister to be completed.

The Pitiless daggers.

The sight of them in such a holy place filled Remy with a dire sense of foreboding. He was tempted to call out, to ask the angel why it was that he had produced the twin daggers, when the angel turned to speak—but not to him.

There was another present—another who hung close to the shadows, watching the birth of the deadly armaments.

Having completed the second of the pair, the angel weaponeer turned, holding the glowing daggers in hand, presenting them to the figure cloaked in shadows. The light shining from the still-white-hot metal dispelled the pockets of darkness within the workshop, revealing the figure that stood there in wait.

As beautiful as Remy remembered him to be, he was adorned in armor the color of the sun's rays, his sharp, noble features looking as though they had been sculpted by a master's hand ... which they had.

He was the first of the angels, and favorite to the Almighty.

He was the son of the dawn ... the Morningstar.

He was Lucifer.

And the Pitiless belonged to him.

Remy awoke with the warmth of the Morningstar's radiance still upon his face.

He was lying on his back upon a plush leather sofa, arms draped across his chest, a Pitiless dagger still clutched tightly in each hand. They were still whispering to him, attempting to pull him back into the visions of their violent glory, but he'd had just about enough of that.

Rising to a sitting position, he forced his cramped fingers open, allowing the twin blades to fall to the Oriental rug on the floor beneath him.

A fire burned cozily in the large marble fireplace across from where he sat, and he looked around the room at the beautiful floor-to-ceiling bookcases that covered three of the walls.

He was in somebody's study; he could at least figure that out. But whose was the million-dollar question.

The back of his head throbbed, and his body ached in places where he didn't think it was possible to ache. The animal ... he'd been fighting the animal when he'd been knocked cold. Remy touched the back of his head, wincing from the tenderness there.

The door into the study opened, and a large, bald-headed man, who Remy could sense was a Denizen, peered in at him.

"Hey," Remy said, having never seen the man before. He was hoping for some answers.

The man didn't respond. Instead he turned to somebody outside the room. "He's awake, sir," the fallen angel said as he stepped back into the hallway.

Remy rubbed gently at the back of his head, trying to make the throbbing pain go away. It wasn't doing much, but the continuous ache was helping to clear away the fog that had settled over his brain.

The bald man appeared in the doorway again, opening the door wider for another to enter, a tall, handsome figure with long blond hair that came down to his broad shoulders. And Remy then knew where he had ended up, but not how he had gotten there. Another heaping portion of mystery, on an already overflowing plate.

Yum.

"Hello, Byleth," Remy said from the couch, eyeing the daggers to make sure they were within reach.

Byleth smiled as he strolled into the study, dressed in dark slacks and sports coat. The bald man came in as well, as did another Denizen lackey. They eyed him with distaste, which Remy could understand. He doubted they had much opportunity to mingle with Seraphim since their fall from grace, and imagined that his presence would likely remind them of things they'd rather remain forgotten.

"It's good to see you, Remiel," Byleth said, using his angelic name. "Or would you prefer that I call you Remy?" he asked with a chuckle.

Remy shrugged. "It's been a long time since the old name actually meant something to me," he said. "You can call me what you like."

Byleth brought a long-fingered hand to his chest. He wore a red silk shirt, the top buttons undone to reveal part of a pale, muscular chest. There were gold chains around his neck. "I actually go by William these days," he said, turning to approach a wooden cabinet in the corner.

"Drink?"

He opened the doors, removed a cut-crystal decanter,

poured one glass, and then another. He delivered one to Remy on the sofa.

"William," Remy said, taking the offered drink. "I wouldn't figure you for a William."

"No?" Byleth asked, taking a sip from his own glass.

Remy drank as well. It was Scotch, a really good Scotch—better than the stuff he'd drunk the other night with Mulvehill.

But would a Satan of the Denizen underworld serve anything less? Remy doubted it.

He'd heard through the grapevine that Byleth had taken the title but had preferred not to give it much thought.

The Denizen crime lord took a seat in the chocolate brown leather wingback chair across from Remy, beside the fireplace. He crossed his legs, resting the glass of fine Scotch on his knee.

"First I want to thank you," he said with the slightest of nods.

"For?" Remy asked.

"You tried to keep my men from getting killed," he explained. "I appreciate the gesture."

"I was mainly looking out for myself," Remy said, taking a small sip from his glass. "Knew that whatever the hell it was would be coming for me eventually, and I wasn't wrong. You wouldn't happen to know how I survived the encounter, would you? Last thing I remember I was about to have my face bitten off."

"One of my people; he managed to empty a gun into the back of the animal's head."

"Kill it?" Remy asked.

Byleth shook his head. "But it seemed to take enough of the fight out of it so that he could bring you here," he said.

"I'm pretty sure it was looking for these."

Remy prodded the knives lying on the rug with the toe of his shoe.

"I think you're right," Byleth agreed, eyes momentarily fixed on the weapons at Remy's feet.

"Any idea what that thing was exactly?" Remy asked. "It smelled like Hell."

"From the description my man gave me, I'm not surprised that it did." The Satan smiled slyly, drinking more of his Scotch.

"No, it smelled like the place," Remy corrected. "It smelled like the place where God sent you and your lackeys when you decided to follow another leader."

Byleth chuckled. "I know what you meant."

Remy wasn't laughing, waiting to see if the fallen angel would give him any more.

"The inmates of Tartarus call them Hellions," Byleth went on, "a form of life especially created by our loving Lord God to hunt down any who might have the good fortune of escaping Tartarus to the wastelands."

The Satan went eerily quiet, his eyes glazing over as he enjoyed more of his drink.

"What's a creature of Hell doing on the streets of Boston?" Remy asked with a snarl, feeling his patience being seriously tested.

"You said it yourself," Byleth commented, and pointed to the twin objects at Remy's feet. "It probably has something to do with them."

"Great," Remy scoffed, taking a large gulp of Scotch to fortify himself.

Byleth laughed out loud. "It's good to see you again, Remiel," the fallen angel said. "It really is."

Remy did not answer, swallowing the alcohol, allowing himself to feel its warmth spread through his chest. And as much as he cared not to, he remembered the last time he had seen Byleth.

When they were still brothers in service to God.

Before Byleth's fall.

*   *   *

Eden, Before the War

"There you are, Byleth," Remiel of the Heavenly host Seraphim said, dropping from the rich, blue sky, his magnificent wingspan spread wide as he slowed his descent to touch down in the lush Garden below him.

"Shh," the angel of the host Virtues hissed as he peered through the thick underbrush at something Remiel could not yet see.

"What is it?" he asked, moving aside the thick vegetation to see what it was that so captivated Byleth.

There were two creatures; the female appeared to be bathing, while the other—the male—lay in a patch of warmth, one of the animal residents of the Garden, a large cat, its orange body adorned in black vertical stripes, lounging beside him.

All appeared at peace in their surroundings.

"A fascinating addition to His growing menagerie," Remiel commented on the bipedal creatures the Lord had named "human." From what he understood, they had been made in His image and designed so that they could replicate, a talent that only the Lord of Lords had been able to perform—until now.

These creatures had been given the gift of creation.

"*Fascinating*," Byleth commented, his eyes never leaving the Almighty's latest works. "Not exactly the word I would use in describing them."

Remiel looked to his friend for further clarification.

"*Dangerous* would be more appropriate, from what I hear," Byleth whispered.

The female waded from the tranquil green waters to lie with her counterpart upon the shore. They truly were fascinating. Remiel saw so much of their own angelic design in their creation, but at the same time they were very different.

"Don't be foolish," he scoffed. "Dangerous to whom? To us? To the All-Father? That's ridiculous."

"I didn't believe it either," Byleth said, "but Lucifer was so insistent."

"What did Lucifer say?" Remiel asked, curious as to what God's most favored had to say about these newest creations.

"He says that these . . . these *humans* will replace us in His eyes."

Remiel watched as the female cuddled beside her partner. He placed his arm around her in a loving embrace, and they held each other by the cool emerald waters of the lake, in the blessed Garden, two separate pieces that together formed one.

The Lord had outdone Himself in their conception.

"Lucifer says that there will come a time when He will love them best," Byleth said.

There was something in the angel's eyes, something Remiel had never seen in their kind.

Envy.

And like the most virulent disease, it would soon begin to spread.

To contaminate.

"It's been a long time," Remy said, the memory of that moment in the Garden fading into the background of his past. He had more of his drink, watching as Byleth . . . *William* slowly nodded. Remy imagined that he was remembering as well.

"Being Satan of your little family of misfits must agree with you," Remy added. The two thugs that had accompanied their boss into the study visibly tensed, looking toward their employer to see his reaction.

Byleth chuckled, letting one of his expensive Italian loafers dangle from his foot. "It's only a title for those who wish to recognize it," the fallen angel said. "There are many Denizens out there who see me only as one of their own, another of those who lost their way doing penance for their sins."

"And some who look at you as the big boss," Remy added. "A leader to guide them in their often illegal pursuits."

Byleth looked at him intensely over the rim of his crystal glass tumbler. "I twist no arms, Remiel," Byleth said, holding the glass to his mouth but not drinking. "They come to me of their own free will. Isn't that right, Mulciber . . . Procell?" He looked to his men, one, then the other. They just smiled smugly.

"There are those words again . . . *free will*," Remy said, swirling the golden liquid around in his glass. "We were so jealous of humanity when He chose to give it to them first." He paused, remembering all the strife that it caused in Heaven, and the tumultuous aftereffects when God at last bequeathed it to them. "But once we had it, we didn't handle it too well. And from the looks of your nasty little family, you're not doing too well with it now either."

Byleth held his glass out, and the large, bald fallen took it from him. "Thank you, Mulciber," he said. His man took the empty glass over to the liquor cabinet and set it down. He then returned to his position on one side of his employer's chair, the second of Byleth's goons on the other. They continued to glare at Remy, genuine hate leaking from their eyes.

"Who's to say?" Byleth responded to Remy's last comment. "It's their choice, and they do with it what they wish. Some choose to live out the remainder of their existence amongst His greatest and habitually flawed creations, waiting for the slim chance that they might be forgiven and allowed back through the pearly gates, while others choose a different path."

Remy polished off his drink, smacking his lips as he placed the empty glass down on the leather couch cushion beside him. "I've always wanted to ask this question: Do you guys actually get some kind of enjoyment out of being bad, or is it all about pissing Him off? Do you think He even cares at this point? I mean, He's already tossed you out; I'd say it's likely that He's written you off by now, wouldn't you think?"

"We can only hope that He's still watching ... seeing how easy it is for even His chosen creations—his beloved *humans*—to fall from grace ... to forget Him and His holy word so easily when the opportunity presents itself," Byleth said with a certain amount of pleasure.

The Denizens reveled in the weaknesses of humanity, taking immense pleasure in leading them down a path of corruption. Drugs, prostitution, gambling; if it could somehow stain the human spirit, they were likely part of the equation, pulling the strings from the shadows.

There wasn't a nicer bunch of guys on the planet.

"It's all we really have left," Byleth offered. "And we take from it what we can."

Remy took the Satan's answer for what it was worth. "Fair enough," he said. He noticed that Mulciber and Procell had stopped giving him the hairy eyeball and were now looking at the area near his feet, at the twin daggers that still lay there. Remy wondered if the knives were somehow attempting to communicate with them as they had with him, filling their heads with their greatest hits.

He leaned forward, picking the twin daggers up from the rug, and watching as all present physically reacted.

"So, what can you tell me about these?" Remy asked. The knives were trying to get into his head again, but he was ready this time, blocking the violent imagery and focusing on the here and now.

"Nothing much to tell, really," Byleth said, uncrossing his legs, planting both feet upon the floor. He was staring at the Pitiless with hungry eyes. "I first learned of them just before my release from Tartarus," the Satan said. "They were whispered about ... their purpose a mystery."

"That was quite some time ago," Remy said, rubbing the flat of his thumb along the hilt of one of the knives.

The weapon seemed to purr, enjoying his attention. "Why the sudden interest now?"

Byleth reclined in the chair and sighed, looking as though he was relaxing, but Remy knew that wasn't the case. "They were supposed to be special, but as far as I knew they were lost, hidden away someplace waiting for somebody to discover them. I never gave them much thought beyond that, really, focusing my talents on building a power base amongst the Denizen community. It was a long, uphill battle, but one I relished, and eventually managed to win."

"Do they give you a special decoder ring, or maybe even some decorative horns when you make Satan?" Remy asked. Obviously he'd been spending way too much time with Francis.

He could see Byleth's men tensing, just waiting for the word to pummel him. But he doubted they'd do it, even if ordered. Remember, he still had the knives.

"You're much funnier than I ever remember you being," Byleth responded with a sickly grin. "Is it something you intentionally work at, or does it come as a result of living with them . . . living as one of them?"

"It was either this or in-line skating," Remy explained. "I went with being funny; it's something I can do all year-round."

The onetime friends glared across the study at each other. Remy could tell that the window for friendly conversation would be closing soon, patience wearing thin, and he needed some answers.

"So what put them back on your radar?" Remy asked, holding the twin daggers up, points to the ceiling. All in the room were feeling it, the daggers' power charging the air.

"Recently released parolees from Tartarus had heard some murmurings from within the prison walls; something big was about to happen and the weaponry was somehow involved."

Remy slid to the edge of the couch. "That was it?

Some parolees talking shit? There had to be more than that."

"They said that there was a change coming," Byleth said, the intensity growing in his gaze.

"And let me guess, you don't like change . . . especially if it involves you. You like things just the way they are."

The Satan smiled, a pale imitation of the beatific appearance he once had when still loved by God. "Exactly," he said. "So I put the word out, that it could be quite profitable to anybody who could find these weapons for me. I figured if they were in my possession, they couldn't do me any harm, and if they were as special as people said, nobody would dare try and fuck with me."

Remy gazed at the knives, stifling the violent urges that attempted to force their way to the forefront of his thoughts.

"They're special all right," he said. He tore his eyes from the sleek, deadly weapons to stare intensely at Byleth sitting across from him. "Do you have any idea what they actually are, or who they were created for?"

The Morningstar's face briefly flashed before his eyes, a surge of rage bubbling up from his center. The Seraphim roared its anger, bucking against the confines placed around it.

"Do you have any idea?" Remy growled, surging up from his seat, letting his arms snap forward, the Pitiless blades spinning through the air before dropping to stick in the hardwood floor before the Satan's feet.

He was glad to be rid of them, the chatter inside his head starting to clear. Byleth's men launched themselves immediately at him, the bald fallen pulling back a fist in order to strike him for what he'd done.

"Don't," their employer commanded, his voice no louder than a whisper.

They stopped midattack, turning to see if their boss was serious.

Byleth had slid from his chair, kneeling in front of the daggers.

"Leave him alone," he ordered, his eyes held to the knives. "He's only given me what I wanted."

Mulciber roughly pushed Remy back onto the couch.

Byleth leaned one of his ears down to the weapons. "I can hear them. . . . They're talking to me." He laughed, reaching out tentatively to one of the blades. "They . . . they want me to hold them."

Remy as well as the two bodyguards watched with curious eyes. He had no idea how the weapons would affect the Satan, if one who had fallen from Heaven would be privy to the visions that had been shared with him.

Byleth's hands wrapped around the hilt of one of the knives, and then the other, tugging them both from the floor. It looked as if the fallen angel had suddenly received a massive electrical shock, his legs sliding out from beneath him as he twitched upon the floor.

The goons made a nervous move toward their employer.

"He's fine," Remy called after them. They turned, staring nervously, unsure if they should trust his word.

"They're just talking."

Byleth thrashed as he rolled onto his back. He held the daggers out before him, a look of absolute shock and surprise etched upon his face. With a sudden groan of exertion, he opened his hands arthritically, the knives falling from his clutches.

His men rushed to his aid, helping him up, returning him to his seat.

"For *him*," Byleth groaned. "The daggers were made for him."

Remy got up from the couch and went to the liquor cabinet. Helping himself, he picked up the crystal decanter and poured another drink. Byleth looked as though he could use it.

"Weapons of the Morningstar," Remy said, handing the fallen angel the glass. Byleth took it from him, slurping loudly at the alcohol. "Weapons crafted for Lucifer's hands."

"It must have been just before the war," Byleth gasped, out of breath from the experience of touching the Pitiless. The effects of the weaponry on the fallen appeared even more severe than they had been on Remy. "Some sort of secret weapons, perhaps."

Remy thought about what Byleth had just said, the idea of weapons as some sort of last-ditch effort rattling around inside his head.

"Secret weapons that were never used."

But if that was the case, why did they end up here . . . on Earth? Remy wondered, not even close to answering the questions that continued to float to the surface of his brain.

"How did you know about my case? How did you know I'd been hired to find what you had been searching for?"

Byleth clung to his glass of booze like it was a security blanket. "Your friend Francis made a few calls for you, asking around. And in turn, those he reached out to got in touch with us. It sounded like we just might be looking for the same thing."

Byleth held out his empty glass. "More," he commanded.

Remy took the glass and poured more Scotch from the decanter.

"Before your involvement, we had been contacted," Byleth said, taking the glass. "Somebody who had heard about my offer to make them rich if they could deliver the Pitiless."

Remy watched the fallen angel drink.

"So you made a deal with this person?" Remy asked.

Byleth nodded. "Arranged for an exchange, but it never happened."

The fallen angel seemed to become even more ner-

vous, getting out of his chair to fix his own drink. His
movements were awkward, a shaking hand dropping the
crystal stopper from the bottle, good Scotch splashing
over the rim of the glass to be wasted as he filled it to
the brim.

"I'm guessing that something besides your seller
standing you up happened."

"You could say that." Byleth laughed nervously, pouring the contents of the glass down an insatiably thirsty
gullet.

Remy urged the Satan to go on with a stare.

"We were attacked," he said. Remy could see that his
hands were shaking, and wasn't sure if it was still the
effect of connecting with the powerful weapons, or this
recent memory. The fallen leader appeared unnerved.

"Rival host, maybe even a Hellion of your very own?
What attacked you, Byleth?" Remy urged.

The fallen angel's eyes got suddenly glassy as he gazed
into the past. Slowly he made his way back to his seat,
swatting away the helpful attentions of his bodyguards.
He lowered himself into the folds of the wingback.

"He dropped out of the sky like a falling star," the
Satan said. "He was beautiful . . . as we all were once."

Byleth looked at Remy, smiling sadly.

"An angel attacked you?"

He nodded. "Something wasn't right about him. He
was enraged, filled with a violent anger, going on and on
about a sin that he couldn't bear anymore."

A sudden twinge of recognition stabbed at Remy,
like a jab from one of the powerful blades.

"Was he a Nomad, Byleth?" Images of the poor creature that he and Francis had rescued from a dissecting
chamber flashed before his eyes.

Remy reached down to grip the fallen's shoulder, to
urge him to answer.

Mulciber immediately grabbed hold of Remy's wrist,
attempting to pull it away. The Seraphim did not take
kindly to being touched by one of *them,* and Remy al-

lowed it to emerge, taking hold of the large man's arm and twisting it violently to one side. Pulling the big man closer, Remy drove his forehead into the Denizen's face.

The fallen grunted, blood exploding from his nose as he dropped to his knees moaning. The other Denizen made his move, but Remy froze him with a stare.

The Seraphim liked this, wanting to make the foolish creatures suffer, but Remy restrained it. This wasn't the time for games.

"Byleth?" he said firmly.

"Yes, yes, he was a Nomad." He tried to have some more to drink, but his glass was empty. "I didn't think of it at the time . . ." Byleth stopped, remembering the details. "But I think he was trying to warn us."

Remy felt his anger flare, the Seraphim right there, eager to be set loose, but he held its leash tight. "But you didn't listen."

Byleth turned in the chair, anger burning in his eyes. "Of course we didn't listen; even though a Nomad, he was still one of them . . . still of Heaven. And he wanted the weapons that we didn't have."

"What did you do?" Remy asked, already knowing the answer.

Byleth laughed, slumping in the chair. "We saw it as an opportunity," he explained.

Mulciber was still moaning, attempting to stifle the flow of blood that poured from his damaged nose.

"We captured him," the Satan continued with a certain amount of pride. "It wasn't easy—he was strong—but at the same time, I don't think he had all his faculties. It was almost as if something . . . some knowledge that he had locked away inside his head had driven him mad."

It took everything that Remy had not to grab Byleth and beat him senseless. "You captured him and you cut him up," he said through gritted teeth.

Byleth smiled weakly, knowing that what he had done was wrong, but still taking pleasure from it. "Normally

I wouldn't have had anything to do with it, but with this one . . . I cut out his eyes."

Remy's true nature fought harder than he could ever remember, and he could feel his skin begin to itch—to heat—as the warrior angel rose to the surface, ready to emerge and destroy these abominations in their nest. And Remy doubted that the unleashed Seraphim would have stopped there, flying into the night, hunting every Denizen it could find and destroying them one after the other.

This might have happened—if there hadn't been a knock at the door.

It was just enough of a distraction to avert disaster.

"Yes," Byleth called.

The door opened and another of his men stood there. He was holding a cell phone.

"It's somebody named Mason," the fallen angel said.

"He says that he's out back and to tell you that he's found what you've been looking for."

CHAPTER TEN

Remy didn't like the sound of that.

Byleth pulled himself together, running his long fingers through his straight blond hair. "It appears to be my lucky day," he said. He removed his sports coat and squatted before the daggers.

"Depends on how you define *lucky,* I guess," Remy said, watching as the Satan wrapped the knives in his jacket. "What are you going to do with them?"

"What do you think?" Byleth asked, a nasty glimmer in his eye. "They were to be Lucifer's. The power of Heaven flows through them. Imagine the clout somebody with these bad boys in their possession would have."

Remy couldn't believe his ears. "You can't be serious," he said. "There's something not right about this whole business," the angel started to explain. "The kind of not right that involves a creature from Hell and an angel driven crazy by guilt. Do you seriously want to wrap this Pitiless albatross around your neck?"

"Losing Heaven nearly destroyed me," Byleth began. "My time in Tartarus was nothing compared to the pain I felt . . . still feel . . . when God took it all away."

The Satan looked to his men.

"Restrain him," Byleth commanded.

Mulciber seemed to have learned his lesson; his face stained with blood, he looked to the floor. But not the other, the one that Byleth called Procell.

Remy had wondered about that one, not at all physically imposing, but there was something about him that flashed caution. He planted his feet, preparing for a physical attack that never came.

The fallen angel Procell lifted one of his hands, and Remy noticed the elaborate tattoos—sigils—that had been drawn upon the pale flesh. He didn't have a chance to react as the Denizen waved his fingers in the air, an incantation of angel magick leaving his lips, cast through the air to ensnare Remy in its ancient power.

It was as if a net had been thrown over him. Remy felt immediately weak, the inner power that he suppressed quieted to an electric thrum. It had been ages since he'd been on the receiving end of angel spell casting, and was amazed that he was still conscious. It was like he'd taken an entire bottle of Vicodin and washed it down with a double-Scotch chaser.

Procell's lips moved, uttering the same incantation over and over again, reminding Remy of buzzing swamp insects on a hot summer's night. His eyes looked as though they'd been covered in morning frost.

"You're making a terrible mistake," Remy slurred, swaying slightly in the grip of the magick.

"I've worked and suffered greatly for what I have now," Byleth said, holding the wrapped daggers close to his heart. "And no one is ever going to take it away from me again. Lucifer's loss is my gain." And with that, he turned toward the door and walked out of the room.

Remy stood there, helpless, wondering how long it would be before they figured out that they didn't need him anymore.

Procell droned on.

"Would it be rude if I asked you to shut up?" Remy said to the fallen angel, who of course ignored the request.

And then his gaze fell on Mulciber. He saw a glint of maliciousness in the fallen angel's eyes. "Gonna give a little bit of this pain back," he muttered through gritted teeth.

Mulciber dug into his pockets to remove what looked like a knife. The blade was short, black, chipped from a larger body of stone. Remy made a mental note to Francis to ask him how the fallen from Tartarus were smuggling the pieces of Hell onto the Earth.

"And you're just gonna stand there and let me hurt you," the injured fallen continued.

Remy looked to Procell for backup. "How do you think your boss will feel about this?" he asked.

Procell just shrugged, repeating the incantation again and again, as Mulciber lurched toward Remy.

"First thing I'm going to fuck with is your eyes," he said.

The fallen angel raised the shark-tooth-shaped blade, making sure that Remy could get a good look. "I've let the blade soak in the blood of one of your relatives," Mulciber whispered, his breath stinking of onions.

"I'll remember that," Remy said, his gaze upon Mulciber's eyes unwavering. "And I'll remember you."

The fallen angel laughed, immediately wincing as a new stream of blood started to flow from one of his nostrils.

He sniffled wetly, wiping his nose with the back of his hand as he moved the blade up to Remy's face. He was just about to insert the point into the corner of Remy's right eye, when Byleth came back into the room.

The Satan's expression at first was excited, a flush of pink on his normally pale cheeks, but it quickly dropped when he saw what was about to happen.

"What the fuck is going on here?" he asked in a husky whisper.

Mulciber lowered the blade but stayed close. "I was about to give him a little payback."

"No," Byleth simply said.

The injured fallen whirled, knife still in hand. "No disrespect, but he should receive some of what he's dished out."

Byleth nodded. "You're probably right, but not now."

Remy breathed a sigh of relief, the fear that he might have to wear an eye patch fading away.

Mulciber stepped in close again, the blade slowly rising.

"Is that disobedience I smell?" Remy asked, barely able to hold back his grin.

"Get away from him," Byleth commanded, and Mulciber backed down, stepping away, the blade disappearing back into his pocket.

"Thanks," Remy said, turning his eyes to Byleth, who'd come a bit farther into the room.

The Satan smiled mischievously.

"I want to show you something."

The hall outside the study was paneled with rich, dark oak. Framed black-and-white photographs—from some fabulously chic up-and-coming artist, Remy was sure—adorned the wood walls on both sides.

He followed Byleth and Mulciber, the still-droning Procell steering him down the hallway. At the end of the corridor, they turned the corner, descending a set of stairs where a heavy metal door equipped with multiple locks stood open. More Denizen lackeys waited by the door, standing up straighter as their Satan returned.

"In here," Byleth said, waving Remy to follow as he passed through the door.

The room was large, filled with multiple shelving units, covered in weaponry of every conceivable design and shape from every time period. It was like the Wal-Mart version of Karnighan's place.

"Oh, I see," Remy said, eyeing the racks.

"False alarms," Byleth said on his way across the room toward another door. "Extreme, I know, but I couldn't be too careful. If I had the slightest inkling that they might be part of what I was looking for, I bought them."

At the back door to the storage room he stopped to look at the arsenal he'd accumulated. "They've come from all over the world," he explained, "and there were times that I actually believed I had finally put my hands on the legitimate items."

He paused before opening the door. "But after tonight, I realize that I was never even close."

Byleth threw open the door into a substantial garage; a limousine was parked over to one side, five trendy sports cars parked in a row on the other. A black van had backed into the center of the garage; its back doors were open wide, and the contents that it had carried were already unloaded.

A folding table had been set up just outside the back of the van; three yellow transport cases—the kind that would be used to allow valuable items to travel—had been laid out upon the tabletop like items at a flea market. Remy noticed that the daggers had been placed, still wrapped in Byleth's suit coat, at the end of the table.

A wheelchair-bound Mason, wearing an Evil Dead T-shirt, drove over to meet them. Julia perched on his shoulder, enjoying some kind of biscuit. "Hey, look who it is," the man said cheerily. "Didn't expect to find you here." A fresh trail of drool trickled from the corner of his mouth.

"I'm a little disappointed, Mason," Remy said, eyeing the objects laid out upon the table. "I thought we had a deal."

"Yeah, about that," Mason said. "With the kind of payday our friend here is offering, I'm afraid I'm gonna have to follow that old adage—deals are meant to be broken."

Julia chattered a greeting to him excitedly in between bites of her cookie.

"Hey, Julia, nice to see you too," Remy said to the monkey. "Did you know that your master is a scumbag?"

The monkey squealed with glee, jumping with her treat down from her master's shoulder to his lap, and then to the floor.

"Julia, come back here this instant," Mason demanded.

Instead she climbed up Remy's leg and onto his shoulder, and tried to feed him her cookie.

"Julia!" Mason screamed, his normally labored breathing sounding all the more difficult.

"Have?" the monkey offered again.

"No, thank you, Julia." Remy smiled.

"Julia, you bad, bad girl. Come to me this instant!" Mason carried on.

Mulciber swatted at the capuchin. "Go on," he barked. "Go back to your boyfriend."

Julia shrieked, baring her tiny teeth, trying equally to avoid the hand and to bite it.

Byleth cleared his throat noisily, not amused by the drama. "Are we going to do some fucking business here, or are we going to continue with this Animal Planet bullshit?"

"Go back to your master," Remy whispered to the agitated animal. "That's a good girl. Go on. That's it."

His soothing tone had the appropriate effect; the monkey crawled down to the floor and then hopped back up onto Mason's lap.

"Don't think I won't remember this when it's time for special treats again," the man complained, obviously jealous of the attention the monkey had shown Remy.

Julia ignored him, her back turned to the threats as she continued to gnaw on the special treat that she already had.

"I believe you've brought something here to sell me?" Byleth prompted.

"Yes," Mason answered, shooting a disdainful look at his monkey before turning his attentions toward Byleth. "Yes, I have, and let me say this time I believe I've outdone myself."

Mason moved the toggle on the arm of his chair, spinning the conveyance around.

They all followed him toward the table.

Remy sensed it immediately, a sudden unease permeating the atmosphere of the garage. He noticed that Byleth was looking at him, that stupid grin that he wanted to smack from his face present again.

"I'm assuming you can feel that?" Remy asked him.

"Isn't it wonderful?" the Satan answered. "That's power you're experiencing," he told his former friend. "You're now in the presence of objects that can initiate change."

Remy wanted desperately to move, to grab the Satan by the front of his shirt and shake some sense into him, but that wasn't going to happen as long as Procell kept on with his muttering.

"You're not seeing the big picture," Remy said. "And I'm sorry to say that neither am I. There's something else going on here besides the fight over ownership of these weapons, but I just don't have all the pieces of the puzzle yet, and something tells me it's gonna be too late once I do."

Byleth dismissed him with a wave of his hand. "I've got all the pieces I need," he said, moving closer to the table, eyeing the transport cases. "Once they're mine, I dare anybody to try and fuck with me."

Remy didn't like what he was feeling. It reminded him of that uneasy sensation that built in the air just before the full fury of an electrical storm was released. He would've bet good money that something was about to happen, and double or nothing that it wasn't anything good.

"Madach, I'll let you do the honors," Mason said, and Remy noticed a lone figure who had been standing by the black van as he came toward the table. He hadn't paid him much attention until now.

He was a fallen, and Remy watched him carefully as he approached the cases. The former angel was nervous, his hands visibly trembling as he undid the latches on the first of the cases.

The way he was dressed—paint-stained jeans and work boots, heavy hooded sweatshirt—was as a working stiff. There was something oddly familiar about this particular fallen angel, but Remy couldn't quite put his finger on it.

"Quickly," Mason urged with a lopsided grin. "I think the Satan here is going to be very happy to see what I've brought for him."

Madach stopped before undoing the last of the latches on the final box. "What we brought him," he said in a firm, yet very soft voice.

Mason glared.

"Excuse me?"

"It's what *we* brought him," the fallen explained with emphasis, to be certain that Mason understood. "You and me. I came to you with the product and you said we'd bring it to him together . . . partners."

Julia leapt up and down excitedly in her master's lap, pulling at her loose-fitting diaper, as if sensing the growing agitation in the room, and maybe something more.

"Of course," Mason conceded, turning his temporarily embarrassed face back to Byleth. "Madach was instrumental in me getting these items."

Byleth nodded, eyes riveted on the cases lying on the table. "I appreciate his efforts," the Satan said. "And perhaps, after the transaction is completed, we can discuss how appreciative I am."

This seemed to satisfy Madach, and he finished with the last of the latches, flipping the lid open, and then moving back to the others to do the same, exposing the special contents to their potential owner.

And it was a look, something briefly expressed in the eyes of the fallen angel, that at last jarred Remy's memory as to where he had encountered this person—this Madach—before.

It had been just days ago, in the entryway of Francis'

Newbury Street brownstone. Madach had been leaving the building as Remy had been coming in. He had reacted strangely to Marlowe, afraid that the dog was going to hurt him. Remy distinctly remembered wondering if that particular fallen would fall in with the Denizens, or lead a repentant life as was expected of him.

So much for being repentant.

Byleth looked inside each of the cases, eyes twinkling excitedly. He stopped, reaching down to remove something wrapped in plastic. Eagerly he tore away the covering.

The Colt Peacemaker glistened like gold in the harsh fluorescent light of the garage. Byleth held the six-shooter before him. Remy could only imagine what that piece of violence had to say.

The Satan examined the weapon's loading chamber, his smile growing so wide that it could split his face.

"It's loaded," he said, aiming down the barrel of the gorgeous weapon.

"Strangely enough," Mason gurgled. "It always seems to be that way, even after we've taken the bullets out."

Like a kid at Christmas, Byleth placed the pistol back inside its case, moving on to the next one. He gasped, and as if carefully reaching for a newborn pup, he put his hands inside coming away with an ancient battle-axe. Byleth hefted the heavy piece, holding it out before him, a crazy person's smile upon his face. As he watched helplessly, Remy was stricken with a sense of dread so immediate that if he had been able to, he would have dropped to the ground and covered his head.

There didn't appear to be anything special at all about the axe, the iron weapon tarnished with age, the edges of the blade stained with something dark that he guessed could've been blood. But like the daggers, the ancient weapon had a voice, and it cried out to anyone with the ability to listen, and it was deafening.

"Something isn't right," Remy warned as he looked around the garage.

Procell remained undistracted from his task, while Mulciber came at him unexpectedly to cuff him on the back of his head, knocking him to the floor.

"Shut your fucking mouth," the bald fallen snarled.

On his hands and knees, Remy felt the floor begin to tremble.

A look of confusion registered on Mulciber's face. Momentarily distracted from Remy, he was feeling it too.

The fallen with the broken nose looked back to Remy with questioning eyes as the vibrations coming up through the floor intensified.

"I told you something was wrong," Remy said.

"Satan?" Mulciber called out to his master, he too sensing that things were not how they were supposed to be.

Byleth ignored him, swinging the battle-axe in the air. Remy could only imagine the slideshow of countless lives cut down in the blade's lifetime playing inside the Satan's head.

Mulciber yelled out, this time a little louder, the vibration at their feet growing worse. Procell noticed now, the chanting of the spell that kept Remy mobilized slowing considerably. And still the Denizen leader wasn't listening.

"Hey, dumb-ass," Remy finally yelled, bringing all the attention to him.

Axe in hand, Byleth snarled. Remy knew what he wanted to do with that killing tool, but he doubted the Satan would get that chance. There were other, more pressing matters, soon to be concerned with.

Remy's outburst finally drew the Satan's attention to the fact that something was wrong. The air was thick with the sense of menace.

"What is that?" Byleth asked, looking about the room. The alarms on the sports cars were triggered, filling the confined space of the garage with blaring horns and flashing headlights.

Remy's eyes were drawn to a section of floor, cracks like bolts of lightning zigzagging across the hard surface before the ground erupted.

Chunks of concrete whizzed through the air as the stink of something awful wafted up into the room in an explosion of dust and dirt.

Remy knew what had burrowed up through the earth—he'd encountered one of them only hours ago.

A symphony of gunfire errupted, mingling with the screams of those dying at the claws and razor-sharp teeth of the animals that Byleth had said were created by a loving God to patrol the environment of Hell.

Hellions, the Satan had called them.

And this time there was more than one.

He could move again.

Remy quickly picked himself up, eyes searching through the concrete dust and chaos unfolding before him.

The screams mingling with the thunderous roar of gunfire were deafening. He glanced briefly to his right, at the sight of the spell caster, Procell, lying on his back on the ground, gazing up toward the ceiling and beyond, his right eye having been replaced with a jagged six-inch piece of concrete flooring. He wouldn't be muttering any more spells for quite some time.

The explosion had pushed Remy away from the focus of the attack, and he moved closer to the center of the storm.

It unfolded before his eyes in a nightmarish blur. The Hellions—there seemed to be hundreds, they moved so quickly, but there were only four—were attacking the Denizens with ferocious abandon. They moved from one kill to the next, Byleth's Denizen followers proving no match for their savagery.

Remy skirted around the gaping hole in the garage floor, the stink of Hell beasts still wafting up from where they'd burrowed. A bellow of rage, conjuring brief elec-

trical flashes of similar cries he'd heard upon the battle-
fields of Heaven, drew Remy's eyes to Mason's van.

Byleth still held the battle-axe, swinging it mightily
before him as one of the Hellions stalked closer, on the
hunt for new prey.

The handicapped Mason was struggling to drive his
wheelchair up the ramp and back into the safety of his
vehicle, as Julia screeched in fear. Madach strained behind the man, pushing on the back of the chair, trying to
move the heavy, mechanized conveyance up the ramp
faster.

The Hellion poised to pounce before the axe-wielding
Satan was suddenly thrown sideways by the force of
multiple bullets entering its red, muscular flesh. The
monster roared, spinning around to face its attacker.
Mulciber, armed with a semiautomatic pistol, sprayed
the monster with more bullets.

"Get away from him!" the loyal Denizen bellowed,
emptying the clip uselessly into the durable flesh of the
abomination.

Remy ran across the body-strewn garage, toward the
van and the overturned table. He was looking for the
daggers. They'd had some effect upon the Hell beasts
before, and would likely do so again.

His gun empty, Mulciber attempted to run, tossing the
now useless weapon at the hissing nightmare. The Hellion, its body seeping thick, yellowish liquid from where
it had been struck, sprang at the back of the fallen. It
landed atop him, driving him to the ground, sinking its
razor-sharp teeth into the soft flesh found at the back of
Mulciber's neck.

Even though the Denizen was an ass, Remy was glad
that it had ended quickly for him. And then he felt as
though he had won the lottery as he found the knives,
still wrapped with Byleth's sports coat. He was removing the blades when screaming close by caught his
attention.

Three of the Hellions were converging on the van.

It was Mason who was carrying on, his wheelchair having moved off the metal ramp, trapping him mere inches from the inside of the van.

"Do something!" the crippled man shrieked as he frantically toggled the hand control while Madach struggled to right the cumbersome chair.

Remy shoved the twin daggers into his back pocket and ran toward the van, jumping up onto the ramp, trying to help Madach get the wheelchair back on track.

"Nice to see that you're not dead, Remiel," Byleth yelled from where he was standing at the foot of the ramp moving the Pitiless axe from hand to hand as the Hellions moved inexorably closer.

"I'm guessing we're going to try to use the van to get the hell out of here?" Remy said, grunting with exertion as he finally felt the chair shift, one of the spinning wheels able to find traction on the rubber-covered ramp.

"I think that's the plan," Madach said, attempting to steer the chair so that it didn't go over on the opposite side.

Remy was about to turn, to see how close the Hellions were, when the monkey started to shriek in warning. At first Remy saw nothing except Mason's chair about to pass over the lip and into the back of the van. But then the growl of a Hellion drew his eyes to the roof of the van, and he knew exactly what the monkey had been screaming about.

"Ah, shit," Remy hissed, pulling the twin daggers from his back pocket.

It happened so quickly. The red-skinned beast dropped down onto the handicapped man, flipping the chair backward and sending Madach flying over the side of the ramp.

The capuchin proved her loyalty to the bitter end, launching herself ferociously at the beast perched upon her master's chest. The poor little thing didn't last long, her entire body snatched up and swallowed in the blink of an eye.

I liked that monkey, Remy thought, charging toward Mason. He had liked her better than he had liked Mason even, but the handicapped purveyor of the bizarre at least deserved an attempt at being saved.

Remy screamed as he jammed one of the blades into the side of the monster's head. He felt the dagger enter the thick, sinewy flesh, hitting against a steel-like skull beneath. The creature bellowed, shaking its head furiously to dislodge the troublesome blade. Angered by its pain, it raked its claws down the front of the struggling Mason, tearing away the flesh to expose the handicapped man's inner workings.

At least his screams were short.

Remy darted forward, jabbing the dagger beneath the Hellion's jaw, into its throat. As the monster wailed, Remy reached across, retrieving the first blade from the side of its head, and used it again, plunging it deeply into one of the Hell beast's loathsome yellow eyes.

The beast toppled over thrashing upon the ground, and Remy turned just in time to see the three remaining Hellions attack Byleth.

Remy was glad to see that the time spent in Tartarus had done little to quell the warrior spirit in the fallen angel. Byleth waded into the battle, swinging the axe with deft precision. The Satan proved to the beasts of the pit that he was not an easy meal and would not be brought down screaming.

"Toss those inside," Remy called as Madach climbed the ramp carrying the transport cases for the remaining Pitiless weapons. "We've got to get out of here."

Remy wished that he could be as positive as he sounded. He strode down the ramp, Lucifer's daggers in hand, to aid his onetime friend and brother who had fallen from grace.

"Who'd have thought after all this time we'd be fighting against a common foe," Byleth said, swinging his axe into the face of one of the Hellions as it surged to strike.

They didn't stand a chance against three of the beasts, but if they could provide enough of a distraction, there was a slim chance that they might be able to escape with most of their skin intact.

Remy heard the van engine turn over and immediately pictured a ticking stopwatch inside his brain. There was very little time remaining before they finally grew tired and fell victim to the Hell beasts' savagery.

The Seraphim was aroused by the smell of death and violence in the air, eager to be called upon. Remy struggled with the idea before deciding what he would do.

"Get ready," Remy said to Byleth, their eyes fixed on the Hellions. The beasts had dropped to a crouch, their repulsive, skinless bodies trembling in anticipation of their next strike.

"What are we going to—" Byleth began.

Remy let the Seraphim free, screaming as he channeled the power of God through one of the Pitiless blades, aiming a blast of divine fire toward the black limousine across the garage.

The fire snaked through the front grille, the intensity of the heat causing the headlights to shatter, before the hungry flame found the gas tank, instantaneously igniting its contents.

The limousine exploded with a deafening roar, spewing flaming wreckage and liquid fire, distracting the Hellish creations. The monsters spun toward the roar of the explosion.

"Move—now!" Remy yelled, grabbing Byleth by the arm and hauling him up the ramp.

But Remy did not stop there. Another blast of Heavenly power flowed from his still-outstretched arm toward the small collection of sports cars, their security alarms still blaring. They too exploded at the touch of the Seraphim's might, filling the enclosed space of the garage with even more smoke and fire.

He was running up the ramp, Byleth ahead of him, when he heard the sound. Remy turned his head to find the Hellions scrambling up the ramp after him; his distraction was less effective than planned.

"Go! Go! Go!" he bellowed, pushing Byleth into the back of the van.

Madach put the van in drive, the tires screeching for purchase on the garage floor. Remy lurched forward, falling down hard on the ramp, grabbing to hold on as the van rocketed forward on a collision course with the closed garage gate.

He'd managed to get a foothold, clambering up into the vehicle as it smashed through the garage door out into the cool, spring night. And then it spun violently as Madach slammed on the brakes.

"What's wrong?" Remy shouted toward the front of the van. He looked back into the garage, through the roiling, oily smoke, to see that the surviving Hellions were clustered together, for some reason not pursuing them.

But how long that would last was anyone's guess.

"What's going on?" Remy asked, jumping out from the back of the van.

"Why are we stop—?" he began, only to stop midsentence as he rounded the front of the van and saw them.

The tiny stretch of back alley that ran behind Byleth's converted church home was blocked by five enormous figures, their features hidden in flowing robes that shifted and moved in a nonexistent wind, shimmering like an oil slick upon the water.

Nomads.

Remy could not help but wonder what had brought them here as he stood with Byleth and Madach in front of the van.

"I'm not too sure that this is the best place to be at the moment," he said as he watched the powerful form of Suroth move to the front of the gathering.

"The weapons," the Nomad leader stated with urgency, eyes burning from inside the deep darkness of the hood that hid his angelic features. "Give them to us before all is lost."

Intimidated by the oppressive power radiating from the fearsome beings, Madach and Byleth cowered in their presence, practically driven to their knees.

"I'm not giving them to anyone," Byleth hissed. "They belong to me." The Satan moved toward the back of the van, and Remy reached out, grabbing hold of his arm.

"Not the smartest thing to do right now," he said.

Byleth fought him for a moment, and then stopped. There were sounds behind them in the alley, low rumbling purrs like the idling of a monster truck. The Hellions had found their way out through the fire- and smoke-filled garage.

"If only there was the time to make you understand," Suroth said, flowing a little closer, as did the Nomads at his back. There were many more of them now.

"How about you try," Remy suggested. "Why should we hand over something so potentially dangerous to you? There has to be some good reason."

The Nomad leader's smile grew from within the shadows of his hood.

"You of all of them should know, brother," he said. "For it was this world, nearly brought to its end, that opened our eyes."

Remy glanced into the side mirror of the van to see one of the Hellions coming closer. He guessed that another was probably coming up on the other side.

Call him dense, but it actually took him a second to figure out what the Nomad leader was talking about. The business with the Angel of Death. He knew that narrowly avoiding the Apocalypse had changed things a bit, but he wasn't quite sure what the Nomad was getting at.

"Answers, Remiel," Suroth stated. "The questions we had carried since the close of the war were suddenly answered."

Another glance in the sideview showed that the Hellion was practically on top of them. It was squatting down now, tensing, ready to pounce.

Remy spun around, facing the creature as it leapt.

"Get down," he screamed, pushing both Madach and Byleth out of the beast's path.

The creature soared over their heads to land gracefully in front of the Nomad leader. The other two beasts slunk out from the other side of the van to join their brother.

The Nomad didn't even flinch.

Suroth extended his hand, and Remy watched in awe as the Hellions cowered. Practically on their bellies, the ferocious beasts crawled toward the Nomad leader.

Something told Remy that things were about to become even more interesting.

"You brought them here?" Remy asked, shock and horror evident in his tone.

"Remarkable beasts," Suroth said, lowering his hand to allow one of the Hellions to sniff at his fingertips. A bruise-colored tongue extended from its skull-like mouth to lick the offered appendage. "And exactly what was necessary to find the weapons of change. It took far less time than you would imagine training them, deceptively intelligent and so very eager to please."

Remy didn't know what to say.

"Sounds like another creation of the Almighty, doesn't it, brother?" Suroth chided.

"You trained them," Remy said, the gears turning and grinding inside his fevered brain. "You trained them to find the weapons."

"We trained them to find the tools of change," Suroth added. "And with them in our possession, the next phase of our plans can begin."

"Why do I have a sick feeling that I don't even want to know what that means?" he asked the Nomad.

"Know that it is all for the best," Suroth said, "and that this time, the true victor will reign supreme in Heaven."

It was as if all sound had been bleached from the air.

Remy's thoughts raced at the speed of light, all the pieces of the puzzle trying desperately to come together. What did the Nomad leader mean exactly—*the true victor will reign supreme in Heaven*? He didn't like the sound of that in the least.

The Hellions jumped to their feet with a grumble, the Nomads advancing toward them.

"Give them to us," Suroth demanded.

The idea was certainly tempting. To be free of the weapons—of the crushing responsibility. For a moment it actually sounded like a pretty good plan.

Until he regained his sanity.

The Pitiless were weapons imbued with the power of Heaven's greatest angel, crafted especially for the Morningstar in his bid to challenge the power of God, weapons that never had been used in the Great War, weapons that fell to Earth in the form of divine inspiration, spurring craftsmen to create these ultimate weapons—these precision instruments of killing.

These Pitiless daggers.

Yep, it certainly would be easy to hand them over to the Nomads, to make them somebody else's problem, but much to his chagrin, Remy just didn't work that way.

"No," he said flatly.

Suroth recoiled.

"Something isn't right here, and I'm not about to hand these bad boys over to you until I feel one hundred percent safe in doing so."

The Nomads said nothing, their heavy robes billowing in a nonexistent wind, shimmering with all the colors of the rainbow, and some that were not.

"What are we going to do now?" Madach asked in a nervous whisper, his eyes still riveted to those blocking their path.

"We drive around them," Remy said, starting to move to the back of the van. "I need to know more, lots more, before . . ."

He was interrupted by Denizens running down the alleyway, stragglers from the slaughter that had occurred inside Byleth's garage.

Remy noticed the guns that they were carrying and the smile on Byleth's face, just before it all went to hell.

It was like something out of the Wild West, the fallen angels coming to the defense of their boss ... of their Satan. Bullets fired from pistols and sprayed from semi-automatic machine guns tore into the Nomads and their Hellish pets.

From their reaction, Remy knew that the ammunition was something special, something likely brought over from the planes of Hell. Man-made bullets would never have had this kind of effect on beings from Heaven.

The Nomads stumbled back, the bullets hitting their wonderful robes in small explosions of darkness. The Hellions squatted at their side, flinching from every bullet hit, waiting obediently for their master's commands.

And then Remy sensed it, the hair on the back of his neck standing on end as the air became suddenly charged with an unearthly power. He reached out and grabbed Madach by the shirt, dragging him up the alleyway, toward a green metal Dumpster. That would have to do.

Bolts of crackling-white-hot energy seemingly pulled down from the Heavens erupted from the Nomads' outstretched hands, forming a single bolt of jagged energy that skewered the front of the van with the most destructive of results.

The van flew into pieces, the vehicle torn asunder by the energy that now coursed through it. Singeing slivers of metal, plastic, and glass whizzed through the air, projectiles of death. Remy listend to the sounds of the shrapnel striking the Dumpster, and the screams of Byleth's Denizens as they were cut to shreds by the razor-sharp debris.

The gunfire was silenced, and Remy peeked out from behind his cover.

"It could have been so easy," Suroth droned, strolling through the smoldering pieces of twisted metal that now littered the alley floor. "But to be expected. Change is often so difficult."

"They're dead, aren't they?" Madach said to Remy, gasping for breath.

The fallen was right; the bodies of Byleth's soldiers lay bloody and torn.

But Byleth was still standing. Chunks of glass and pieces of the van stuck out of his body, making it look as though he was wearing some bizarre suit of armor. He had found the axe again, drawing strength from the powerful weapon to remain standing.

"Come at me, then," he growled, blood dripping down from his mouth in a slimy trail. He spun the axe in his hands, swaying from side to side. "I've killed your kind before and am not afraid to do so again."

Remy and Madach watched as some of the Nomads drifted about the wreckage of the van, retrieving the yellow transport cases. He felt Madach tense beside him and reached out to grab hold of his arm.

"But we can't . . ."

"That's right," Remy agreed, turning his attention back to Byleth's fate.

"It saddens me that you could not be made to listen to reason," Suroth said to Byleth.

The Hellions stalked toward the Satan, stopping as he swung the axe at them.

"I've lost everything that's ever mattered to me," he grunted, stumbling toward the Hell beasts, swinging the axe in a wide arc that almost caused him to lose his balance. "And I'll be twice damned if I lose this as well."

The Nomads dropped the battered yellow cases at their master's feet. One of them knelt down, opening a case and rummaging around inside. He carefully removed a pistol and handed it to his master. Even in the faint light of the darkened alleyway, it glistened like the most valuable thing in all the world.

Suroth admired the weapon, hefting the weight of it in his hand.

"The humans certainly do have their talents," the angel said, pointing the weapon at a startled-looking Byleth.

"At least your suffering will be at an end," the Nomad leader said as he pulled the trigger, firing a single shot like a clap of thunder into Byleth's forehead. The Satan flipped backward to the ground, hands still clutching the body of the battle-axe.

The Nomads quickly moved to retrieve the weapon from his corpse as the Hellions darted forward and began to feed upon the bodies that littered the alley.

"That's our cue," Remy whispered, nudging the fallen angel by his side into action. Clinging to the shadows, they exited the alley, and Remy saw that he recognized where they were.

On Massachusetts Avenue they stayed in the cover of shadows, desperate not to be noticed. They had to get as far away from their attackers as possible before they could stop and catch their breath, maybe figure out their next step without the threat of being killed.

It was good to have something to aspire to.

CHAPTER ELEVEN

Remy couldn't believe it; something actually seemed to be going his way.

"Would you look at that," he muttered, leaving the sidewalk, much to Madach's surprise.

"Where are you . . . ?" the fallen started to ask, but then decided to simply follow.

After everything he'd gone through that night, Remy had never expected this. His car was parked in a vacant lot along with the black SUV that Byleth's gang had been driving.

With all the sports cars, and the limousine, of course there wasn't enough room in the underground garage for anybody else's vehicles, he thought, moving toward the Toyota, hoping that whoever had driven it here had left the keys. The thick, acrid smell of fire was prominent in the air, and he was glad at the moment for Byleth's automobile indulgences.

"This is yours?" Madach asked as Remy opened the door and got behind the wheel. He leaned over and unlocked the passenger-side door, allowing the fallen angel to get in, then crossed his fingers and pulled down the driver's-side visor. His keys fell into his lap.

Breathing a sigh of relief, Remy turned the engine over, flinching at the sudden explosion of noise. Someone had taken some liberties with the radio, a country-western station blaring from the speakers. He reached out, quickly turning the volume down to nothing.

They sat there in silence, the only sound the gentle purring of the car's engine. Remy glanced down at himself. He was a mess, his pants torn and stained, one of the sleeves of his jacket and shirt charred black and crumbling from the release of his inner power.

He looked over at Madach, who sat with his eyes closed, head leaning back on the headrest. "You all right?"

Madach nodded. "Fine. Should've figured it would turn out something like this," he said. "I knew it would all turn to shit the minute I listened to them."

There was a bit of a chill in the air, and Remy jabbed the button to turn on the heat.

"Listened to whom?"

Madach laughed before answering. "The weapons," the fallen said, eyes opening. "I was working a job—house painting—a few weeks back, when I first heard them."

The whirling bits of information in Remy's mind suddenly began to click into place.

"You were working at the Karnighan house in Lexington."

This made the fallen angel sit up a bit straighter in his seat.

"Yeah," he said. "How could you know that?"

"Small world," Remy answered. "I was hired to find the stuff that you ripped off."

"That's right; you're a detective," Madach said with a nod. "Mason had said something about a Seraphim that was also a private investigator looking for the Pitiless."

"That would be me." Remy nodded.

"I would have given them away to anybody who would've taken them off my fucking hands," Madach added. "But Mason saw dollar signs when I approached him. He said we could make a fortune . . . that there were plenty of buyers for what we had."

"When I saw you leaving the brownstone on New-bury Street," Remy said, "did you have them with you then?"

At first Madach didn't seem to know what Remy was talking about, but realization quickly dawned. "That was you," he said, forcing a simple smile. "You had the black dog." He started to pick at the skin around one of his fingernails, peeling away some paint that had stained his flesh. "Don't really care for dogs," he said before laughing nervously. "After the garage, you can probably figure out why."

"Marlowe's much nicer than that," Remy said.

"That's good to know. And yeah, I did have them with me."

"So the weapons called out to you while painting Karnighan's house and you decided to break in some night and steal them? Paint me a better picture."

"They didn't just call out to me ... they *called out to me.*" He struggled with the explanation. "They seemed to know me ... to want me to take them." The fallen fidgeted in his seat as he remembered. "I tried to take them that very day, that very moment, but there was something that kept me from entering the room no matter how hard I tried ... something special to keep somebody like me out."

"Meaning a fallen angel?" Remy suggested.

Madach nodded. "I think so. The security lock was nothing. I figured out the code in a matter of minutes, but I couldn't get past the doorframe."

Angels and their puzzles, Remy thought, recalling Francis' Sudoku books. Now why somebody like Karnighan would have security specific to angels in the first place was another question entirely.

Remy drummed his thumbs on the steering wheel.

Unless he knew more about the Pitiless than he was letting on.

"How did you finally end up getting them?"

"I brought help," Madach said. "Human help. One of

the guys that I worked with had a little history, and it didn't take all that much to convince him to give me a hand."

"The guy that helped you," Remy asked. "He live on Huntington Avenue by any chance?"

"Yeah," Madach answered with a nod.

"He's dead, you know," Remy offered.

"That doesn't surprise me," Madach said. "He stole the daggers from the Pitiless stash, replaced them with some of the other antique knives that he'd taken from the house. I think he figured they were more valuable than the other shit just by watching how I acted around them." He paused, working on the skin around the nail again even though the paint was gone. "How did he . . . ?"

"The dogs . . . the Hellions got him."

Madach seemed to physically react. "Nobody should go like that," he said with a furious shake of his head. "After a few days I could sense that those things were around, stalking me, stalking the weapons. At first I thought I was cracking up, traumatic stress syndrome or something like that. I didn't even think it was possible for them to leave Hell, never mind track me down. I think they could smell them . . . the Pitiless."

"As soon as the weapons left Karnighan's house, they became aware of them," Remy said. Once again he was faced with the concept that there was more to Karnighan than met the eye.

"You say *they,*" Madach commented. "You're not talking about the Hellions, are you? . . . You're talking about the ones who are controlling them."

Remy nodded slowly, examining nuggets of information still floating around inside his head.

He thought of his recent dealings with the Nomads, focusing on the incident involving the angel that he and Francis had freed from the Denizens. He remembered some of the dying Nomad's cryptic words of warning.

The deceivers live on, the black secret of their purpose clutched to their breast.

I could bear the deceit no longer . . . my secret sin consumes me. . . .

We should be punished. . . . Oh, yes, we deserve so much more than this.

We're no better . . . than those cast down into the inferno.

And how Remy had tried to explain it all away as insanity brought on by countless millennia of guilt, but now . . .

"They're called the Nomads," Remy started to explain to the fallen angel. "At the beginning of the war they decided not to choose sides, opposing the nightmarish struggle that they were certain was about to unfold."

Madach nodded in understanding. "In Tartarus they're called the Cowards."

"Didn't seem too cowardly to me tonight," Remy responded. "Because of their stance during the war, they call no place their home. They're able to walk between the worlds, just as comfortable in the wastelands of Hell as they are here on Earth, or in Heaven."

"And now they have the Pitiless," Madach said.

Suroth's words echoed inside Remy's mind, madness at the time, but now taking on new meaning.

And with them in our possession, the next phase of our plans can begin.

Know that it is all for the best, and that this time, the true victor will reign supreme in Heaven.

"I think we need to go see Francis," Remy said, putting the car in motion, driving across the uneven dirt surface of the makeshift parking lot.

"What do you think is going on?" Madach asked him. "Why would the Cowards—the Nomads—have any desire to possess weapons with that kind of power?"

Remy left the lot, banging a sharp left onto Massachusetts Avenue, heading toward Newbury Street and Francis' brownstone. He didn't answer the fallen angel, not wanting to curse the situation—to give it strength—wanting so desperately to be wrong.

They rode the few blocks in silence, the tension inside the car becoming nearly palpable as the traffic closer to Newbury Street became thicker, cars stopped in the middle of the street, seemingly refusing to move.

"Is it a breakdown?" Madach asked, craning his neck to see through the windshield.

"I don't think so," Remy said, rolling down the window just as the sensation hit him.

His hands started to shake, his body breaking out in a chilling sweat. He looked across the seat to see that Madach was staring straight ahead, his body trembling as if the temperature in the car had dropped to subzero levels.

"I'm not even going to ask if you're feeling that," Remy said.

The strange sensation, an aura of undiluted menace, pulsated in the air, creating an invisible barrier that caused the people walking the streets, or driving in the vicinity, to have no desire to go any farther, making everything come to a complete stop.

He had an idea as to the cause but hoped he was wrong.

Turning around in his seat to check the rear window, Remy put the car in reverse. He beeped his horn to get the traffic piling up behind him to move so that he could back the Toyota toward Commonwealth Avenue, where he took a left, heading away from the chaos.

"Thank you," Madach said though chattering teeth.

"Don't," Remy stated flatly, his eyes scanning the street for the first sign of an open space. He found one that would require an amazing feat of parallel parking, but he wasn't deterred.

"What are you doing?" the fallen angel asked, panic growing in his voice.

"What does it look like?"

"You can't," Madach stated. "You can feel it in the air as much as I can, and you know what it is." He hugged himself as his body became wracked with painful-looking spasms. "It isn't right," Madach yelled through clenched teeth. "You're not supposed to be able to feel it here."

Remy shut the engine off, pulling the keys from the ignition. As he opened the door, preparing to get out of the car, Madach's hand shot out, grabbing hold of Remy's shoulder.

"We're not supposed to feel Hell here."

"You're right," Remy said, shrugging the hand away and climbing out of the car. "We're not.

"And that's what makes me so goddamn nervous."

As much as it frightened him to admit it, the essence of Hell had indeed come to Newbury Street.

Steeling himself against the feelings of utter despair, fear, and hopelessness wafting down the street at him like a bad stink riding on a gentle summer wind, Remy forced himself forward, fighting his way toward Francis' brownstone.

The sidewalks and street were filled with people, lying where they had fallen—first affected by the waves of misery leaking out from the nether regions, some trembling and crying, others so sickened, so traumatized by what they were experiencing, that they had fallen into a kind of coma, puddles of vomit pooling at their heads.

The closer Remy got to the brownstone, the harder it became for even him to continue. His mind became crowded with thoughts of failure—of the crimes he'd committed against his own kind in the name of God. He saw the death of his enemies—his brothers—his sword cutting them down. With each strike of his sword—each death—the journey down Newbury Street became more difficult.

Remy stopped, pummeled by the memories, the guilt, of his ancient past. Violently shaking his head, trying to force away the overpowering thoughts, he glanced at Madach there beside him.

The fallen angel hugged himself, tears streaming down his face as he gazed fearfully ahead.

"I can't go back there," he said shaking his head. "I've done my penance and I won't go back—I can't go back."

The miasma of anguish that enveloped them was nearly suffocating; Remy felt his legs begin to grow limp, and he was tempted—oh, so tempted—to lie down on the street, curling up into the tightest ball that he could imagine, to escape the sensations he was experiencing.

Anything of importance had left his mind; all he could think about, all that he could dwell upon, was the failure to his own, to his Lord God Almighty.

To Madeline.

It was as if he'd a received a shot of pure adrenaline directly to his heart, the image of his wife's smiling face, like the rays of the sun, burning away an oppressive fog. Thoughts of her loss, and of how he had failed her on so many levels, niggled at the edges of his memory, but they had not the strength to dampen the joy and love he felt for her still.

Remy straightened, focusing on his surroundings. They were less than two blocks away.

Madach had dropped to the street. He sat there rocking back and forth, head buried in his hands.

"Get up," Remy said, reaching down to haul the fallen angel up by the arm.

"I can't . . . ," he complained.

"You can and you will," Remy stated firmly, using this moment of clarity to propel himself and his companion forward. "If it wasn't for you, this wouldn't be happening. You're coming with me just in case I need a hand."

He pulled the struggling Madach along, maneuvering him through the body-strewn street until they finally reached the steps of the brownstone.

Wave after wave of sensations, the likes of which Remy had never felt before, washed over him. Hell had indeed come to Earth and it was leaking from the brownstone.

Madach was a quivering wreck, trying to sit down on the building steps, to hide from the destitute feelings that threatened to cripple him.

"I . . . I just can't," the fallen said, his voice a pathetic squeak. But Remy would not allow him to sit down, holding on to his arm and dragging him up the stairs toward the door.

The fallen angel's complaints fell on deaf ears, Remy's only concerns being that he get inside before he himself was reduced to a quivering pile of jelly. He had to know what was going on. He had to know the fate of his friend.

Remy opened the heavy wooden door and pushed Madach in ahead of him. The inside foyer door was open and Remy dragged Madach through the lobby to the door to the basement and Francis' apartment.

Reaching for the doorknob, he felt the pulsations of the infernal place radiate from the crystal knob, a warning of what he was likely to find on the other side.

Again he steeled himself with the memory of Madeline, and like a suit of armor, it protected him against the relentless onslaught of the dispiriting atmosphere.

He took the knob and turned it, pulling the door open and letting it bang off the wall as he stood in the entryway looking down the stairs. Voices drifted up from the room below, voices that sounded familiar.

Madach shuffled closer. "We're going . . . we're going down there?" he asked, gulping noisily as he stared down the steep set of steps that led to the living area below.

The voices continued, followed by some menacing music that strangely enough seemed to fit the situation. Eerie pulses of light caused bizarre shadows to dance around what little they could see of the room waiting at the bottom.

"Looks like it," Remy said, already beginning his descent.

He stopped momentarily to give Madach a look, making sure that he wasn't going down alone.

The fallen angel pulled his act together, using the banister as he leaned against the wall, taking each of the descending steps slowly.

They were closer to the source. It was all Remy could do to keep from blacking out with the intensity of malevolence that hung in the air like smoke.

"We've got to keep it together," he told Madach, who didn't appear to want to leave the next-to-the-last step. He stood there, body rigid, petrified.

"You're doing fine," Remy told him, walking into the living space. "Don't make me haul you off those steps."

His words having their desired effect, Remy listened as Madach descended the remaining stairs and followed at his back.

Nothing appeared abnormal. The strange, shifting light and the sound of voices were caused by the television set. Remy took note that Francis had been watching *Jaws*. There was a half-eaten sandwich and cup of coffee sitting on the table, next to Francis' chair.

"Where is he?" Madach asked through trembling lips.

Remy didn't answer, approaching the television and turning the volume down to nothing. He hated to do it. His favorite scene was on: Quint's speech about being on the *Indianapolis*.

But it didn't become completely quiet.

He saw that Madach was carefully looking around the space, zeroing in on the source of the additional sound.

"It's coming from over there," he said, pointing with a nearly lifeless hand at the narrow corridor that ended with the worn door to Hell.

Remy moved down the hallway, the noise growing louder the closer he got to the door.

"I don't think . . . I don't think you want to go down there," Madach said at his back, and Remy had to agree.

He didn't want to go there, but there really wasn't much choice.

Madach stopped at the edge of the darkened corridor as Remy continued.

The door was closed, but a radiance of palpable hopelessness emanated off the paint-blistered surface of the wood, and the sounds coming from the other side—he hadn't a clue how to describe them. They were like the raging of a powerful storm, the sounds of nature's fury muffled only by the fragile barrier that kept the storm at bay.

Something was wrong on the other side of that door.
Horribly, horribly wrong.

Remy wanted to quit, to drop down to the floor, allowing the sins and failures of his very long life to wash over him, to drag his body out into an ocean of anguish but Madeline helped him to fight, her memory urging him on.

The doorknob was both excruciatingly hot and numbingly cold in his grasp. As he was about to turn it, he looked to the end of the hall to see Madach standing there. The fallen looked as though he had aged twenty years, his body stooped from the Hellish emissions that pummeled them.

"Don't," he begged, a plaintive hand reaching out trying to convince him not to do what Remy knew had to be done.

He had to find out what was going on, and what fate had befallen his friend.

He had to know about Francis.

Remy turned the knob, throwing open the door to a blast of intense, lung-shriveling heat, followed by suffocating cold.

Through watering eyes Remy gazed in horror at the sight before him. Francis stood upon the bridge of writhing, fallen angels in the midst of battle, a bloodstained sword in one hand, a gun in the other. From out of the icy prison streamed a steady flow of prisoners, their mouths open in ululating screams of madness and rage as they attempted to put him down, fighting to get past the only thing preventing them from making their way toward the exit and the earthly plane beyond.

Remy stared, frozen in place by the sight of the former Guardian angel as he dispatched wave after wave of his attackers. He was relentless in his defense, as were the fallen in their attempts to remove him from their path. For every fallen angel that fell beneath the boom of gunfire, or was cut in two by the bite of his sword blade, there seemed to be four more scrambling over the decimated corpses to take their places.

"What's going on? What do you see?" Madach cried, temporarily distracting Remy from the disturbing scene playing out before him.

Remy glanced to the end of the hall and then back through the doorway. He had to do something; the number of fallen angels spilling out from the prison onto the bridge was growing unmanageable, many of the pale-skinned attackers tumbling over the side of the bridge of angel flesh to the Hellish landscape waiting for them below.

He started onto the bridge, the bodies of the fallen that comprised the structure quivering beneath the heel of his shoes.

"Francis," Remy yelled.

The Guardian turned and his face twisted at the sight of Remy.

"Get back!" he screamed, quickly returning his attention to the marauding fallen, cutting down five more before looking back. "Get back into the fucking apartment!"

Remy hesitated, not sure what he should do. It wouldn't be long before his friend succumbed to the ever-increasing number trying to escape.

He started forward again, feeling the stirring of the Seraphim within. He would have to let it out if he was going to be of any significant help to Francis in holding back the ravening hordes emerging from Tartarus.

Francis turned back again, his favorite suit tattered, spattered with blood, his horn-rimmed glasses missing.

"Don't you fucking listen?" he bellowed, shoving the handgun into the waistband of his pants and reaching inside his jacket pocket to remove something that chilled Remy more than the frigid air radiating from the frozen prison at the bridge's end.

Francis held a grenade, something that he'd likely picked up wholesale from one of the many weapons suppliers that he did business with.

"I said go back." And with those words he pulled the pin on the round, olive green explosive device, rolling it across the uneven surface of the flesh bridge, where it became trapped within one of the open mouths of the angel-damned.

Remy knew what was about to happen and turned quickly, running back toward the open door.

The force of the blast propelled him through the doorway, face-first into the corridor wall, the deafening roar of the explosion and agonized screams of the fallen angels that made up the bridge suddenly cut off by the slamming of the door behind him.

CHAPTER TWELVE

Remy rolled awkwardly onto his back, the metallic taste of fresh blood filling his mouth. He leaned his head back against the wall of the narrow corridor, and gazed at the dilapidated door, listening to the sudden silence.

Slowly Madach moved down the hallway toward him. "What happened?" he asked, cautiously eyeing the closed door.

Remy scrambled to his feet, his human form aching in more places than he could count. He ran a hand across his mouth and nose, wiping away the blood there.

"He closed it."

Remy took hold of the doorknob again, experiencing none of the extreme sensations he had before. The emanations from Hell had stopped completely. Throwing the door wide, he gazed upon a utility closet; the most menacing things inside were an ancient mop and a plastic bucket.

"He closed it," Remy said again, looking fitfully to Madach. His mind was on fire. Something terrible was happening in Tartarus, and he was almost certain that the Nomads were responsible, and that it all revolved around the Pitiless weaponry.

A spasm of cold went up his back, so powerful that it nearly broke his spine, Suroth's words again echoing in his ear.

This time the true victor will reign supreme . . .

He liked the sounds of them even less now.

Pushing past the fallen, Remy went out to the living area, his brain humming as he tried to piece together every piece of information he'd gathered and form it into something he could act upon.

But there were still too many gaps.

"So what now?" Madach asked, much calmer now since the radiation from Hell had stopped.

Remy dropped down heavily upon the couch. "Good question," he said, throwing up his hands in frustration. "I'm stumped." He strained his fevered brain even more, staring at a particular section of pattern on the carpet beneath the coffee table until it blurred.

"The Nomads took the Pitiless for some kind of purpose," he said aloud. "And from what I just saw, it has something to do with Tartarus and the prisoners there."

Madach leaned against the doorframe. "They're going to break them out," he said suddenly.

Remy looked up, urging him on with his eyes.

"They're going to use the power of the weapons to free all the fallen angels still being punished in Tartarus."

A sick sensation began to grow in the pit of Remy's belly, something horrible and malignant expanding in size as he realized how close Madach likely was to being right.

"They're going to free all the prisoners," Remy muttered, again hearing the Nomad leader's chilling words.

This time the true victor will reign supreme . . .

Tiny pinprick explosions of realization erupted all across the surface of Remy's brain and suddenly he knew the horrible, deadly truth.

He bolted up from the sofa, going to the closet in the corner of the room adorned with the original poster from *The Wild Bunch*. He grabbed the latch and gave it a pull. As expected, it was locked, but he couldn't—wouldn't—allow that to stop him. He gave the handle a forceful twist followed by a tug and listened as the lock broke, pieces of the mechanism clattering around somewhere inside the closet door.

Remy pulled open the door, exposing Francis' treasure trove of violence: everything from bladed weapons to guns of almost every caliber, shape, and size. It was a closet filled to the brim with instruments of death.

"Was your friend expecting to fight a war?" Madach asked, coming to stand beside him.

"He liked to be prepared," Remy said, reaching for one of the handguns—a Glock—hanging from a peg. He hoped that Francis had a hefty supply of the special ammunition he would need to deal with the kind of threat he believed he was going up against.

Madach reached for one of the handguns too.

"You don't have to do this," Remy said, finding the ammunition in a small wooden box and loading a full clip. Even touching these special bullets, created from materials mined in Hell, made him feel sicker than he already did.

"Yeah, I think I do," Madach answered. He took a gun, staring at it in his hand. "You said it yourself. If it wasn't for me, none of this would have happened."

Remy slipped the loaded clip into his gun.

Madach helped himself to some of the special bullets, doing as he'd watched Remy do. "Who knows," he said with the hint of a sad smile, "if I do some good maybe I'll get time off for good behavior, and I'll be able to go back home all the sooner."

Remy scowled, not even wanting to think of Heaven. If what he suspected was going on, he was disturbed to see its lack of involvement. It just proved to him again how dramatically things had changed, and not for the better.

"So what now?" the fallen asked, carefully loading his weapon.

"I had some dealings with the Nomads a few days ago," Remy said. "Only thing I can think of right now is to check out where I found them last and hope they've left clues as to where we go next."

Madach stared at him blankly.

"I know, the plan sucks, but it's all I've got right now."

His phone started to ring and he reached inside his coat pocket to retrieve it.

"Hello," he said, placing it to his ear.

There was a long pause, and Remy was about to hang up on the call when he heard the unmistakable sound of labored breathing. He almost laughed, an obscene phone call at a time like this, but then the caller managed to speak.

"Mr. Chandler," it gasped, and he recognized the voice.

"Karnighan?"

"Come to Lexington, Mr. Chandler," the old man wheezed, sounding as though he was teetering at death's door.

"Karnighan, I certainly will be coming to Lexington. You've got a lot of questions to answer, but right now . . ."

"Come to Lexington, Remiel," Karnighan interrupted, using Remy's angelic name as if he'd known it all along. "It's time you knew what is going on."

Mulvehill wasn't picking up, so Remy left a message.

"Hey, it's me," he started, leaning back against his parked car. He wanted to be sure to phrase what he had to say right. He didn't want to frighten his friend, but how else could he explain that he might not survive the next few hours? "Listen, I've got a favor to ask."

Remy glanced back up the street toward Mass Avenue. Things looked as though they'd returned somewhat to normalcy. He was sure the multiple fire trucks and police cars and hazmat teams were still milling about upper Newbury Street. As he'd left the brownstone, he'd heard murmurings about some sort of weird gas leak.

Whatever helps them make it through the night, he thought.

"Things have gotten a bit intense," he started to explain into the phone. "Not sure how much deeper I'm going to be sucked into this and I was wondering if you could . . . if need be . . . take care of stuff for me."

He felt a raw, painful surge of emotion that he was more than willing to blame on the residuals of the Hell leakage, but deep down Remy knew that it wasn't the case. These were the emotions he'd suppressed—pushed down deep—since Madeline's death. They bubbled to the surface now, hot . . . burning.

Infuriating.

It was a product of that damn humanity he'd worked so hard to achieve. All part of being human.

"I know you've said you're not good with dogs, but . . . if something should happen to me . . . would you take care of him . . . of Marlowe?"

He thought about his animal friend, feeling guilty about how much the simple creature had had to endure over the past few months.

"I'd really appreciate it if you would do that for me." Remy paused, not knowing how to go on. He really didn't have anything more to say.

"Thanks, buddy," he finally added. "Take care of yourself and . . . well, I hope to see you later."

He thought about telling Mulvehill how much his friendship had meant to him over the years, but decided that in the long run it wouldn't have been worth the punishment. If he managed to survive what was ahead, and had left a message pretty much professing his love for the man, any moment spent afterward with the homicide cop would be unbearable, the teasing that he would have to endure more painful than the tortures of Hell.

Why take a chance?

He pocketed his phone and got into the car.

"Everything all right?" Madach asked, staring straight ahead with unblinking eyes.

"Had to put some stuff in order, just in case."

Remy slipped the key into the ignition and turned the engine over. Pulling out of the parking space, he

drove down Comm Avenue, trying to get as far from the
commotion surrounding Newbury Street as possible. He
swung around the Public Garden, then past the Common and the State House, tempted to stop and see Marlowe one more time. But as usual, time was wasting. He
picked up 93 by Haymarket and headed north out of the
city. It was a roundabout route but it would eventually
get them to Lexington and Karnighan's mansion.

They drove in silence, Remy lost in his thoughts, trying to recall every minute detail of the case, carefully
picking through the information in search of something
he might have overlooked.

"What did you see back there?" Madach asked, his
voice startling in the quiet of the car.

Remy glanced briefly at the fallen angel, both hands
upon the wheel as he drove up Route 2 in light traffic.
"What do you mean, what did I see?"

"Back when we were walking to Francis' place," Madach explained. "When Hell was leaking out onto the
street. What did you experience?"

Remy thought about how to answer the question.
He finally just shrugged. "A lot of things I regret,"
Remy stated, eyes fixed to the road. "Things I wish
I could have done differently, but at the same time I
know there really wasn't much of a choice."

"Choice," Madach repeated, laughing a bit sadly. "It
was all about choice . . . and so many of us making the
wrong one, y'know?"

"But you had to have believed that what you were
doing was right," Remy added. "No matter how mis-
guided, you were fighting for something you believed
in."

The fallen angel laughed all the harder. "I don't even
remember anymore," he said. "I was just overwhelmed
with this sense of utter desperation."

Remy felt his stare, so intense that it was hot upon
his cheek.

"I was filled with hatred and sadness over what I had

done," Madach finished. "I still am. I should never have been released from Tartarus."

"But you were," Remy said, taking note of the exit signs. "I can't see many mistakes being made there."

"Yeah, I guess. And look how I repaid that faith," he said, shaking his head in disgust.

"Not the best of moves," Remy added, flipping on his signal as he moved over to the right-hand lane to exit. "But maybe you'll have a chance to redeem yourself tonight."

"Or maybe I'll just make the wrong choice again."

They rode the remainder of the way in silence, a knot of apprehension forming solidly in the center of Remy's belly as he drove through the gate of Karnighan's home, and up to the house.

Remy opened the car door, reaching down to release the latch that would open the trunk. Going around to the back of the car, he removed the duffel bag stuffed with weapons that they had taken from Francis' home.

"What are you bringing those for?" Madach asked.

"Just in case." Remy slammed the trunk closed and waited, looking around the property.

"What's wrong?" Madach asked, standing beside him.

"Karnighan has dogs, but they don't seem to be around."

"I let Dougie deal with them," Madach said. "Guess he ground up some sleeping pills and put it in hamburger. I wanted them asleep before I even got out of the car."

Remy walked toward the front door, slipping the strap of the heavy bag over his shoulder. "I doubt they're asleep now," he said as he reached out to ring the doorbell, but then he noticed that the door was ajar.

"Shit," he hissed.

He pressed his fingertips against the heavy wooden surface and pushed; the front door silently swung wide, exposing the empty foyer.

The lights were on, but there wasn't a sign of Karnighan.

"After we dealt with the dogs, we got in through a side door in the garage out back that I had left open the day before. We knew that the old man wouldn't be around because he specifically told the foreman that we shouldn't work on Friday 'cause he'd be away on business. It was the perfect opportunity—the one Dougie and I'd been waiting for."

They stepped into the foyer and Remy closed the front door. Everything seemed pretty much the same as he remembered.

"Doesn't sound like you had to twist Dougie's arm all that much to get him to help you," Remy said, speaking in almost a whisper, gesturing for the fallen to follow him. He was tempted to call out Karnighan's name but decided against it. No need to call attention to their arrival; the old man knew that they were coming.

"We got in and went right to the room downstairs," Madach continued. "Dougie wanted to have a run at the whole place, but I wouldn't let him. We'd come for the weapons, and that was it."

Madach swatted his arm, getting Remy's attention.

"That should count for something, don't you think?" the fallen asked. "If I'da let him, Dougie would have ripped him off blind."

"You'd think," Remy acknowledged as they passed through the room that was being painted the last time he'd been there. The job had been completed since then, the ceiling now a robin's egg blue, the trim painted white. There was a baby grand piano in the corner, and a leather couch and sofa positioned around a long coffee table, its surface covered with large hardbound art books. It was like something out of a home design magazine, Remy observed as they passed through and approached the corridor that ended with the elevator.

"We headed down in the elevator and I worked on the combination for a while," Madach said.

"Puzzles, right?" Remy asked. "You're good at solving puzzles?"

The fallen angel nodded. "You should see me with a Rubik's Cube."

The aroma floated lightly in the air, and could easily have been lost amongst some of the other scents of the spacious home, but it snagged Remy's attention, filling him immediately with dread.

"Down here," he said, taking a right at the top of the corridor, away from the elevator, following the smell down another hallway to Karnighan's study.

"Smell it?" Remy asked, approaching the study.

Its doors were open wide, inviting them to enter.

Madach bent his head back and sniffed at the air. "What am I supposed to be smelling? All I'm getting is new paint."

Remy had forgotten how much the fallen had lost from their original states of being; senses once so acute that they could smell the stink of sin had been dulled by their plummet from grace. They'd had so much taken from them, it was no wonder the Denizens had turned against the Lord God and all that He stood for.

This is where he and Karnighan had shared coffee and talked about their business arrangement.

It hadn't smelled of blood then.

The odor was nearly gagging in its intensity as Remy entered the room, and there was little doubt now as to what it was. He stopped, eyes darting around for the source. A lone reading lamp in the far corner of the room provided the only light and there Remy saw someone crouched upon the bare hardwood floor within a circle of blood.

The man worked busily, painting with gore. The body of one of Karnighan's guard dogs—*Daisy*—lay just outside the circle, her stomach slit open vertically, exposing her innards. The man dipped one of his hands within the dog's stomach for more to paint with. The room was in disarray; the furniture and priceless Oriental rug had all been pushed away to the sides of the room, giving the mysterious figure room to work.

"What's going on?" Remy asked, his anger aroused. He'd liked Daisy quite a bit.

The man, who was dressed in a long, oversized bathrobe, flinched at the sound of his voice.

"Remiel," the artist croaked, as if his throat was choked with dust. "I didn't hear you come in."

At first he was startled at the use of his angel name by this stranger. He watched as the kneeling man slowly turned himself around within the circle of blood. Then with the aid of a cane that Remy had not noticed lying on the ground beside him, he rose unsteadily.

And he was a stranger no longer.

"Karnighan?" Remy asked, not believing his eyes.

The sight of the man was disturbing to say the least, nothing but paper-thin skin and bones, the heavy bathrobe threatening to swallow his entire skeletal form. It was like looking at an Egyptian mummy Remy had once seen at the Museum of Science, brought to life by some kind of dark, powerful magick. There was no way this mockery of a man should have been alive.

But he was.

The living cadaver nodded tremulously, leaning upon its cane. "Yes, for now," Karnighan croaked, the sound of something wet and loose rattling somewhere in his throat. The figure swayed like a Halloween decoration in a cool October wind.

"What's happened to you?" Remy asked.

Karnighan jerkily stepped closer, a crooked grin that might have been a smile but was more likely a grimace of pain on his cadaverous face threatening to tear the paper-thin skin. He looked down at his bloody work.

"All part of the story that I need to share with you," he said, leaning upon his cane to lower himself back down to the floor. "I'll have to talk and work at the same time," he wheezed. "I'm not sure how much time I still have . . . how much we all have, really."

He could still reach Daisy's corpse, and stuck his fingers into the wound again.

"What's going on?" Remy asked as the old man added details to what Remy—on closer inspection—realized were sigils of angel magick.

"They're going to try and use the Pitiless to free him," the living corpse said. The scent of death hung heavy in the air, and Remy wasn't sure if it was the body of the dog or Karnighan himself.

Though he'd hoped to be wrong, Remy's suspicions were correct, and he felt the world drop away from beneath him. All the pain and suffering—the penance—it was all going to be for nothing.

It's going to start again.

"Lucifer," Karnighan spat, furiously working, his face mere inches from the floor.

"They're going to set the Morningstar free."

"Why would the Nomads do that?" Remy asked the living skeleton kneeling beneath him.

"The Nomads," Karnighan repeated, stopping briefly, his breath coming in short, ragged gasps. "Is that who they are? The ones who managed to acquire the weapons?"

Remy gave Madach a sidelong glance, then looked back to the old man. "In a roundabout way, yeah."

Madach came closer, no longer a figure in the background. "I stole them," he confessed. "I was working in your home when I heard them. . . . They . . . they called out to me . . . and with the help of a friend, I took them from your house."

Karnighan rose from his work, looking at the fallen through squinting eyes. "I was going to ask who you were, but I recognize you now." He pointed at Madach with bloodstained fingers. "You painted in the den." The old man nodded, knowing that he was right about where he'd seen the man before. "You say that they called to you?" he asked.

Madach nodded. "I tried to ignore them, but it was impossible. I would've gone nuts if I hadn't done something. It's no excuse, but . . ."

Karnighan returned to his work. "I'd say it was impossible. I thought I had silenced the weapons' voices cloaked their very presence in this house by all manner of angelic sorcery, but here you are confessing to the act."

The old man reached deep inside Daisy's stomach, pulling something from the slaughtered animal. Squeezing the crimson moisture from it, he began to draw again.

"Curious."

"What's happened to you?" Remy asked again, still starving for answers.

Karnighan dropped down closer to the floor to add some detail that seemed to be going around the inside of the circle. "It was a deal I made a long time ago," he started to explain while he toiled. "They promised me a long, long life if I did what they asked of me, swore my allegiance to them, and performed the task they set before me."

"They?" Remy questioned, but the old man was on a roll.

"It was on my deathbed in the summer of '17. I'd made my living traveling from town to town with my collection of oddities; I'd traveled the four corners of the world in pursuit of the strange and bizarre. Anything that I imagined separating a country hick from his two bits was worth acquiring for my road show. It was a good life while it lasted, but I'd come to the end of the line. Cancer. On a road between Arkansas and Texas, I came to the painful realization that I wouldn't make my next engagement, that the curtain was about to fall on Karnighan's Traveling Show of Rarities and the Bizarre."

Karnighan paused, straightening slightly, the vertebrae in his back snapping and popping like fireworks on the Fourth of July.

"I was afraid as I lay alone in the back of my wagon, surrounded by the objects that had been almost like family to me. And as the time of my inevitable demise came closer, I began to pray."

The old man laughed wetly and started to cough.

The cough soon became worse and Remy moved closer to the circle and to the man within to see if he needed help, but Karnighan raised a spidery hand and waved him away.

"I'd never had any religion. I was raised by the most resolute of atheists," he gasped as he caught his breath. "But at that moment as I lay dying alone, I decided to give praying a chance, just in case there was some-body . . . something out there listening."

He chuckled again, but managed to keep from coughing.

"There was, as I'm sure you already know, and they communicated with me by using one of the artifacts in my exhibit. I listened as they told me they were emis-saries of Heaven, speaking through the mouth of the most moth-eaten of stuffed gorillas, explaining that they required the services of an earthly soul and had heard my pleas for continued life. They said I was exactly who they were looking for."

For a moment, Karnighan was clearly back in the past. He gazed out over the study as if he was seeing it all play out again.

Again Remy asked who *they* were, but the old man either ignored the question or did not hear.

"They wanted me to continue with my life as it had been, traveling the globe in search of objects of won-der, with one difference. I was to look for weapons, but not just any weapons—these weapons had been shaped from the stuff of Heaven, dangerous and powerful be-yond anyone's wildest dreams. I was to find them, collect them and hold them in my possession; and as long as I did that, I would live, forgoing the passage of time."

Madach swallowed with a wet-sounding click, drawing

attention to his presence there. "But when the Pitiless—
the weapons of Heaven—were stolen, the years . . . the
cancer came back for you."

Karnighan's skull bobbed up and down on its stalk of
a neck. "Now you can see why I was so desperate to get
them back," he said. "The longer they are out of my possession, the faster the hungry years claim what has long
been denied them."

Remy shook his head slowly, realizing once again that
he'd been drawn into the machinations of Heaven, and
those who followed God's holy word.

"These . . . Heavenly emissaries," Remy asked. "Tell
me about them."

"Oh, you're quite familiar with them, I believe," Karnighan answered. "As they are with you . . . Remiel of
the host Seraphim. They told me that you were a great
warrior of Heaven who had lost your way, and that by acquiring you to search for the Pitiless, I would help you to
find your way back home."

Remy knew of whom Karnighan spoke even before
the old man uttered their names; roiling spheres of
Heavenly fire, adorned with multiple sets of all-seeing
eyes.

God's personal assistants.

"The Thrones believe that you are the only one who
can help us to avoid disaster," Karnighan said. "They
gave me what I needed to procure your services."

After he had helped to prevent the Apocalypse, Remy
had refused their offer—*God's offer*—and rejected a return to Heaven. It seemed, however, that they still had
plans for him.

"They'd always known the intention of the Pitiless,"
Remy stated.

"Which was why they were so eager to have them
all collected, and hidden away," Karnighan explained.
"They knew that the possibility always existed that
powers still loyal to the Morningstar would attempt to

obtain these weapons forged in the fires of Heaven, and use them for that nefarious purpose."

"You mentioned angel magick," Madach said. "That special spells were used to hide their existence from any that might be looking. How was it that I could hear them? That they spoke directly to me?"

Karnighan thought about the question, a hand sticky with blood slowly making its way up toward his shriveled mouth.

"Perhaps the magick had degenerated over time, or perhaps something happened in the ether to weaken the spell's strength," he suggested.

Remy immediately thought of the disappearance of the Angel of Death and the consequences that had followed, and wondered if that could have had something to do with the weakening of the magick that had hidden Lucifer's armaments.

"A mystery for another time," Karnighan said, bending forward to continue with his work. "There are more pressing matters to attend to."

Remy hadn't thought it possible, but in the brief time that they were there, Karnighan's physical appearance seemed to have become even worse.

"I must finish what I've started," the old man croaked, reaching into the animal's body again and moving his hand around.

"Would one of you be so kind as to bring me another?" Karnighan asked, pointing to an area of shadow in the far corner of the room where more dog bodies lay.

Madach responded to the request, probably figuring it was the least he could do after causing such problems. "I don't have a problem when they're dead," he said, grabbing the corpse of a dog by its collar and dragging it across the floor over to the circle.

"Did they have to die?" Remy asked.

The old man sighed, laying a crimson hand consolingly upon the dead dog's rib cage. "As much as it pained me, yes."

Madach pulled Daisy's body away.

"Angel magick is based on loyalty and sacrifice to the art," Karnighan explained, spindly fingers exploring the insides of the second once-faithful animal. He continued to draw the tiny intricate symbols along the inside of the circle. "The blood of the faithful is pertinent to the completion of this magick, pertinent to stopping the Nomads from completing their heinous objective."

"What are you doing?" Madach asked, squatting down just outside the circle for a closer look.

"I'm constructing a new doorway," Karnighan replied. "If all has gone according to plan, all the doorways leading to the earthly realm have been closed."

The memory of Francis tossing his grenade, and the devastating explosion that followed, replayed in Remy's head.

"Is that smart? Opening a new doorway?" he asked. "If Tartarus was breached, that means the prisoners have been freed and . . ."

Karnighan looked up from his art to glare at Remy. "Then how else will I get you there?"

Deep down Remy had known that it was likely to come to this. As much as he despised being drawn into the affairs of Heaven and Hell, he'd suspected that there would be a chance he would have to go there to avert disaster. And then there was Francis. He would need to check on the safety of his friend as well.

"You'd think the Thrones would have a better handle on this," Remy groused, walking to the study's entryway and kneeling beside the duffel bag they'd brought from Newbury Street.

"I believe they know exactly what they're doing," Karnighan said, having just about completed the circle of sigils painted with the blood of innocents.

Remy removed a short sword from within the bag,

hefting its weight. He then removed the Glock that he'd loaded earlier, at Francis' place.

"So I'm guessing they want me to cross over into Hell, and do what I can to prevent them from releasing Lucifer," Remy said.

Karnighan surveyed his bloody work with a tilt of his head. "That sounds like the plan," he answered. "My final instructions were to bring you here and to open a doorway."

Madach knelt by the bag and began to rummage.

"What are you doing?" Remy asked him.

"Picking weapons," he said as he withdrew a fearsome knife with a six-inch blade.

"No," Remy stated. "You've helped enough."

"I can do more," Madach urged. "I'm responsible for this mess, and I should help to clean it up."

With the help of his cane, Karnighan shakily rose to his feet and carefully stepped from the circle.

"You've already done your time in Hell," Remy said, watching as the old man shuffled around the blood circle. Double-checking to make sure everything had been written down correctly, he imagined.

"You've helped me come this far, and I appreciate it. Go back to your life now; continue with your penance; stay away from the Denizens. Live a good life and maybe, depending on how all this works out, it'll be looked at as just a minor bump in the road."

Madach laughed. "Being the main reason why Lucifer was set free as a bump in the road." He stuck the knife he'd chosen through the loop of his paint-stained jeans. "For some reason I just can't see it."

Karnighan leaned upon his cane, looking as though a gentle breeze could carry him away. "All is in place," he said, looking first at Madach and then at Remy. "Now all I need to do is turn the key."

He turned around to the circle, an incantation not meant for human mouths spilling from his withered lips.

Slowly he raised his scrawny arms, cane still clutched in one of his hands. Karnighan's voice seemed to gain in power as he continued to recite the arcane words of the first fallen sorcerers.

Remy felt it before seeing it, a sense that the floor beneath his feet was falling, reminding him of that final, stomach-flipping sensation just before an elevator reaches its destination. He gripped his weapons tighter, the Seraphim essence fully aware that it might be called upon.

But in this instance, he really didn't mind, suspecting that the angelic nature caged inside him would be a necessity if he wanted to survive.

Karnighan wailed, extending the cane before him, waving the end around like a magician's wand. There was a moment in which it was as if all the sound had been somehow sucked from the room. Then the hardwood floor in the center of the circle became like fluid, sucked down into the opening punched through the fabric of reality into Hell. It sounded like the world's largest drain cleared of an obstruction.

Karnighan teetered on the brink, his frail, ancient form almost pulled over the rim of the conjured opening by the vortex.

Remy moved to help the man, to keep him from being yanked into the yawning breach. Wailing winds as well as screams and moans of another kind wafted up and out into the room as Remy took the old man's arm.

A Tartarus Sentry emerged from the center of the new doorway, like a whale breaching. The armor of the giant—forged in Hell from the stuff of Heaven—was tattered and tarnished, covered in the gore of battle. It was missing a wing, the single appendage flapping uselessly, its armored feathers falling like autumn leaves.

Two Hellions crawled upon the prison guard, their powerful claws and teeth tearing away chunks of armor and the angelic flesh beneath as they climbed his body.

It all happened so fast.

The Sentry thrashed in defense of itself. In one of its massive hands it held a medieval cudgel, swinging it wildly as it attempted desperately to remove the ferocious attackers that tore at its body.

Remy watched in horror as the cudgel swung out, gliding through the air in slow motion, missing its intended prey and connecting with the upper body of Alfred Karnighan. There was a wet cracking sound, followed by a fine spray of crimson mist, as Karnighan's body took the full brunt of the impact. The old man was launched across the room, hitting a back wall before dropping, broken and shattered, to a collection of furniture that had been moved there to make way for the conjured doorway.

Remy considered going to the man, but his eyes were drawn to the crimson stain high upon the wall. The old man's point of impact dripped with blood and fragments of other matter, and Remy knew that there was nothing he could do.

The Sentry roared, his mournful cries muffled by the helmet that covered his face and head. One of the Hellions had managed to reach its prey's neck, digging its fangs beneath the lip of the helmet and tearing out chunks of the divine flesh beneath. And as quickly as the mighty figure had erupted from the newly opened doorway, he was gone again, dragged away by the savage beasts that prowled the wastelands of Hell.

Remy stood at the edge of the yawning hole torn in the fabric of space and time, weapons clutched in his hands. Images of past battles, like the staccato blasts of machine-gun fire, flashed within his head, and he wondered if there would ever be a time that it was all just a memory, or if violence would always be a part of what he was.

But that rumination was for another time, the angel thought, when the affinity for bloodshed wasn't a necessity for his continued survival.

The Seraphim clamored excitedly, the stench of Hell

rousing it to attention. It was only a matter of time before it was free again.

Madach appeared beside him, knife in hand, a snub-nosed pistol stuffed in the waistband of his pants. Their eyes touched briefly, before both looked down into the sucking void that had been punched through reality, an oppressive blanket of hopelessness and despair being draped upon the shoulders of both men. The sounds of combat mixed with those of intense suffering, escaping from the entrance, a symphony of misery foreshadowing what was likely to come.

"Hear that?" Madach asked, raising his voice to be heard over the wails and cries. "They're welcoming me back."

And with those words, the fallen angel jumped down into the hole, disappearing within roiling, rust-colored clouds that stank of death and desperation.

Remy tensed, ready to join Madach, when he sensed them.

In the corner of the study they hovered, rolling balls of fire that watched him with multiple sets of unblinking eyes.

They didn't even have the common decency to wish him luck.

CHAPTER THIRTEEN

They'd been married only a very short time.

Marlowe had yet to enter their lives, and they were living in an apartment in Somerville. Their life was good together—better than good, really.

The love he felt for her, and she for him—it was like nothing he'd ever known. But that was a lie, for he had known the intensity of a love like it when in the presence of God.

And he could not help but feel a bit ashamed—and even a little astonished—that a love so great had been so easily replaced. But when he looked at her, lying beside him in bed, or typing up invoices in the office, he knew how it could be possible, for the Almighty had given humanity a piece of Himself, and it radiated through so much more brightly in some than in others.

Madeline shone like the sun, and Remy was powerless not to be drawn to the warmth of her love, which made her sudden statement that cold Sunday afternoon all the more disturbing.

They'd been making dinner together. She was preparing a roast and was about to finish up by using the greasy drippings of the beef to make the gravy. He'd been in the process of opening a bottle of red wine when she made the statement. It was sudden—unprompted—the meaning devastating to him.

"I'm probably going to Hell when I die."

She had just placed a few tablespoons of flour into the pan of drippings and was stirring it; she wasn't even looking at him.

"What did you just say?" he asked with a chuckle, stopping the turning of the corkscrew midtwist.

He could see that she was suddenly upset, her eyes appearing puffy as tears began to roll down her ruddy cheeks. Remy set the bottle upon the countertop and went to her.

"What's wrong?"

He'd come up behind her and put his hands upon her shoulders. There was the faintest of trembles there. It was chilly in the old apartment, but he knew that this had nothing to do with the cold.

She laughed, wiping away the tears running down her face as she continued to mix in the flour she'd added to the pan.

"You're going to say I'm stupid," she said, turning her gaze up to him. "At least I hope you do."

He waited patiently for her to continue, rubbing his hands lovingly up and down her arms.

"Making the gravy made me think of my nana Sarah— my dad's mom," she said. "This was her recipe. She taught me when I was a little girl . . . before she got sick."

He still wasn't quite sure where she was going, but he kept silent, allowing her to purge whatever it was that was bothering her.

"She lived with us after she was diagnosed with emphysema," Madeline explained as she crushed the balls of flour that floated in the bubbling mixture. "Sarah had a two-pack-a-day habit—Camels unfiltered—and it killed her to stop, even though she was so sick and could barely breathe. We fixed up a spare room, moving her in so that we could take care of her."

Madeline had continued to stir the light brownish mixture, as if stirring up the memories of the past.

"At first it was sort of fun having her around all the time, but as she became sicker it got tense and sort of scary. Both my mother and father had part-time night jobs and would leave me home alone with Sarah . . . even after she'd become really bad."

Madeline set the spoon that she'd been using down and just stood there silently.

Remy said nothing, but continued to rub her shoulders, encouraging her to continue with his silence.

"I can remember sitting in the kitchen at night . . . sometimes for hours, listening to her in her bedroom down the hall gasping for breath . . . waiting for something . . . something horrible to happen. I grew to hate her for what she was putting me through."

He started to turn her around toward him. At first she fought, but she soon succumbed, melting into him as he put his arms around her.

"It must have been very hard for you," he said understandingly. "And not the sort of responsibility that should be dropped on a kid."

He felt the dampness of her tears seeping through the fabric of his shirt.

"You really didn't hate her; you hated the situation you'd been put in—the illness that was taking away the woman you loved."

Madeline's body became rigid within his arms, and she lifted her face up to him. Her eyes were red and swollen, cheeks damp and flushed with pink.

"One night sitting alone in my kitchen, listening to her struggle to catch a breath, I wished that she would die—for God or whoever to come and take her so that I wouldn't feel so scared anymore."

Remy knew what had happened then, and how it had played on her childlike psyche, growing into an overpowering obstacle of guilt that she had carried with her to that day.

"She died, Remy," Madeline had told him, her voice shaking with sadness and shame. "I wished my grandmother dead—I wished so hard that it killed her. And that's why I'm probably going to Hell."

Madeline pushed her face into his chest, and he felt her body shudder pathetically with sadness. He tried to comfort her, stroking the back of her head and rocking her gently from side to side.

He wanted to tell her that it was impossible to wish someone dead—to think that there was some great power out there listening, waiting to respond to such random requests—but then he remembered the life that his love had been not all that long ago indoctrinated into: an existence where a human woman had married an actual being of Heaven.

And he could see how a belief such as this didn't seem quite as silly as it once had.

That was when he'd told her about Hell—about Tartarus—and why it existed, and that even if she had managed to somehow wish her grandmother dead, she wouldn't have gone to Hell when she died.

Hell was not a place for humanity; it was for those who had rebelled against the glory of Heaven.

For those who had sinned against their loving God.

These were the thoughts that instantaneously danced across the surface of Remy's mind as he clung to a precarious outcropping of ice, Karnighan's doorway swirling and sputtering in the air above his head.

The old man's spell had torn a hole in the air above Tartarus, and as Remy had fallen through, he'd lost his weapons as he'd frantically clawed for purchase on any surface that could break his fall. The ice numbed his hands to the point where his fingertips had cracked and started to bleed, staining the ice crimson.

Hanging on to the jagged protrusion of ice, Remy studied the area around him, searching for a sign of Madach, or any possible hint as to how dire their situation actually was.

The air of Hell was filled with swirling clouds of noxious fumes that partially obscured his vision and poisoned his thoughts with the taint of fear and desperation. But there wasn't time for such things; he was to somehow thwart the Nomads' plans. How this was to be accomplished, and why it had become his responsibility, were mysteries he would have to deal with another time, when there were less pressing matters to concern himself with.

There was no sign of Madach, and not having the luxury to worry, Remy began his dangerous journey down the side of the ice prison, bloodstained hands searching for any crack, edge, or divot that could be used to assist his descent.

The filthy sky above his head trembled, and he chanced a look upward to see Karnighan's passage begin to falter. The nexus began to sputter and pulse, the magicks used to hold it open beginning to fail. Remy quickened his descent, the sharpness of the icy surface cutting into his fragile flesh, the blood from the cuts making the frigid exterior slicker than it already was.

There was suddenly a roar like thunder, followed by a powerful expulsion of air that tore him from his perch upon Tartarus' surface and tossed him into oblivion.

Remy tumbled down, the fetid air of the place rushing to fill his lungs with its corrosive stench. The ground flew up to meet him with alarming speed, the essence of the divine imprisoned inside the cage of humanity shrieking to be loosed. But he waited too long, dreading the release of the Seraphim.

Remy struck another outcropping of ice on the way down, and the world went temporarily dark. Struggling to regain some semblance of consciousness, he found himself continuing to fall, the punch line to an old joke echoing inside his head as he waited for the inevitable.

It's not the fall that kills you, it's the sudden stops.

He landed atop something that partially cushioned his fall. It wasn't as if he'd landed on a big pile of pillows, or even bags of trash, for that matter. It was like landing on a sack full of doorknobs: a little bit of give-and-take as he connected, and then he found himself bouncing off, only to sail through the air again, eventually landing on a cold, rocky surface.

Remy's head swam with pain, a steady throb of agony that pulsed with every rapid-fire beat of his heart.

But he'd survived, not that he really had much of an option.

The atmosphere of Hell was working its magick, trying to convince him to curl up into a ball and give up, but he knew that wasn't going to work for him. He'd landed on his back, and eventually forced his eyes open, focusing on the looming image of the icy prison before him. He had a rough idea as to where Karnighan's doorway had dropped him off, and was disturbed to see the distance he had fallen.

Remy started to sit up, the sensation of bone rubbing against jagged bone causing blossoms of color to appear before his eyes. He lay back down on the ground, willing the agony pulsing through his damaged body to subside.

Counting to three, he managed to force himself up into a sitting position, focusing on the locations of his extreme discomfort. One of his legs appeared to be broken, lying twisted and useless upon the inhospitable earth at the base of Tartarus.

"Shit," he hissed, pushing himself backward toward the formation of ice that jutted up from the ground. Again he saw a universe of stars, the grinding of his bones apparently caused by some broken ribs.

He leaned back against the ice, breathing through his nose, waiting for the pain to subside. A rust-colored mist hung thick, like smoke, making visibility difficult until a powerful belch of fetid air—likely from the heat-blasted landscape located in the deep valleys and ravines below the prison of ice—helped to improve the visibility momentarily.

He wished it hadn't.

As far as he could see, the frosty ground was strewn with the dead. Broken corpses of fallen angels, Hellions, armored Sentries, and even some of the cloaked Nomads littered the ground. This was what had broken his fall.

He recalled the fields of Heaven during the war, the corpses of those slain in the conflict that pitted angel against angel. Remy had hoped to never see anything like it again.

The sight sickened him, reminding him of why he had abandoned the celestial for the earthly comforts of humanity.

The thick, sulfurous mist was stirred by a shifting breeze, temporarily obscuring his view of the dead, and he was grateful. He lay back against the foundation of Tartarus and thought about what he had to do, although in his current condition, his choices were limited.

Out of the corner of his eye he thought he saw something move. Hoping that it was a merely a trick of the mist, Remy squinted, watching the toxic fog for any sign of life. He saw it again, followed by other shapes moving stealthily about, trying not to be seen, and knew immediately what had found him.

Hellions. A small pack of the Hell-born animals had found his scent, preferring living prey over the dead.

Great, Remy thought, *the day just keeps on getting better and better.*

He could hear their claws clicking on the rocky surface, the low rumbling growls of anticipation as they zeroed in on his scent.

Bracing himself, Remy pushed back against the ice, forcing himself up onto his good leg. The pain was worse than before, and he knew then that he must prepare for the inevitable. Hell was a cruel and vicious place, and not at all accommodating to the frailty of human flesh.

He knew he was going to have to give in, to shed his guise of humanity, and to once again resume his true form. The pain made it difficult to concentrate, the wildness of the angelic nature fighting him, as if trying to make him pay for its imprisonment.

Through pain-hazed eyes he saw at least three of the

Hellions converging. Remy let go of his humanity, opening the mental gates that held the nature of Heaven at bay, allowing the Seraphim its freedom.

But it didn't come fast enough.

The Hellions pounced, their hungry jaws clamping down on one of his wrists, another sinking its fangs into his injured leg. Remy cried out, falling forward to the ground. He could feel the Seraphim rising to the surface, but it seemed to be taking its time.

At last his flesh began to heat, to bubble and steam, as the radiance of God's power began to emerge. The Hellions seemed excited by the physical transformation, as if somehow aroused by the taste of his change.

They climbed up on him, fangs snapping at his flailing hands as he tried to keep them from his throat. His covering of flesh was melting away to expose his angelic form, but the Hellion attack was savage, relentless, their ferocity more than he could handle at the moment.

He actually began to consider the fact that he might die, when his thoughts were interrupted by a blast of gunfire, followed by the yelp of an animal's pain. Remy took note of one of the beasts, its head flipping back sharply to one side as it dropped heavily to the ground.

The remaining two Hellions ceased their attack, their bony heads suddenly moving in the air as they searched for signs of the threat.

Again there came a clap of artificial thunder, another of the Hell-hounds shrieking wildly, turning tail, trying to slink away dragging a now useless leg behind it.

Another shot finished the fleeing beast, leaving only one of the attacking Hellions alive.

Remy tossed his head back in an awful mixture of sadness and euphoria, crying out as the last of his humanity was excised, and the Seraphim completely emerged.

Now healed, he climbed to his feet, golden wings unfurling from his back to beat the sulfurous air. His angelic form was still adorned in the armor of war, the armor that he had worn when he had killed his brothers in Heaven.

Through angelic eyes he watched the last of Hellions as it tensed, the exposed muscle and sinew of its body bunching together, readying to pounce upon Remy's savior as he emerged from the shifting haze.

Remy leapt, dropping down into the Hellion's path. The monster roared, but before it could strike, Remy lashed out with one of his wings, the strength contained within the feathered appendage swatting the Hell-hound against the side of an unyielding Tartarus.

The animal roared its anger, thrashing upon the ground before returning to its feet.

He was about to go at the Hellion again, but another shot rang out, catching the beast in the eye and dropping it onto its side, dead.

"I was wondering where you'd gotten to," Remy said, relaxing his wings, assuming that it was the fallen angel Madach who had come to his aid.

And then he gasped, watching the man stumble as he emerged from the thick, shifting fog, the gray three-piece suit hanging on his form in tatters.

"Francis," Remy said, springing into the air, his newly birthed wings carrying him the short distance to catch his friend before he could fall to the ground.

"You're going to be all right," Remy said, never even considering Francis' condition. His friend had to be all right.

He didn't want to consider the alternative.

"Nomads," Francis gasped, in between gulping breaths. "Didn't think they had it in them."

His friend's body shivered and Remy held him just a bit tighter.

Francis was hurt badly, the extent of the wounds that Remy glimpsed, casually checking out his friend's condition, grave: gaping cuts, bullet holes, and sixth-degree magick burns.

It was a wonder that he was functioning at all.

"Could have kicked all their asses . . . and then some, but . . ."

The former Guardian stopped, the expression on his face telling Remy that he was experiencing a great deal of pain.

"Don't talk," Remy told him. "Lie here; rest. I have something that I have to do, and if things don't turn to absolute shit I'll be back to bring you home, and we can see about—"

Francis' eyes opened wide, a bloody hand reaching out to grab hold of Remy's shoulder. "They have the Pitiless, Rem," he croaked.

Remy nodded. "I know that; it's part of the reason I'm here. They're going to try and use the weapons to set him free . . . the Morningstar."

Francis swallowed hard, closing his eyes. "Fucking thought so," he hissed, slowly shaking his head. "Idiots."

He shifted his weight, slowly bringing up his other hand—still holding the gun. "Managed to drop one of the hoodies with this," Francis said, poking fun at the Nomads' attire.

Remy looked at the weapon, knowing at once what it was. The Pitiless pistol shone seductively in the muted light of Hell.

"Nice gun," Francis croaked. "I'd probably be dead if it wasn't for this."

They were both looking at the old-fashioned Colt Peacemaker, mesmerized by the stories that it whispered, the many lives it had taken. When it had left Heaven, it was nothing more than a shapeless blob of Heavenly matter, falling through the universe to Earth, where it nestled—resting—until it was mined from the earth and processed, found by a master craftsman and shaped into something with the mastery over death.

The last times the Pitiless Colt was fired flashed within their minds. Remy saw it all play out, Francis, his clothing torn, covered in the gore of his enemies, attacking the Nomad who wielded the weapon—disarming him bloodily—and using the pistol to shoot out both the angel's eyes. Energized by the weapon in his possession, he continued to kill, the Peacemaker shaped from the power of the Morningstar giving him the strength to vanquish foe after foe.

"It wears you out after a while," Francis said, interrupting the violent scenes playing inside Remy's mind. "Inspires you to kill until you just don't have the strength anymore."

Francis laughed, pushing the weapon toward him.

"It wants to go to you now."

"Hold on to it," Remy told him. "Defend yourself until I get back."

The Guardian shook his head. "No," he stated flatly. "I'm done."

"Don't talk like that. Keep the gun, use it if necessary, and I'll be back to take you out of here just as soon as—"

"I said I'm done," Francis said, silencing him with an icy stare. "And you don't have a chance of doing anything against the Nomads if you don't have something of equal strength."

He took Remy's hand and forced the pistol into it. "You need this if you're going to do what you have to do."

Remy's mind was immediately flooded with the images of those slain by bullets spat from the gun throughout the years as his hand wrapped around the sandalwood grip.

"That's it," Francis said with a sigh, his body growing limp. "Time to go."

"Don't talk like that," Remy barked angrily, his aggression stimulated by the weapon in his hand.

"What are you going to do? Shoot me?" the Guardian asked, and started to laugh, which turned into a nasty, wet-sounding cough.

"You've survived worse; you're going to be fine,"

Remy stated. He found himself distracted by the gun in his hand, the urge to kill stronger than he'd ever experienced before.

"I did it, you know," Francis stated.

Remy looked away from the gun, not sure what his friend was talking about. "You did what?"

"I revealed myself," he said, a limp hand rising to his mouth to wipe some blood away.

Remy couldn't resist. "And did the grown-ups at the playground call the police?"

Francis laughed again, wincing in pain. "Asshole," he managed, in between coughing spasms. "I showed myself to Linda . . . the waitress at the Piazza."

Remy found himself smiling. "Wow, what moment of weakness inspired that?"

Francis closed his eyes. "Something in the air, I guess," he said. The Guardian's voice seemed to be getting weaker. "There came a moment when I knew I should do it . . . or I'd never get the chance."

"Something to hold on for," Remy said to him.

"No, something to do before it was over."

"I told you not to talk like that."

"And when did I ever listen to you?" Francis asked. "You should really think about getting in there." He motioned limply with his bloody hand toward Tartarus behind them. "Not sure what it's going to take to set the asshole free."

Remy was torn; he knew his friend was right, but he didn't want to leave him, especially like this.

Francis must have suspected how he was feeling.

"Get the fuck out of here," he snarled. "I don't need an audience for what's coming." He started to push Remy away from him. "Go on, get inside and blow their asses away. Show them the consequences of picking the wrong side."

The Guardian pulled away, curling into a tight ball upon the ground.

"Francis, I—" he began, but he wasn't given a chance to finish.

"You were a good friend that I didn't deserve. Thank you."

Remy slowly stood, staring at the body of his friend lying upon the cold, frost-covered ground in front of Tartarus. "You were a good friend too," he said, straining to suppress his anger—to hold back the rage he was feeling toward those who had hurt his friend. "And besides, I felt sorry for you."

Francis remained very still and quiet upon the ground, unresponsive to the verbal jab.

A steady, reverberating, pounding noise began to flow out from the melted opening in the front of the prison, capturing Remy's attention. He could only begin to imagine the source of the sound.

He chanced one more look at his friend, and realizing that there was nothing more that could be done for him, turned toward the entrance. The pounding thrum intensified, sending vibrations through the ground beneath his feet.

Starting toward the prison, Remy stopped short as he heard the sound of his friend's weakened voice.

"What was that, Francis?" Remy asked, turning back.

"Just talking out loud," the fallen Guardian angel said. "Was wondering when it comes time for me . . . was wondering if I'll get back to Heaven."

Remy didn't know what to say.

"Yeah, I didn't think so either," Francis said, his final words trailing off to a whisper.

Remy left his friend.

The Seraphim nature was glad to leave the fallen one behind. It was eager to fight, to destroy the unclean as it had done so very long ago.

It missed the violence. The killing.

Remy held the Pitiless pistol in a grip as tight as the one he had on his fleeting humanity. He didn't want to lose it completely, but now that the nature of the angel had taken control, it would be so very easy to let it go.

To release the hurt along with the memories, to let it all evaporate away to where it would mean nothing.

But he would not allow that; Madeline would not allow that.

Remy entered Tartarus, passing beneath jagged stalactite teeth that had formed when the opening was made. If he'd thought the feelings of desperation and misery were bad outside, within Tartarus it was a different story entirely.

Protected within the breast of the Seraphim, his humanity shied beneath the heavy atmosphere of oppression. If he hadn't yet shed his human guise, it would have instantly withered upon entering this place of penance.

It's even larger on the inside, Remy thought, his golden-flecked eyes looking about the cavernous chamber as he walked deeper inside. There was death everywhere he looked, both fallen and angel Sentry alike. There was no separation here and now, the sinners' blood mixing freely with that of their jailers.

At the end of the body-strewn circular corridor that appeared to have been bored through solid ice, Remy found the room.

For a moment, it was like being back in Paradise.

He imagined that it was a kind of testament—a monument—to why a place such as Tartarus existed. At one time, before the stink of death had infected it, this place would have been special, a tiny pocket of Heaven floating within the depths of the inferno.

The huge concave walls, now spattered with the blood of conflict, showed another such struggle; they showed the story of the Morningstar and those who had followed him, moving moments captured from long ago depicting how they had waged war against the All-Father.

Leading to their fall.

These disturbing moments of betrayal and carnage would be the first things the prisoners of Tartarus would have seen upon their arrival, as well as the last when it came time for their release. A grisly reminder of the wrong they had done.

Remy wanted to look away from the horrific scenes of warfare as they were played out but found himself held by the sight.

Is it possible that it was even worse than I remember? he thought, watching as the two opposing angelic forces clashed upon the golden fields of Heaven, and in the open sky above.

Remy stepped over the bodies that littered the ground of the entryway into the Heavenly chamber, drawn closer to the images of the Great War and the end of a way of life that had been denied him forever because of it.

The battle depicted upon the curved wall of the vast chamber went to white, the searing brightness nearly blinding. Remy lifted a hand to protect his sight.

A face suddenly appeared upon the wall, the resplendent light emanating from around his beatific features. Remy had forgotten how beautiful the Son of the Morning had been, which made what Lucifer had done all the more offensive.

He had been God's favorite—the chosen son—the first of them all.

Remy felt an undying anger overtake him as the Seraphim was stirred by the sight of its most hated enemy. And deep inside, buried beneath the fury, his human nature bowed its head in sorrow over the enormity of what had been lost on account of this being.

Deciding that he'd already wasted too much time on things long past, Remy was prepared to go deeper inside the formidable structure, when his eyes caught sight of movement at his feet.

What he believed to be the corpses of dead fallen angels shifted suddenly, giving off the illusion of life. Remy spread his wings, propelling himself back out of harm's way as something emerged, exploding with a bloodcurdling shriek up from beneath the bodies of those vanquished in battle.

It had once been one of his own, an angel of Heaven, but now it appeared as something else. Its robes clung wetly, the gore of those slain in combat making the angel raiment stick to the body like a second skin.

Through the scarlet taint Remy suddenly recogn ed the face of Uriel, the warden of Tartarus.

His wings had once been snow-white, but now were flecked with crimson. Eyes huge and wild, the warden surged at him, a sword forged from the elemental forces of Heaven crackling in his hand. Uriel raised his weapon but paused in his attack when he saw that it was a Seraphim there before him.

The niggling voice of the Pitiless pistol screamed, to be used inside Remy's head; he could actually feel the metal of the trigger gently caressing his index finger, attempting to seduce it into action, but Remy stayed his hand, forcing the weapon down by his side.

"I've come to help," he told Uriel, watching the blood-stained expression turn from one of absolute panic to one of surprise.

Slowly Uriel lowered his weapon, head tilting from one side to the other as he studied the angel before him. It was as if he truly didn't believe his eyes.

"I'm Remiel," he said, hating the sound of his angel name. After all these centuries, it still sounded wrong—*dirty*—coming from his mouth. "Of the host Seraphim. I'd learned of your situation here and have come to—"

He never got the opportunity to finish the sentence.

"Lies!" Uriel screamed, his blood-covered face twisted in unabated fury. He came at him then, sword humming like a swarm of angry bees as it cut a swath through the air.

Remy quickly moved out of the way. If not for his wings propelling him back, the arcing blade would have split him in two.

The angel was beyond talking to, the madness of this place—of Hell—having taken root. He was lost to sanity.

The warden's blade buried itself in the cold floor of the prison lobby, passing through the bodies of the dead that littered the ground, as insubstantial as smoke.

Again the ornate pistol clutched in Remy's hand begged to be used. It showed him how deadly it could be: multiple blasts of gunfire, multiple victims falling to the weapon's voice.

So many victims.

"So many lies," Uriel bellowed, tugging his blade free. "We believed it was over—the indignity perpetrated upon us by one of our own—but it was all a lie."

The warden charged with a roar, the blade in his grasp sizzling as it cut the air in search of Remy.

Remy leapt above the sword, his wings taking him up toward the cathedral-high ceiling. From the corner of his eyes, he saw projected upon the wall of the chamber the final act to the most disturbing of dramas, the powerful Morningstar brought down by the legions loyal to the Almighty.

He saw Lucifer driven to his knees, wings shackled in restraints of gold. There was a calmness in the features of God's adversary, an expression of peace that spoke nothing of defeat.

Of surrender.

Uriel had taken to the air, his blood-colored wings pounding as he erratically came at Remy.

"How could we have been so blind?" the warden wailed. "So complacent? Did we learn nothing?"

The burning blade descended. Reflexively, Remy lifted his gun hand, halting the sword's arc with the barrel of the old-fashioned pistol. The weapons collided with a blinding flash, and Remy was thrown back by the powerful concussion.

Landing in a roll, he quickly got to his feet, blinking his eyes furiously, attempting to clear away the sunbursts

that blossomed there, obscuring his sight. He was ready
for Uriel's next attack, but the warden was nowhere to
be found. As his vision began to clear, he saw that he
had been knocked into another area of the prison by the
force of the blast.

He was in an enormous chamber composed of the
same icy material that formed the structure of Tartarus
itself. It reminded him of the inside of a hive, the walls
honeycombed with circular cells. He was dwarfed by the
vastness of it all, and it made him feel incredibly small.

As he was drawn farther into the room, Remy could
see inside the honeycomb-like apertures. He could not
help but stare in rapt amazement at the frozen shapes
of the fallen angels within. Some of the chambers were
open, what had once been contained inside having been
freed.

How many have the Nomads managed to release? the
Seraphim wondered, nearly overwhelmed by the sheer
number of cells that dotted the walls. This was an awful
place, and Remy now understood why Uriel had not followed him in here.

The fallen were very much alive within their icy cells,
reliving their moment of betrayal over and over again
for an eternity.

Or for as long as He deemed fit.

Standing there, surrounded by all this pain and sorrow, Remy again questioned the concept of a loving
God. And cursed how far Lucifer had caused them all
to fall.

The voice of the warden drifted out from somewhere
in the room, and Remy realized that he no longer held a
weapon, the Pitiless pistol having been lost in the explosion that had propelled him into the prison chamber.

Uriel flowed from the darkness, his Heavenly sword
poised to strike.

Remy whirled to meet the attack, his hands catching
Uriel's wrist, preventing the burning blade from falling.

The warden was screaming, insane ramblings of a

mind shattered by the magnitude of his failure. What had happened here would affect all reality, all the way from Earth to the gates of Heaven itself.

Wings beating mercilessly in combat, the two took to the air.

The Seraphim wanted to destroy its foe, to vanquish anyone who dared stand between it and the task that it had taken on.

The Morningstar cannot . . . will not be released.

Perhaps it was his humanity that still held on by a thread, but Remy could not bring himself to fully succumb to the angelic nature's thirst for death. He found himself holding back, acting only in defense against Uriel's shrieking onslaught.

The angels flew up and backward, their struggling bodies colliding with one of the cells, the impact so great that it shattered the icy covering that sealed the fallen angel inside. The fallen came suddenly awake with a scream.

The disgraced creature of Heaven wailed its displeasure as it pushed away the shattered fragments of its prison to grab at them. With ragged, clawed hands it reached out, grabbing hold of Remy's wings, attempting to pull him inside the cell to share in his misery.

Remy beat his wings furiously while attempting to fend off Uriel's attempts to kill him.

The warden took advantage of this distraction, freeing his hand long enough to thrust his sword, the burning tip penetrating the breastplate of Remy's Heavenly armor with a flash and the stink of ozone. Remy roared, driving an elbow back into the face of the Tartarus prisoner, and with his wings freed, furling them tightly against his body, allowing himself to drop like a stone.

The pain was incredible, a burning sensation spreading across the flesh beneath his armor. Disoriented, Remy spread his wings to slow his descent, but landed hard, rolling across the icy surface.

The pain beneath the armor intensified. On his knees

he tore at the straps holding the armor in place. It came away in two pieces, clattering to the ground. Remy gazed at the wound, the flesh around the point of penetration angry, a mottled redness starting to spread across his shoulder and down onto his chest. If not taken care of, the infection caused by the wound could prove deadly.

But this was the least of his problems at the moment, listening to the sounds of flapping wings growing closer.

The warden was coming.

He sensed the angel bearing down on him, and spun around to confront the latest attack.

Uriel dropped, gore-spattered wings fanned out to slow his descent, his sword raised in preparation to strike Remy dead.

Remy tensed, isolating the pain in his shoulder, hoping that he had what it would take to survive this moment.

Two gunshots rang out, tearing away a portion of the angelic warden's face, a third removing the top of his head.

The angel dropped down atop him, deadweight driving him to the ground. Remy struggled out from beneath the corpse of the warden, his hand searching for the sword Uriel had dropped. He found it, shrugging away the angel's body as he rose in a crouch to deal with this latest obstacle.

The fallen angel Madach stood in the shadows, a strange golden light emanating from the Pitiless pistol in one hand, and from the Japanese sword clutched in the other, forming a kind of halo around his bedraggled form.

"If we want to get this done, you better follow me," the fallen angel responsible for setting this chain of events in motion said.

Remy gripped Uriel's sword tighter as he watched Madach turn away to be swallowed up by the darkness of Tartarus.

He had no choice but to follow.

Come to find out, not only did Madach now have the Pitiless sword and the Colt, but as Remy followed him into the inky blackness, he saw that the fallen angel had—sticking out of the back pockets of his blood-soaked jeans—the twin daggers as well.

"How?" Remy called after him.

They were descending a winding path made of ancient yellowed ice. The walls around them—these too were peppered with the honeycomb cells, some with prisoners still intact, others shattered and empty.

Madach stopped briefly, turning around to speak.

"It's weird," he said with a laugh. "Seeing you that way."

He pointed at him with the barrel of the gun.

"This place changes you," Remy said, painfully aware of his angelic form. His shoulder throbbed, the infection caused by the sword wound continuing to spread. "And not for the better."

Remy wanted to be human again, but he wasn't sure if that could ever be possible again.

Something had happened to Madach as well. Remy could see that this wasn't the same fallen angel that he'd first come in contact with. There was an air about him, the way he carried himself.

Almost as if he were somehow comfortable with the Hellish environment. As if he belonged.

"The weapons," Remy said eyeing each of the pieces in the fallen angel's possession. "How did you end up with them?"

Madach gazed down at the weapons, an expression on his face as if seeing them for the first time.

"I came through Karnighan's passage into the middle of a battle," the fallen said, eyes glassy as he recounted how it had been. "The Sentries were fighting Nomads just outside the entrance." He went silent, continuing to admire the accursed weapons he'd acquired.

"I don't remember," Madach then said, managing to

pull his gaze from the Pitiless to stare at Remy. "I'm not sure how that's possible, but the next thing I knew, I was inside Tartarus . . . and then I found you."

"And the gun," Remy said, his own gaze fixed upon the weapon that he'd lost in his struggle. There was a part of him that wanted it back, that wanted to hold death in his hand again.

Madach looked at the gun with loving eyes, rubbing a smudge of soot from its body against his pants leg, smiling when he saw that it was clean.

"It's as if I'm drawn to them," the fallen said. "Maybe it's because they know that I'm the one responsible for all this . . . for freeing them," he said.

Remy could just imagine what it was like for Madach, having them in his possession, chattering away inside his head, the images of past violence and death they were so eager to show him.

The air became filled with an echoing, pounding sound, like the one he had heard earlier that had drawn him inside the icy citadel. The vibrations that followed shook the very foundation, rubble raining down on them from above.

The sound was coming from somewhere below.

"It's the axe," Madach said, his voice barely audible over the powerful noise.

It was the one weapon of the Pitiless that Madach had yet to recover, and the fallen turned away from him, hurrying down a descending path that led deeper into the bowels of the prison.

"What is it?" Remy asked, following.

"We have to hurry," Madach answered. "The axe is being used. There isn't much time."

The words were enough for him to ignore the aching pain in his shoulder, and to drive him on. If they were too late the end result was more than he had the ability to comprehend at that moment.

They rounded the corner, their movements illuminated by the eerie yellowish glow that emanated from inside the still-occupied fallen-angel cells.

A memory from Remy's human past flitted through his mind's eye: a Sunday visit to the New England Aquarium with Madeline. She loved the penguins, perfectly happy to skip any of the other exhibits to watch the tuxedoed birds waddle about in the artificial environment that imitated their natural habitat.

He was suddenly, profoundly disturbed, the memory vivid right down to the penguin-house smells, but there was something horribly missing.

Madeline's face.

Her features were blurred, as if she'd moved unexpectedly as a picture was being taken—or as if the memory of her was slowly fading away. It was something that he couldn't tolerate, that he wouldn't—*couldn't*—allow to happen. As his humanity was squelched, pushed deeper and deeper into a smaller and smaller place inside him, his memories—the memories of his human life—were gradually being discarded, seen as useless by the angelic nature that had at last regained dominance. These fragile human remembrances were not what were needed at this time.

Now it was about the battle, the fighting skills, the fury. These were the memories that would allow him to vanquish his foe, to serve the Lord God Almighty to his fullest capacity. There was no reason for compassion, kindness, and love in a place like this.

His humanity was dying, and Remy realized that it wouldn't be long before all the precious experiences and memories that he'd collected over the centuries he'd lived as a human would be gone.

But there was no other choice. If this was the sacrifice required of him to prevent this most heinous act from happening, then it was the price he would have to pay.

He returned his focus to the job at hand, descending farther and farther into the bowels of Tartarus. The air had become even thicker with despair, the lower levels where the least repentant of the Morningstar's minions were kept.

He did not want to look at them, curled fetal-like within their small, icy cells, but could not help himself. Remy had known these creatures. *No, it was Remiel who had called them family,* his brain quickly corrected. But nonetheless, they had been part of his world at one time, and here they were confined to an eternity—*or more*—of suffering for their actions.

Remy had tried not to think of what had occurred after the rebellion had been thwarted, after he had left Heaven for the earthly planes. He knew it would be bad; how could it not? The Lord of Lords—the Creator of all things—had been challenged by His own creations. How could *He* not punish them?

Remy knew it would be bad, but he never imagined anything like this.

They rounded yet another corner, the pitching of the floor beneath their feet making it ever more precarious as they descended deeper and deeper into the prison's lower depths.

From the corner of his eye, Remy believed that he'd seen movement from inside one of the cells. His gaze moved over the frozen wall, looking for what he'd seen, and he was about to dismiss it as a trick of the poor light when a section of cell wall to his left suddenly cracked, sounding like the snap of a bullwhip, and then exploded outward.

Remy and Madach reared back, immediately on the defensive as they were showered with razor-sharp fragments of prison wall. At first he believed it to be more of the fallen angels escaping, but he quickly came to the realization that it was something much bigger, as even more of the wall crumbled and gave way to reveal multiple Tartarus Sentries pouring into the winding corridors, locked in furious combat with recently escaped fallen prisoners.

The Sentries roared through their blood-streaked helmets, unleashing the full fury of their Heavenly weaponry as they attempted to beat back the prisoners that attacked them.

They were like locusts, swarming through the jagged break in the wall, attacking the guards in a frenzied rage. The Sentries swung their crackling swords wildly, the burning blades decimating their enemies with every swing, flaming body parts strewn into the air, but still they kept coming.

The Sentries' attempts to defend themselves grew more frantic as the fallen numbers continued to grow unabated. Soon Remy could no longer see the giants, their armored forms covered in writhing bodies slick with the grime of confinement in Hell.

The corridor trembled from the ferocity of the struggle, chunks of ceiling dropping down to shatter at their feet.

"Go!" Remy yelled to Madach, pushing him farther ahead. But their way became blocked by one of the Sentries, who dropped to his knees to reveal fallen angels wielding jagged pieces of their prison walls like daggers, clinging to their keeper's back like hungry ticks to a dog.

And the walls continued to shudder from the enormity of the struggle, more and more of the prison breaking away. Remy was certain the passage was about to come down on their heads, and knew that if they were going to continue on their mission, he had to make this fast.

Leaping in front of Madach he raised the sword that he had taken from the warden Uriel, lashing out at the fallen that swarmed atop the giant Sentry.

The prisoners screamed, leaping back from the devastating blade, shielding their eyes, sensitive from a millennia of shadowed confinement, from the emanations that leaked from the Heavenly weapon.

With a grunt, the Sentry clamored to his feet, reaching out to destroy anything within reach. Realizing that they too were targets for the giant guard's rage, Remy and Madach tried to push past the Heavenly Sentry. The being's movements were wild, out of control, as he slammed his bulk against the wall, his flailing, razor-sharp wings cutting through the air, their sharpness devastating to any who got too close.

Madach dove past the Sentry's uncontrolled movements with Remy close behind.

They were barely able to keep their footing as they skidded down the winding, circular corridor. Remy looked over his shoulder briefly, the curve of the wall hiding most of what was occurring behind them.

There was a sudden roar and a flash of blue light, and Remy watched as the area behind him started to disintegrate. He turned away from the horrific sight, the sound of devastation at his back. He spread his wings, springing off the ground that had started to crack and crumble beneath his feet, reaching for Madach. He grabbed the fallen angel beneath the arms, lifting him from the path and into the air.

He wanted to believe that there was still a chance they could survive this. If there was one thing living as a human being had taught him, it was to believe.

There was always a chance.

No matter how bleak the circumstances.

"It doesn't look good for me," the man he would know as Steven Mulvehill had said, leaning back against a gray concrete parking garage support.

There was a growing patch of crimson on his belly where he'd been shot, and he was looking at one of his hands. It had been stained red with his blood.

He was dying.

Remy did not know this man; the two had not yet established their special bond.

Two cases: one that he had been hired to investigate—

a possible kidnapping—had somehow intersected with that of another investigation being carried out by the homicide division of the Boston police. Revelations were made, motives revealed, and guilty parties attempted to flee justice, no matter the price.

It had been three a.m. on a rainy Sunday in a Logan Airport parking garage. A suspect in both their cases was preparing to leave the country. Mulvehill had been confused; some pieces of the individual's story just didn't seem to fit. He had some questions for the man—some niggling inconsistencies that needed to be clarified before he felt safe in allowing this man to leave.

Those same inconsistencies had aroused Remy's interests as well, bringing him to the same Logan parking garage.

Mulvehill had been the first to arrive, catching the man as he unloaded a suitcase from the back of his metallic blue BMW. All the homicide cop wanted was to talk, to have a few of his questions answered, some gaps in logic cleared up, and then the individual would have been allowed to go on his way.

The violence was unexpected, the weapon hidden somewhere in the trunk. And it was the one shot fired from the handgun—the single thunderous clap that reverberated off the concrete walls and ceiling of the parking garage—that had led Remy to the man who would later become his friend.

He had found him alone, slumped against the support column, the stomach area of his shirt stained red from blood. The man was dying, and Remy found himself drawn to act.

"It doesn't look good for me," Mulvehill had said, looking down at the expanding stain. There was fear in his voice, fear of the unknown that awaited him if he were to die.

It was in Remy's nature—as a being of Heaven—to comfort, and to ease the dying man's fears. He had knelt beside the terrified man, taking his bloodstained hand in his, lending him some of his divine strength to either pass to the Source or hold on until help arrived.

He had told the man—told him that no matter what happened he would be all right. And to further ease his fears, Remy did something that he had not been inclined to do since his revelation to Madeline.

Remy could never quite figure out why it was this man, this dying individual's fear, had inspired him in such a way to reveal his true nature.

Holding the man's hand tightly in his, Remy had dropped the human facade to reveal the being that he truly was, and again he had told him that no matter the outcome, he would be fine.

The homicide detective seemed to relax, all the tension leaving his body. A smile slowly formed on his paling features, as he looked up into the eyes of a servant of God.

"What a relief," he'd whispered as his life force continued to ebb away. "This makes it easier."

The eerie sounds of police and ambulance sirens filled the parking garage, their piercing wails urging him to hang on.

The dying man seemed to be at peace, and as his eyes began to close, his grip upon Remy's hand weakening as he succumbed to unconsciousness, he spoke the words that could very well have been his last.

"I thought I was going to Hell."

CHAPTER FOURTEEN

The memory of how his friendship with Steven Mulvehill had been born was viciously snatched away and replaced by the painful reality of the moment, as Remy was startled back to consciousness.

He remembered the pulsing blue light the Sentry's power unleashed and the corridor turning to rubble around him.

He gasped, eyes snapping open, as he pushed himself up from where he lay, the horror of the current situation reminding him that the danger was still ridiculously high.

Looking about the darkened subchamber, he came to the realization that he was not alone. They squatted around him, the fallen that had survived the Nomads' liberation, insanity and desperation burning in their once-divine eyes.

Seeing that he was now awake, they reached for him, spidery fingers eager to connect, to remind them of what had once been theirs. They were all around him, moving as one, drawn to his divinity.

Their hands were eager, desperate, clawing at his flesh, hungry to be as he was again. The touching soon went from cautious to demanding, jagged fingernails digging into his flesh as they sought to possess a piece of what they had lost to sin.

Sure that he was about to be torn apart, Remy cleared

his mind, reveling in the power that was his to control. The Seraphim became aroused, and it flexed its Heavenly might. Remy's flesh began to glow, the power of Heaven radiating outward. The fallen gasped, stumbling away from the divine light that emanated from his every pore.

But they were starving for Heavenly power, and soon surged at him again. Greedily they engulfed him, their filthy, emaciated bodies suffocating the light as they forced him down to the frozen ground with their rapacious mass.

He tried to fight, to push them away, but there were just too many. It was like attempting to hold back an ocean wave, and it wouldn't be long before he was drowned in their hunger.

The Pitiless pistol roared. Remy knew the sound, the timbre of its voice.

"Get away from him," a voice that he recognized as Madach's yelled.

The fallen recoiled, allowing Remy to scramble to his feet. But his body still glowed with its Heavenly light, and the fallen angels could not help themselves, again surging toward him.

Madach aimed the pistol, firing into the advancing swarm. Remy watched them go down, one after another. At least ten of them had to die before the others got the idea, running off to hide in the deep shadows of the cavern, until their courage was again restoked by his divine light.

Madach looked about as good as Remy felt. He leaned awkwardly to one side, almost all exposed skin stained a horrible blackish red.

Remy was pretty sure he looked no better.

"Those things certainly do come in handy," Remy said, pointing at the Pitiless weaponry still in Madach's hand.

"Fire with fire," the fallen angel said, turning slightly toward another tunnel at the far end of the vast subterranean chamber.

A succession of loud, nearly deafening pounding sounds drifted out from the tunnel mouth, sounds that suggested something very tough being broken into. This is what they had heard in the upper levels of the prison, what they had been drawn to.

"We need to go in there," Madach said, pointing with the tip of the samurai sword he held.

Remy saw that the fallen were becoming brave again, the pathetic creatures coming out from hiding, their hands extended toward him like they were beggars on a street.

"Then, let's go," he said, being the first to move toward the cavern entrance. "But I'm going to need a weapon."

They stood at the opening, Remy waiting to see if Madach would share his arsenal. *If not, I suppose I can always use a heavy rock,* Remy thought.

Madach hesitated, but then handed the Pitiless Colt over, turning the pistol around to hand it to Remy butt first.

The gun felt hot in his hand, and Remy let the images of past violence wash over him unhindered.

The earsplitting noise at the end of the tunnel continued, sounding more furious and frantic.

"Don't want to jinx it, but we might not be too late," he said, leading the way into the cavern.

"With the way my luck runs, we might want to hurry, then," Madach said, tight at his back.

The cavern passage dipped down in a precarious slope, deeper and deeper into the innards of Hell.

In the distance there was a flash of light, the sharpness of the flare nearly blinding in the darkness of the cavern. Before each spark there came the distinctive clanging sound of metal striking something even harder.

They moved toward the flash, toward what they sensed to be their ultimate destination. The Seraphim was content in its natural state, eager for the conflict that it would soon be facing. Remy wasn't sure if it would even be possible to repress the angelic nature again—to put it back inside its box. But that was a worry for another time, a worry that he would be lucky to have, because it would mean that he had managed to survive the impending confrontation.

Cautiously he and Madach emerged from the cavern passage out into the larger chamber, their eyes fixed upon the vision before them. The chamber was vast, its walls made from the same miles-thick icy substance found throughout the prison of Tartarus.

Only here it was melting.

It was like coming out into a torrential rainstorm, water from the melting ice raining down upon them from miles above. In the center of the vast water-soaked chamber there stood what could best be described as a sarcophagus. Remy had seen things similar in his extensive lifetime upon the planet, as well as in his many visits to Boston's museums of science and fine arts. Only this had been built not to house the dead, but to imprison and punish the still living.

Remy couldn't believe what he was looking at. He'd heard whispers of Lucifer's pall but had never expected to see it. It was strangely beautiful to behold, the front of Lucifer's place of confinement adorned with the intricate sculpture of a beautiful winged warrior clutching a flaming sword to its breast. Carved above the sculpture, written in the language of the Messengers, it read, HERE IS THE SON OF THE MORNING, THE MOST BEAUTIFUL OF THEM ALL, WHOSE BETRAYAL HAS SHAKEN THE PILLARS OF HEAVEN. MAY HE SOMEDAY LEARN THE ERROR OF HIS ACT.

The stone case shuddered violently, a flash of bluish light filling the chamber as it was struck from somewhere behind.

Slowly a figure emerged from behind the standing coffin of the Morningstar, dragging an enormous battle-axe crackling with the power of Heaven behind him. He was looking for damage in the surface of the stone case, not paying attention to anything else in the chamber.

Remy knew the figure at once, despite the Nomad's haggard appearance. Suroth continued to walk around the case, unaware that he was no longer alone. The Nomad leader moved in closer to the sarcophagus, reaching out to run his hand over the surface, searching for any flaws that could be taken advantage of.

With a roar, he raised the Pitiless axe up over his head and brought it down upon the pall's front. Again there was an explosion of sizzling blue, and the Nomad scrutinized where the weapon had struck.

It might have been a trick of the light, but Remy thought that he might have seen the beginning of a crack.

"Suroth, stop!" he bellowed, scrambling across the slippery surface, Pitiless pistol in hand. "This has to end now."

The Nomad had raised the axe to strike at the coffin again but stopped, turning toward the angel.

At first Suroth appeared enraged, gripping the hilt of the battle-axe tighter, prepared to deal with the interloper, but his features softened as he recognized who approached.

"Remiel?" he asked, a smile forming on his haggard, blood-flecked features. "Can it be true?"

Remy stopped beyond the reach of the axe.

"It's true, Suroth," he said. "You have to stop this."

The angel looked around, his wide, insane eyes taking in every bleak detail of the chamber in which they stood.

"Yes, you're right. I have to stop this."

With incredible speed and a roar of indignation, Suroth lashed out with the axe again, this time the wide blade causing visible damage in the surface of the great stone burial case.

Remy saw the wound appear as the blade struck, and reacted instinctively. This couldn't be allowed to happen, no matter the cost, and he found himself raising the gun that he held tightly in his grasp. He listened to the chattering of the weapon, its promises to stop his enemy—*all his enemies*—forever and ever.

Remy fired the gun, hoping to injure the Nomad enough so that he would drop the axe and step away from the sarcophagus. The Colt Peacemaker roared like a lion, the muzzle flash illuminating the chamber in its celebration of violence.

But the unthinkable occurred.

As he fired, eyes squinting down the barrel of the weapon, Suroth moved, the arm holding the mighty axe placing the blade in the pathway of the bullet, deflecting the shot.

It was as if the Nomad leader had planned it.

The bullet ricocheted off the axe blade with a petulant whine, the shot then striking Lucifer's pall close to where the previous blow had made its wound.

Suroth smiled.

"Thank you for the assistance, brother," he said. "I'll be sure to tell the Morningstar of your efforts."

Tendrils of angel magick erupted from the Nomad's free hand. The force lifted Remy from the ground and threw him backward against the nearby wall of ice.

The world exploded colorfully, and a curtain of black fell. Remy forced himself back to consciousness, listening as the gun begged him to fire again, to blast the smile off Suroth's smug features, but he held back, hesitating to inflict any more unwanted damage.

"For millennia we stood on the sidelines, waiting with our decision," Suroth said, eyes riveted to the break in the sarcophagus' front. "He'd come to us—before the beginning of the war—knowing our feelings, our hurt over what was about to occur in the most holy of places."

The Nomad leader turned the axe in his hand, deciding where he would strike next.

"He understood that we would not stand with him, but he told us that there would come a time when we would know who was right and who was wrong. And then it would become our job . . . our sacred duty to act on the side of right."

Suroth's eyes were suddenly upon Remy, holding him in place with their intensity.

"It's time, Remiel."

As if sensing Remy's quandary, Madach launched his own attack, charging across the slick surface, sword poised, ready to strike.

The Nomad leader barely acknowledged the fallen angel's presence, swinging the axe toward the damage already wrought in the surface of the coffin.

The sound of metal striking metal sounded in the chamber, and Remy was stunned to see that Madach had blocked the axe strike with the katana.

"No more," he stated as Suroth withdrew his weapon with a growl.

"Can't you see that I do this for you . . . for all who made the choice and have suffered for their decision?" Suroth stated, magickal discharge sparking from the tips of his fingers

Remy pushed off from the wall, raising the Pitiless Colt to fire. He had to take the chance; their options were dwindling by the moment. Pain was his latest foe, threatening to drag him down deep into numbing oblivion as he took aim.

"Get out of the way!" Remy screamed at Madach as he fired the gun. The fallen angel reacted, but not fast enough. The pistol discharged just as Suroth unleashed another blast of magickal fury. Madach was picked up and thrown viciously against the sarcophagus.

Remy couldn't be certain, but he thought he might've heard the sound of multiple bones breaking upon impact.

Suroth gripped his shoulder as blood erupted from between his fingers. "I thought you, out of all of them, would understand," the Nomad stated.

"I understand that this isn't the way it should be,"

Remy stated, still managing to stand while aiming down the barrel of the gun. "We need to get past this . . . past the horrors that we inflicted upon one another. It can never go back to the way it was."

"But it can be made better," Suroth urged.

Remy shook his head. "No, the war is over."

The Nomad leader stood a little bit straighter then, removing his hand from the bullet wound in his shoulder.

"Not over," he said, just as Remy sensed movement behind him.

The fallen prisoners of Tartarus spewed from the nearby tunnel mouth. Remy spread his wings, attempting to take flight over them, but there were many and they moved too fast. They gripped his ankles, his legs, pulling him down into a sea of them.

"Only a brief interlude before the final act."

From between desperate, clawing fingers, Remy watched as Suroth moved closer to Lucifer's pall, and to Madach lying broken before it.

The fallen moved like a single organism, preventing Remy from raising his arm and firing the gun. It wasn't long before it was wrenched from his grasp, disappearing somewhere into the mass of them.

"It will be the dawning of a new angelic age," the Nomad said, kicking away the samurai sword that the injured Madach was straining to reach. "The Creator surpassed by His creations—order brought to a universe in the throes of chaos."

Suroth reached down, picking Madach up by the throat and hauling him into the air.

"*He'll* be proven right," Suroth said, pulling Madach in close to speak into his ear. "And the Lord God Almighty will be forced to bow before a new and glorious master."

From beneath the overwhelming weight of the fallen, Remy watched as Madach's hand fumbled at his back pocket, slowly withdrawing one of the Pitiless daggers that had managed not to be lost in their violent struggles.

Still dangling from the Nomad's grasp, Madach struck, the arc of the blade directed toward Suroth's throat. But the Nomad leader moved faster, the Pitiless axe dropping from his grip as he captured Madach's wrist before the blade could bite.

Suroth twisted the dagger from the fallen angel's hand, and tossed Madach away.

Suroth studied the blade.

"Amazing to think that this was crafted by one of *His* special monkeys," he observed, admiring the craftsmanship of the piece. "I seriously doubt a Heavenly craftsman could have done better."

He brought the blade closer to his ear, closing his eyes and listening to the voice of the weapon.

"It's waited a very long time for this," he said, "to at last be reunited with its master."

And with those words, Suroth attacked the case, digging the tip of the dagger into the imperfection that he'd cut in the face of the sarcophagus. Again and again he jammed the blade into the stone, digging and twisting the metal, breaking away sections of the stone lid.

Remy watched, horrified, as the broken pieces of the coffin fell to the ground. He struggled in the grasp of the fallen, but their grip on him was firm. They were sapping his strength, their voracious number feeding on his inner light.

All he could do was watch.

The knife wasn't doing the trick fast enough, and the Nomad tossed it aside, going in search of something to quicken his work.

Having already used the axe, Suroth reached for the katana.

Madach screamed out, throwing his broken frame across the blade.

"Don't do this," the fallen angel begged.

Suroth extended an arm, using his magickal abilities to yank the injured Madach up into the air. The fallen still clung to the sword, his face twisted with the agony of his injuries.

"Please don't," he pleaded. "If it starts again ... if the war resumes, all the pain and suffering we went through ... it'll all be for nothing."

The Nomad leader approached the fallen, who hung in the air, grabbing the hilt of the sword and ripping it from his grasp. "Think of it as a precursor to victory," Suroth said, admiring the blade before, with a wave of his hand, he cast the begging fallen aside, sending him flying through the air to land in a shattered heap across the chamber.

"All the pain and suffering is fuel for what is to come," Suroth said, gripping the hilt of the Japanese sword in both hands. "A victory in the making."

He spun around with a blurred swiftness, the sword blade cutting into the surface of the sarcophagus with an explosion of fiery blue.

Still held in the grip of the escaped Tartarus prisoners, Remy flinched, as if the sword had bitten into his own flesh. He watched with disbelieving eyes as more pieces of Lucifer's pall broke away.

Remy tried one last attempt at breaking free.

"Suroth!" he screamed, giving it everything he had, flexing his wings with enough force to temporarily toss off the fallen, allowing him to achieve flight.

He had only one thought inside his head: to stop the Nomad leader. He hurtled toward Suroth, at the last second, spreading his wings, using the sudden resistance to slow his progress and drop to the ground. The Nomad spun toward him, sword in hand as Remy grabbed for a weapon, snatching up the Pitiless axe.

"Of all of you, I thought you were the one that would understand our plans," Suroth said, attacking with the skill and ferocity of the ancient samurai.

Pitiless metal struck Pitiless metal, arcs of hissing energy exploding out from where the weapons kissed.

"I understand them just fine, Nomad," Remy said, swinging the axe wide, hoping to drag the razor-fine blade across his enemy's midsection, severing him in two. "The problem is, they're completely insane."

Suroth jumped back and sprang into the air. Remy watched as, with a cry sounding of both pain and pleasure, the angel sorcerer unfurled wings that had likely not seen light since before the war in Heaven. They were impressive things: a dark, almost chocolate brown, with a texture that reminded him of velvet.

"To what do we owe the occasion?" Remy asked, springing up to meet his foe in flight.

The Nomad seemed almost euphoric, his powerful feathered appendages beating the air.

"The celibacy of flight has come to an end," Suroth stated, reveling in each and every flap of his mighty wings. "I fly for all my brothers now."

Remy rushed the Nomad, raising the axe to his shoulder, ignoring the intensity of the pain radiating from his infected shoulder wound.

Shrugging off his happiness like a cloak, Suroth met his attack like the warrior that he was, the millennia of not using his wings seemingly having little effect upon his aerial combat skills.

The Nomad was just as ferocious in the air as he was on the ground, driving Remy back as he lashed out with the Japanese sword. Avoiding the blade's bite, Remy cast his gaze up toward the chamber's vast ceiling. Leaping above the Nomad's attempt to separate his head from his body, Remy flapped his wings furiously, soaring up to the chamber's highest regions.

As he had hoped, Suroth followed.

On the roof of the chamber, resembling the teeth of some enormous mythical beast, there hung huge dripping stalactites. A quick glance below and he saw the

Nomad leader leering up at him, his eyes glistening with a madness that would not be satisfied with anything other than Remy's death.

Remy flapped his wings all the harder, increasing his speed, seemingly on a collision course with the ceiling fangs. Straining against the increasing pain in his shoulder, he lifted the Pitiless axe, swinging the razor-keen blade into one of the hangings of ice as he passed alongside. Darting between the chunks of falling debris, Remy struck at the next, and one after another, huge pieces of the ceiling ice rained down on the ascending angel.

At first Remy thought his efforts had failed, the Nomad leader able to maneuver through the falling rubble as he continued to ascend. But one of Suroth's powerful wings was struck by a large chunk of ice, sending the Nomad leader spinning into the path of other pieces of debris. It wasn't long before the Nomad leader plummeted to the chamber floor.

Remy dropped, following the rain of debris to the chamber floor. He hovered just above the ground, searching for Suroth's body, imagining it buried beneath the tons of ice. Bodies of fallen angels who had been killed by pieces of the falling ceiling littered the ground. He could see others peering out fearfully from patches of shadow, having escaped their brethrens' crushing fate.

He doubted it would be long before they were again drawn to him.

Touching down, Remy suddenly realized how weak he was, his legs barely able to support his weight. He dropped to his knees upon the ice, looking around the chamber.

His eyes touched upon the body of Madach, lying bloodied and twisted upon the ground, protected from the falling rubble by Lucifer's pall.

Remy pushed himself to stand, stumbling over the shattered pieces of ceiling ice to reach his reluctant partner in this insane endeavor. The battle-axe slipped from his grasp, but he did not bother to retrieve it. He lowered himself to the ground, pulling Madach into his arms.

"Hey," he said, giving the fallen a gentle shake. "Are you still with me?"

Madach's eyes flickered open, looking into Remy's fearfully.

"It's all right," Remy reassured him. "I think we might've actually averted the disaster."

Remy chanced a look toward the sarcophagus; though large chunks were missing from its surface, none of the blows had actually managed to break through to the inside.

He felt Madach's body stiffen in his arms.

"No," the fallen angel stated, shaking his head. "No, it's not all right at all."

The explosion immediately followed upon Madach's words. Remy watched as the blood-covered form of Suroth rose from the rubble of the broken ceiling.

Steam wafted up from his soaking robes, his features twisted in a combined grimace of rage and agony. In his hand he still clutched the hilt of the Pitiless katana. The blade had been snapped about midway down, but Suroth had still managed to hold on to his weapon.

Twisting away from the still-thrashing Madach, Remy scrambled for the battle-axe. Maybe this was what Hell was for him, one countless battle after another, feeling his humanity slipping away inch by inch.

Suroth opened his mouth to speak, his jaw hanging crookedly. It looked quite painful as he forced the words from his mouth.

"With the end . . . I bring about the beginning," the Nomad croaked and extended the sword, pointing the broken blade at Remy.

Remy tensed to fly and was shocked when Suroth changed the direction of the blade, pivoting to point it at the sarcophagus.

Snaking arcs of angelic power emerged from beneath

the angel's wet and tattered robes, tentacles of magick that snaked down the length of his arm, flowing into the hand that clutched the broken sword.

A blast of angel fire, far stronger than anything the Nomad had conjured yet, struck the front of Lucifer's personal prison.

The chamber was filled with a searing blue light, a magickal energy continued to flow from some vast reservoir within the Nomad leader.

Remy knew what was happening, and that it was now too late to stop it.

Suroth was sacrificing his angelic life force and adding it to the magick his kind had mastered so many millennia ago. The once-mighty Nomad leader had begun to wither, his body mass dwindling away to nothing before Remy's eyes.

Lucifer's pall had begun to glow white, the intense heat radiating from the stone prison causing the moisture from the melting ice to evaporate, filling the chamber with a roiling steam that made it nearly impossible to see what was happening.

Remy was drawn to the sarcophagus, flapping his wings aggressively to disperse the hindering mist. He was at least three feet from the pall when the magick pouring from Suroth abruptly ceased. A thunderous blast followed as the case exploded, lifting him off his feet and tossing him through the air.

The silence that followed was deafening.

Knowing that the unthinkable had occurred, Remy stood.

The steam had begun to fade, a roiling layer of fog undulating like something alive close to the chamber floor. He moved toward where the stone coffin had once stood, broken pieces now scattered about the floor.

As he moved closer, he saw kneeling amongst the fog and rubble, the form of a man. Remy froze, staring at the shape that suddenly stood and turned to face him.

It was Madach who stood in the remains of the sarcophagus.

Remy's angelic instinct was immediately on alert. *Something is wrong—horribly, horribly wrong,* he thought as he strode closer, ignoring the pain that attempted to cripple his body.

Standing beside Madach, Remy scanned the ground, finding only the broken pieces of the Morningstar's imprisonment.

Lucifer was nowhere to be found.

Remy felt their presence just as the screaming began.

Horrible shrieks and wails echoed through the prison chamber, and he turned toward the cries of misery.

The Thrones hovered in the air, their round, roiling bodies crackling with repressed Heavenly power. Tendrils of humming energy leapt from their bodies, lashing out at any and all who dared come too close.

The fallen screamed as they died. They came en masse, unable to stop themselves from rushing toward the creatures of Heaven, hands outstretched, desperate to once again touch the light of the Almighty.

As the fallen were killed, their once-divine forms exploding into clouds of ash, the Thrones paid little attention to their demise. All eyes—each and every one of the large, piercing orbs that covered the seething masses of power—were fixed upon Remy.

He could feel their gazes burning into his flesh and then he heard their roaring command.

"End his life."

Their voices were overwhelming, like every sound in existence—the beautiful and the harsh, the melodic and the earsplittingly painful, all combined to give them voice.

Remy immediately dropped the battle-axe at his feet, bending forward, covering his ears with his hands, though it did him little good, for the Thrones spoke inside his head as well.

"I . . . don't understand," Remy cried. It took every bit of strength he had remaining to stay on his feet.

"Do as we command before it is too late," the Thrones cried. It was like having an atomic weapon set off inside his skull.

Still bent over, Remy looked up into the multiple eyes of his tormentors, squinting through their radiance as he attempted to understand what they wanted of him.

"I don't . . ."

The orbs of divine power surged closer, tentacles of energy moving across the ground, bodies of dead fallen exploding to drifting bits of nothing at their pernicious touch.

"There was always a fear that something of this magnitude would occur," the Thrones announced. *"So he was removed. Placed where he would no longer be a threat . . . where he could do no harm."*

"I have no idea what you're talking about," Remy screamed, the coppery taste of blood filling his mouth. His nose and ears were leaking from the Thrones' assault, and he wanted it to stop, but most of all he wanted to understand.

"He was never supposed to return here."

"Tell me who you're talking about!" Remy cried, lurching toward the emissaries from Heaven.

"There is no time!" the Thrones wailed, one of the snaking appendages of fiery energy touching something on the ground and hurling it at him.

Remy caught the object, surprised at the sudden wave of familiarity he experienced on contact. He gripped the pistol tightly in his hand, the familiar voice of the weapon present inside his head again.

Kill him!

The eyes were looking past him, focusing on the object of their obsession, and Remy slowly turned to gaze at the pathetic form of Madach. The fallen angel stood slump-shouldered, his body beaten and lacerated, his clothes hanging from his broken shape in bloodstained tatters.

He seemed to be in a sort of trance, staring down at the shattered remains of Lucifer's pall.

"Him?" Remy asked, turning back to the Thrones. "You want me to kill Madach?"

The Colt became euphoric, not because of the why or whom it was to be used upon, but because it had the opportunity to do what it had been created for. It urged Remy on, telling him in a hissing voice like radio static to do as he was told.

Remy ignored the Pitiless, waiting for some sort of answer, something that would make sense of the murderous act that the Thrones were demanding of him.

And then Madach began to chuckle.

Remy turned away from Heaven's emissaries to look at the fallen angel.

He was hunched no longer, standing perfectly straight, with his hands hanging down at his sides.

"Madach?" Remy questioned, not seeing the humor.

"It's all clear to me now," Madach stated, smiling so wide that it seemed to split his face.

Do it! Do it! Do it! Do it! Do it! Do it!" the Thrones shrieked inside his head. Through eyes tearing with pain, Remy watched Madach.

"I'm free," he said, his eyes glinting a golden yellow.

A million questions filled Remy's head, but he knew that there wasn't time for a one of them.

The wounds—the cuts and abrasions—that the fallen had received during his tribulations in the underworld had begun to glow. An eerie white light starting to seep from somewhere inside him.

No longer trusting Remy to do what they asked, the Thrones made their move. Their spherical bodies began to glow like miniature suns, as they merged their masses to form one enormous globe of eyes and fire.

A tentacle of fire grew from the burning surface,

lashing out like a whip. Remy barely avoided the ferocious attack, his wings smoldering with the intensity of
the heat as he leapt from harm's way. He rolled onto
his back, extinguishing the unearthly fire eating at his
wings.

Shielding his face and eyes, he peered through the
searing brightness, barely able to make out the shapes
of the sunlike Throne and its enemy.

Questions raced through his mind as he watched and
waited for the inevitable outcome.

Then the horrible screams of the divine erupted in
the air.

Remy crawled to his feet, stumbling back, trying
to escape the oppressive sound that was exploding all
around and inside him.

It was the Thrones. Somehow, the Thrones were
screaming.

There was a burst of light. Remy reacted instinctively, looking away just in time, before his eyes could
be burned black in their sockets. When he turned back,
through vision obstructed with dancing black spots and
expanding circles of color, he saw the most disturbing
of sights.

The fire of the single, great Throne had been extinguished, and the Thrones had returned to their individual states. But no longer did they float above the ground,
spinning and turning, casting off tongues of fire. Now
they simply lay upon the ground like spherical lumps of
cooling volcanic rock.

But most horrible was what had happened to their
eyes.

Their eyes were now no more than smoldering wet
craters dripping with a viscous fluid that formed steaming puddles on the cold ground of Tartarus.

All except for one.

Madach had left each of them a single eye, and those
eyes watched him now, filled with something the Thrones
had likely never known.

Fear.

For Madach wasn't Madach anymore, and Remy stood paralyzed by the mind-numbing realization.

The fallen angel's damaged skin had begun to slough away, revealing new, bronze-colored flesh beneath. He was still smiling—even wider than he had been before—wiping the old, loose skin from the new, muscular form beneath.

Madach isn't Madach anymore.

Magnificent wings as black as the night unfurled from his back, languidly teasing the air, flexing powerful muscles that had not been used for so very long.

Remy stared with wonder. He'd always thought that the Lord God Almighty had ripped those impressive black appendages from his shoulders before casting him down to Hell.

And then Madach ripped the mask of flesh from his face, and even though Remy already knew who it was that now stood before him, he still gasped at the sight.

In awe of *him*.

In awe of the Morningstar.

CHAPTER FIFTEEN

The Thrones' cryptic words finally made sense.

He was never supposed to return here.

And now Remy knew why they were so desperate for him to have killed Madach.

What he'd feared most had happened, not exactly in the way that he thought it might, but it had happened.

Lucifer was free.

Remy hadn't a clue what he should be doing, and so he stood, frozen in place, watching as the Son of the Morning looked about him, like a new tenant surveying the empty space of an apartment, deciding where the furniture should go.

And then his golden-flecked eyes fell upon Remy.

Remy met that gaze without fear, remembering a time when this powerful being once stood at the right hand of God, but also recalling the rebellion that the Morningstar had perpetrated. The Seraphim nature remembered the battles and the bloodshed as well as who was ultimately responsible, and it would not wither before the angel's commanding stare.

Sensing no imminent danger, Lucifer looked away, his awesome wings unfurling completely from his back. The dark angel leapt into the air. Hovering above the chamber, he raised his arms, fingers extended. Head tossed back in a cry of effort, the Morningstar began to exert control over his surroundings.

The ground began to tremble, a slight vibration at first, followed by tremors so great that it was difficult stay upright.

Remy felt helpless. Certainly he could have listened to the urgings of his angelic nature, flying up to confront the first of the fallen, but he knew that it would make little difference.

Lucifer was free, and Hell was his to command.

From beneath the dead, the Pitiless emerged. The weapons created from the Morningstar's essence flew up into the air of the prison chamber to hover before their true owner. Their master.

"These have served their purpose well." Lucifer's voice boomed, and Remy watched as the weapons began to lose shape, becoming like smoke that swirled around the Morningstar, eventually being absorbed into his golden body, as he took back the power he had cast off so very long ago.

His already perfect form seemed to become even more immaculate, glowing like a star—*a morning star*—and bathing the once-icy chamber in his radiance.

The walls began to creak and groan, large portions of ancient ice sliding from the walls to shatter upon the floor.

"They sought to keep me from . . . this." Lucifer's voice carried above the rhythmic beating of his awesome wingspan.

And with those words, the Son of the Morning threw out his arms, accepting his environment. The ground writhed like ocean waves; the walls crumbled.

Remy was forced to the air, and he watched in growing horror and awe as the ceiling of the chamber fell away to reveal the tarnished sky of Hell.

Tartarus was crumbling.

Remy flew through the air, dodging huge sections of the ice prison as they came hurtling down at him.

In the icy rubble below he saw them begin to appear, fallen angels that had not been freed in the initial attack.

They crawled out from beneath the remains of their prison cells, haunted faces turned toward the heavens of Hell.

Up toward their lord and master.

The light of the Morningstar bathed the Hellish landscape, and like the spread of the most virulent disease, it too began to writhe and change. The ground shook, its dry, blighted surface beginning to crack, huge, miles-long fissures zigzagging like bolts of lightning across the surface. New mountains surged up from the ground where there had been none.

Riding the powerful updrafts of air, Remy watched with a mixture of wonder and horror as the land was transformed with little regard to those below. The fallen skittered about for safety, many of them falling victim to the shifting ground and the hungry fissures that would swallow them whole.

Hell has to eat if it is to change, to grow into something else.

Remy listened to their screams, their pleas to a god that flew above them, but their cries fell upon deaf ears.

Outrage spurred him on, and before he knew what he was doing, Remy was flying toward the Morningstar; the closer he got, the greater his rage.

There had been the slightest bit of hope, a kernel of chance that the countless millennia of imprisonment had done something to change the attitude of God's once favored, that he had learned from his monumental error in judgment.

That he was repentant.

Remy hadn't a clue as to what he would do once he reached his opponent, weaponless except for the brute strength of his kind, but he could not stop himself now.

Here was the being responsible for the event that had changed his existence—changed the very nature of Heaven and what it meant to be a servant of God.

Lucifer's hand wrapped around Remy's throat in a

grip of iron, stopping the Seraphim's attack with bone-jarring ease.

That glimmer of hope, that kernel of chance was quickly dispelled as the first of the fallen looked down into his eyes. And all Remy could see reflected in that golden-flecked gaze, was a seething fury, anger barely held in check.

"I could end you with the merest flick of my wrist," Lucifer said, his voice a soft whisper, nearly lost in the cacophonous sounds of a Hell in transition.

Remy felt the grip on his throat grow tighter, the pressure inside his skull so great that he wondered if the top of his head might explode.

"But something prevents me." Lucifer drew him closer, studying Remy's straining features.

"You meant something to the being I was," the Morningstar stated. It was as if a door inside his mind had been suddenly opened, revealing the secret contents held inside, the experiences of a fallen called Madach.

"You believed in my repentance."

The fingers around Remy's throat opened, releasing him, and he swam backward through the air, away from his foe.

"For that belief you shall live," Lucifer said, looking down at the morphing landscape of Hell. The cries of the fallen as they fought to survive drifted in the air like a perverted birdsong.

"And with this gift, I give you purpose."

Lucifer extended a muscular arm, his long, delicate fingers splayed.

Remy felt the air around him immediately charged. He tried to escape by dropping down to the chaotic terrain that twisted and changed below, but he was held fast by the Morningstar's will.

"You will be my messenger," Lucifer said. "You will tell them of my return, that their best-laid plans were for naught, and that they will pay for their transgressions against me."

The air around him began to crackle, the fabric of Hell's reality beginning to tear.

Lucifer was opening a passage.

But to where?

"As to when, that will be for me to decide."

The portal opened with a terrible sucking sound, and Remy found himself pulled into the blistering cold of its infinite darkness. He tried to stop himself, to hold on to the sides of the puncture made in the sky above Hell, but the pull was too great, and he slipped into the void, the final, chilling words of Lucifer Morningstar sending him on his way.

"For I have a kingdom to build."

Remy was deposited before the Gates, the stink of Hell radiating from his angelic form.

He fell to his knees as the wound in time and space healed behind him. Eager to breathe in anything other than shadow, he gasped, taking in hungry lungfuls of the suddenly hospitable environment.

He felt the soft earth beneath his knees, the golden-colored grass that tickled the palms of his hands, the fragrant, nearly intoxicating smell of the air; it had been a very long time since he'd been to this place.

But it was impossible to forget.

A fine haze covered the golden plains of grass, but then a gentle breeze stirred, moving aside the curtain of mist to reveal the Gates. Two enormous posts that looked to be fashioned of finely polished bone, or as said some who'd managed to catch a glimpse of the magnificent sight, and remained alive to speak of it, pearl.

Remy rose to his feet upon wobbling legs, lurching forward, drawn toward the magnificent sight.

Toward the only thing that separated him from the kingdom of Heaven.

He could see it there in the distance, through the intricate metalwork that hung between the awesome posts.

Flashes of memory were stirred, and he recalled

when last he'd passed through this gateway. It had been at the close of the war, and he thought it would be the last time.

He had abandoned Heaven, or more accurately, Heaven had abandoned him.

Remy stood before the shuttered Gates, a glimpse of Heaven partially obscured by the blowing mist beyond them, and knew a serenity that he'd not felt in a very long time.

His Seraphim nature was calmed by the return, sedated by the sight of the golden kingdom beyond the entrance. And deep inside, a little bit more of the humanity that he'd worked so hard to create died.

He reached out, prepared to push the Gates open and stride toward the vast city of light, to deliver the message given to him by its most fallen son.

His hands had barely touched the warm metal when there was a brilliant flash and he was repelled. He lay on the ground stunned, his entire body numbed as if by a million volts of electricity. Gradually, feeling returned, and he cautiously climbed to his feet.

Have I been barred from Heaven? His thoughts raced as he again readied to approach the gateway. *Is this some sort of punishment for my leaving after the war?*

Off in the distance, above the spires of the Heavenly kingdom, Remy saw that it had grown dark, as if storm clouds now hung over the city and were spreading across the skies of Heaven.

But soon he realized that it was not clouds at all.

A great army flew through the sky toward him.

An army of angels.

Heaven's air was filled with the sound of pounding wings as they approached—swarming across the sky, descending on the other side of the Gate that separated them.

"Hail, Remiel," an angel at the head of the flock cried, the first to touch down.

He was adorned from head to toe in intricate armor

of gold, as if the rays of the sun had been used to create the ornate adornment for him, and for all the angelic soldiers that landed behind him.

As the leader strode closer to the Gate, he removed his helmet, and a sick feeling writhed in the pit of Remy's belly as he recognized this angel.

"Greetings, Michael," Remy said, bowing his head slightly in respect for the leader of the mighty Archangels.

The Gates parted, and the Archangel strode through them. "Heaven knows of your involvement in the most delicate and dire of matters," the warrior angel stated, stopping before Remy. "Your arrival here before the Gates, stinking of the pit, implies that a great danger to Heaven, and all of creation, has not been averted."

Remy studied the angel before him, and all those that had descended with him from the sky. They were clad in the armor of war, a telling sign that they were very much aware of what had transpired.

"The Thrones are no more," Remy said, watching for some sign that this was a surprise. There was nothing; the sharp angular features of the angelic warrior remained passionless. "Destroyed by the newly awakened Lucifer Morningstar."

A violent shudder ran through Michael's brown-speckled wings, the only sign that he was affected by this news at all.

"I suspected no good would come from their scheme," the angel stated, obviously referring to the Thrones' plan to remove Lucifer from Tartarus. "They used forbidden magicks to make him forget who he was . . . what he was," Michael continued with disdain. "And then they made him believe he was another . . . another of the lowly, absolution seekers that had sinned against the All-Father."

The Archangel paused.

"What we feared most has occurred." The angel

turned to the army that stood beyond the Gate. "But we stand ready to deal with this impending threat."

"So it's war again?" Remy asked, an oppressive sense of sadness sweeping over him, replacing the euphoria of his return.

Michael turned, revealing the most disturbing of expressions. The Archangel wore a smile, and there was a glint of excitement in his piercing eyes.

"War," he repeated as he reached down and drew the sword hanging from the scabbard at his side. "For the kingdom and the glory of Heaven."

He raised the blade high, and all those behind him did the same.

Remy's warrior nature was aroused by the sight before him, eager to join their number, to again wield a weapon in service to the Lord God Almighty.

But there was also a part troubled by the sight, by a nagging voice from somewhere deep in the recesses of his mind that warned the coming war would make the first pale in comparison.

"You haven't learned a thing," Remy said to the armored Archangel.

Michael scowled. "We've learned that the battle is never truly over until your enemies are utterly vanquished."

"And the grace of mercy?" Remy asked.

"Mercy," the Archangel scoffed. "You see now where mercy has brought us."

And Remy saw exactly where it had brought them. There had been no healing since the conflict that altered the very nature of Heaven; in fact, he believed the wound caused by the war now festered with infection.

He hadn't the slightest idea what could be done to cure this illness, and, to be honest, was unsure if it wasn't already too late. Looking about, he saw what he had not noticed before, the patches of tarnish that stained the shiny surfaces of their armor, the gray haze that hung over the city in the distance like an abandoned spider's web, a hint of something sickly sweet lingering in the breeze that could very well have been decay.

"Will you fight with us, brother?" Michael asked, holding out the blade of his sword toward Remy.

The pounding of flapping wings filled the air again, and two angels not of the warrior class flew down to land on either side of the Archangel. Each was holding a pitcher of fragrant water and watched Remy with wary eyes.

"Allow them to cleanse the stain of Hell from your person," Michael said as the two angels slowly stepped forward. "Then you will once again be allowed to pass through the Gates of Heaven."

Remy started to move away and the advancing angels looked nervously back to Michael.

"What is it?" the Archangel asked. "Is there something wrong?"

Remy slowly nodded. "There is," he said. "And the sad thing is, there is nothing I can do to fix it."

The Archangel sheathed his weapon. "You do understand that you are to be welcomed back into the fold," he explained. "That your desertion of duty is to be overlooked as restitution for the services that you performed in the service of Heaven."

Remy shook his head. "I don't want to come back," he told the warrior. "I was given a task by the Morningstar ... to deliver the message that he was free, and the sad fact that the war isn't over. I've done that now, and now I'm through here."

Michael gripped the hilt of his sword tightly. "How does it feel to abandon everything that you are?" the Archangel asked, malice dripping from each and every word.

It couldn't have hurt worse if the angel had driven his blade through Remy's chest.

"I've changed," Remy told him. "It isn't what I am anymore."

He couldn't stay. The war in Heaven had nearly destroyed him once; he wasn't about to give it the chance to do so again.

"What are you?" the Archangel Michael asked of him. "What are you if not of Heaven?"

He'd believed that it was dead—or at least close to being that way—but he had been mistaken. Remy felt his humanity, weak and buried so very deep, but still alive. It fluttered at the question, finding the strength to fight.

To survive.

And with the realization that it still lived, he turned away from the gathering of angels, from Heaven itself.

Feeling the pull of Earth upon him.

The pull of the world that had become his home.

The journey from Heaven to Earth was a long one.

Remy lost track of time as he drifted in the void between worlds, descending from on high, moving through one plane of reality to the next.

Some of these were dreadful worlds, full of dreadful creatures that would have liked nothing more than to feed upon the flesh of the divine. And through those fearsome worlds Remy traveled, avoiding conflict when he was able, and, if he needed to, vanquishing any challenger that dared try and prevent him from reaching his destination.

The journey was long and hard, but the promise of what awaited him at the end of this long journey was enough to sustain him.

In a vast sea of black, waiting for the gentle tug of the world he so longed for, Remy floated, wrapped within his wings of golden brown.

Fragments of memory that he believed lost rose to the surface of his resting mind. He hadn't lost them. They were still there, just buried very deep. And as he floated in the darkness of the void, continuing the long journey home, he carefully stirred them to the surface.

Reacquainting himself with his humanity.

*   *   *

"So it wasn't like ... a hallucination, since I'd been gut shot and all," Steven Mulvehill said as he raised his cup of coffee to his mouth, all the while watching him.

Remy gazed out over the city of Boston from the patio of Massachusetts General Hospital, where the homicide detective was still recovering from his gunshot wound. He almost hadn't made it.

Almost.

"Would you believe me if I told you it was?" Remy asked him.

Mulvehill barely took a sip of his drink, the intensity of his stare showing that he was seriously thinking about the question, and its answer.

"No," he said finally. "Even though I know it doesn't make a lick of fucking sense, I know what I saw ... what I experienced."

"I could deny it," Remy answered. He was watching the birds fly above the city, missing the glorious feel of wind beneath his wings. "Who's going to believe that you actually saw an angel, other than the truly devout, and some others that have a tendency to skip their meds?"

Remy tore off a piece of bagel and placed it in his mouth.

"But you're not going to?" the detective asked. "Deny it."

"Not to you," he answered, chewing his breakfast. Remy picked up his napkin and wiped stray crumbs from his mouth. "Nope, I made my bed and now I have to lie in it."

Mulvehill's face screwed up. "What the fuck's that supposed to mean, *Plato*?"

Remy laughed.

"Means that I've got to deal with what I've done. I showed you what I am, and now we both have to live with it."

"You thought I was gonna die, didn't you?" Mulvehill

asked. "You didn't think you were gonna have to deal with this."

Remy shrugged, having some more of his coffee.

"How many others know ... you're like that?" the detective asked.

"My wife, my dog, some business associates, but they've got some interesting qualities of their own," Remy answered. He'd finished his coffee and didn't want any more of the bagel.

"Do you want the rest of this?" he asked Mulvehill.

The detective shook his head, turning the wheelchair slightly to look out over the city. They were both quiet, wrapped up in their own thoughts.

"They say I'll probably be going home Friday," Mulvehill said.

"That's good, right?" Remy asked him. "You're ready to go home, aren't you?"

The man nodded once, looking back to the angel sitting across from him at the patio table.

"Yeah," he said, and paused. Remy could see him reviewing his next words carefully. "But what happens after that?"

Remy leaned back in the chair, folding his hands on his stomach. "I guess it all depends on how long it takes for you to get back on your feet. After that, you'll go back to work ... light duty at first, slowly working your way back to where you were."

Mulvehill leaned in closer to the table so that others wouldn't hear.

"You don't get what I'm talking about," he said to the angel. "Knowing what I know now ... that something like you actually exists ... it changes everything."

"I guess it does," Remy agreed. "And for that I'm sorry. I just didn't want you to be afraid."

"I'm afraid now," Mulvehill said, his gruffness suddenly pulled away like a curtain to reveal a man confronted with the reality of something so much bigger than himself.

"And here I was thinking I was doing you a favor. The next time you get mortally shot, remind me to look the other way."

The detective at first appeared stunned, but as the smile began to form on the angel's face, the two of them began to laugh.

The pull on Remy was stronger now, the current that he traveled through the void bringing him closer to his destination. He had no idea how much longer he still had on his journey, or even how long it had been thus far. All he knew was that it was a distance that must be traversed in order to return home.

Still swaddled within his wings, Remy floated through the void, the memories that continued to rise to the surface making him all the more hungry for the existence he had left behind.

Somewhere in the darkness the puppy whimpered.

Not really asleep, but in that weird resting state that he'd eventually learned to put himself in while Madeline slept, Remy rose from bed, careful not to wake his wife, and went in search of the animal.

It had been only a few days since Marlowe had come to live with them, and the young canine seemed to be adjusting quite well to his new environment.

Or at least that was what Remy believed.

He found the pup downstairs, in the corner of the shadowed living room, sitting in a patch of moonlight beneath the open window.

"What's wrong?" Remy asked the animal, keeping his voice soft so that he did not awaken his wife.

"Miss them," the puppy said, staring at him briefly with large, seemingly bottomless dark eyes, before he turned his snout back up to the breeze wafting in through the window.

"Who do you miss?" Remy asked him, sitting in the

chair not too far from where the Labrador puppy sat. "Your pack brothers and sisters?"

"Yes."

"As you have done, your brothers and sisters have gone to live in new places, Marlowe. With new families," Remy started to explain. "We are your pack now."

The dog looked at him with sad eyes, ears flat against his small, square head. *"Not same. Miss them."*

Remy moved from the chair, and sat beside the animal on the floor beneath the window. "Yes, it's sad," he told the puppy. "But that's the way it works. First there is the pack, and then the pack is broken up, each of you going off to find a new pack."

Marlowe crawled up into Remy's lap, plopping down with a heavy sigh.

"The way it works?" the Labrador pup asked.

"Afraid so," Remy said, beginning to stroke the dog's short, silky-soft fur.

"You leave pack?"

"Yes, I did."

"Find new pack? Happy now . . . not sad?"

"No, not sad," Remy told him, as he gently patted the young dog until he drifted off to sleep.

"Happy now."

He was nearly there.

Remy could feel it in the sea of dark, just beyond his reach. It was the tug of the familiar, a promise of the warmth and love of companions.

They were not his kind, but still they had recognized and accepted what he was, and in turn he had made them his own.

Rousing himself from a sleeplike stasis, Remy spread his wings and listened to his senses, homing in on the place that called out to him.

The world that was his home.

*   *   *

They climbed the stairs to the rooftop.

Madeline carefully pushed the door at the top of the stairway open and stepped out onto what would soon become their rooftop patio.

She held his hand in hers, drawing him out onto the tar-paper surface for a view of the city beyond Beacon Hill.

"This will be fantastic," she said, looking around at the space. A stack of empty and broken clay flowerpots sat in the corner, along with a punctured bag of potting soil. "We can put the table just about there, with the chairs around it. . . . This is going to be great."

She spun around and hugged him tightly.

"Are you happy?" she asked, her faced pressed to his chest.

This would be the first night in their new home on Pinckney Street. They had spent the entire day—since early that morning—painting and doing some fixing about the brownstone. The phone man had been there, as had the gas man.

Remy wrapped his arms around his wife and hugged her close.

Am I happy?

Since making this world his home, he'd slowly acclimated himself to the concept. He was a creature of Heaven; there was no time for happiness or the opposite. His existence had been to serve the Almighty.

He guessed there had been happiness in that, but now he couldn't truly be sure. The war had taken so much from him, bleached away the colors of what had once been such a glorious rainbow.

But this world, this earth, had given him back some of the color.

In retrospect, he saw the happiness had grown. The more acclimated he became, the more human, his joy had increased.

And it had reached its zenith with the love of his wife.

"I'm happy," he said, kissing the top of her head.

She looked up at him.

"Really? Are you really?"

He smiled at her. "What are you getting at?" he asked. "I can hear that sound in your voice. You're fishing for something."

She laughed as she broke away from his embrace, going to the edge of the roof. "I don't know," she said, leaning on the brick edging that bordered the roof space. "Sometimes I get to thinking about the reality of what you are, and where you came from."

Remy came up from behind, wrapping his arms around her waist, and pressing against her. "I don't understand what that has to do with . . ."

Madeline turned around in his grasp, gazing into his eyes.

"You're an angel from the kingdom of Heaven," she stressed. "Isn't all this . . . with me . . . I don't know . . . boring?"

Remy looked deep into her inquisitive stare as she waited for his answer. She would know whether or not he was lying; it was a gift that she had.

Slowly he lowered his face down toward her, his lips eventually meeting hers. They kissed softly at first, and more eagerly soon after that.

Before leaving the roof to descend the stairs to their new home, where they made love on an old down comforter they'd used as a makeshift drop cloth, Remy broke their passion to answer her question.

"All this . . . you . . . this is Heaven," he told her.

This is Heaven.

He emerged from the void into a darkness of a different kind, this one illuminated by a multitude of stars, twinkling in the galaxy like jewels strewn upon a covering of velvet.

Hanging in space, he found his bearings, moving through the vacuum, at last, toward his destination.

He had no idea how long he'd been gone, feeling the heart within his chest swelling in size as he beheld the planet he had so come to love hanging there, as if waiting for his return.

The angelic nature was displeased, attempting to exert dominance, to suppress the humanity that had emerged from hiding as he'd traveled the void toward Earth, growing in size and strength at the joy he had found in the recollections of being human.

There was nothing the angelic essence would have loved more than to withdraw completely, leaving him frail and unprotected in the killing coldness of space, eager for him to beg to be something more.

Remy held the reins firmly, controlling the troublesome aspect of his being as he entered the Earth's atmosphere, the sudden friction of oxygen upon his flesh causing it to heat, threatening to burn. His body beginning to glow white-hot with reentry, he gritted his teeth, spreading his wings wide to help slow his descent.

The angel dropped out of the night sky unnoticed by the city below, which was as he wished it to be.

Dropping through a thick bank of clouds, Remy emerged over the city of Boston. A smile appeared on his face and his naked flesh tingled. It had been scoured a bright red as a result of his journey. It would all heal eventually, he thought, flapping his wings furiously, pushing his speed to the maximum in order to return home. He had no idea how long he'd been gone, time moving differently in travels from one realm to the next.

He just hoped it hadn't been too long. That he hadn't been forgotten.

Remy soared above Faneuil Hall, Government Center, and then the golden dome of the State House on his way to Beacon Hill . . . to Pinckney Street.

To his home.

The rooftop of his building appeared below him, and he was suddenly overtaken with a feeling of absolute exhaustion. He swooped down from the night sky, aiming for the rooftop patio below.

As his bare feet touched down upon the blacktop, he collapsed, pitching forward, the stinging warmth of his face and body now pressed to the cool tar-paper roof.

Unconsciousness threatened to take him, but he managed to fight it, not wanting to surrender to the darkness again. He'd spent far too much time in the womb of oblivion, and would prefer not to return there.

In the distance he heard a noise, growing louder, more persistent as it came closer. It was the barking of a dog—*his dog*—and he wasn't sure if he'd ever heard a sound so beautiful.

Marlowe was saying *hurry*, over and over again in the rough voice that he had. And Remy couldn't have agreed more.

Hurry.

He heard the door to the roof open, the distinct voice of his friend speaking to the insistent animal.

"If these are friggin' pigeons again, you're not getting your snack tonight. You think I'm joking? Try me. If you brought me all the way up here in the middle of the freakin' night again to . . ."

Marlowe knew he was there, somehow sensing his arrival.

He was a good boy, a really good boy.

The barking turned higher, almost a squeal of pain, as the dog found him. Remy could feel his excited approach. The Labrador pounced and began licking his face, his head, his shoulders, repeating his name over and over again. Remy wanted to sit up, to throw his arms around the neck of his animal friend and tell him how much he was missed, but he couldn't move, couldn't even open his eyes.

"Jesus Christ, Remy," he heard Mulvehill say. "I thought you were dead. When I got that phone message I didn't know what to think. . . . I didn't know if you needed my help. . . . I thought you were dead. . . ."

Mulvehill knelt upon the ground, and Remy's bare skin stung as his body was gently raised, held in the arms of his friend.

Marlowe had not stopped kissing his face. It felt good, cool and sort of slimy on his tender flesh.

"Look at you," Mulvehill said, holding his friend close. There was worry in his voice, and Remy wondered how bad he actually looked.

"You hang in there, okay?" he said. "You're going to be fine. It's my turn now," Mulvehill said. "There's no reason to be afraid. . . . Everything is going to be all right."

And with those words, Remy managed to crack open his eyes, staring up into the man's worried face.

His friend was right, he thought, as he felt his eyes begin to close, eager oblivion rushing in to steal him away from this moment of happiness.

At the moment, there was *no* reason to be afraid; everything *was* going to be all right.

And as exhaustion threatened to take him, he saw his wife's beautiful face as she again asked him the question.

Are you happy?

And he completely surrendered to the moment, taking her into his arms, the two of them drifting down, down, down into the darkness.

Yes.

EPILOGUE

It had taken him time to heal, the damage far more extensive than he would have originally believed.

Hell certainly had its dramatic effects; his shoulder still ached where he had been wounded, his flesh still peeling in places, the remaining manifestation of his angelic form sloughing off like a snake shedding its skin.

It itched like hell.

Remy stood in the foyer of Francis' building on Newbury Street, listening to the sounds of the empty building. The fallen that had lived here were gone, leaving to go elsewhere when the passageway between this world and Hell was severed.

It is not such a bad thing, he thought, there being one less entry point from the netherworld, especially now.

The jingling of Marlowe's collar distracted him from his musing. The dog was at the end of the hall, sniffing around an old radiator.

"What did you find?" Remy asked.

"Mouse smell," Marlowe said, lifting his head to answer, a large wad of dust sticking to his wet black nose.

Since Remy's return, Marlowe had become his shadow, refusing to let him out of his sight. He believed the dog had thought that he had died, leaving him like Madeline had. It would take some convincing, but he was sure that the animal would soon start to relax again.

Malowe padded down the hallway toward him.

"Want to get going?" Remy asked him, reaching out to pat his head and wiping away the dust and dirt that still clung to his nose.

"Park?" the dog asked.

Remy reviewed his day. It was Saturday, and there really wasn't all that much planned.

"Sure, I think we can squeeze in a run to the Common," he said.

Marlowe's tail wagged happily.

Fishing the building's keys from his pocket, Remy noticed Marlowe now sniffing around the door that would take them down into what had been Francis' place.

"Where Francis?" Marlowe asked with a tilt of his head.

He really didn't know how to answer the animal. To tell the Labrador that his friend was dead would have likely been a lie. Francis had been a Guardian angel in service to the Lord God who had betrayed his station by joining Lucifer's rebellion against Heaven. He had realized the error of his ways, begging the Almighty's forgiveness, and had been given penance.

"Francis had to go away," Remy told the animal.

And until that penance was completed, until the Lord of Lords bestowed forgiveness, there would be no release.

"Coming back?" Marlowe asked, inquisitively tilting his head to one side.

"I don't know," Remy answered truthfully. "I really don't know."

The former Guardian must have suspected that something had been wrong in the netherworld, putting things in motion in the material world that put Remy in charge of all his financial holdings. Remy had been stunned when he'd received the letter from the lawyer's office explaining that he was now the sole owner of the property on Newbury Street, until the original owner's return.

"C'mon, let's go to the park," he said, opening the

foyer door out into the entryway. Marlowe bounded ahead of him as Remy took a final look.

They'd blamed the results of Hell leaking out from the Tartarus passage on a gas leak, city workers tearing up the street in front of the brownstone, as well as the basement, in search of the problem pipe.

Nobody ever really said if they'd found what they were looking for, but things returned to normal, and the building was again deemed safe to be lived in.

Not wanting the now vacant building to sit there empty, Remy had contacted a real estate company and was going to rent the apartments out. There was no danger now, the passage to Hell having been permanently closed, but Francis' apartment would remain locked and unrented just to be on the safe side.

Remy left the building, the details over what had transpired in both Hell, and later in Heaven, nearly dominating his thoughts. He had no idea what the future would bring, the concept of a war breaking out between the forces of Hell and Heaven making him feel very afraid. He knew that a war such as that would not stay within the combatants' borders.

Marlowe barked, snout pointed at the door as he waited patiently to leave.

"All right, pal," Remy said, pushing open the outside door. "We're going."

The dog leapt out onto the front landing, bounding down the steps with increased excitement.

Heading straight toward the lone woman standing at the bottom of the stairs.

"Marlowe, no!" Remy yelled, hoping to put the brakes on the dog's excitement, but it didn't do much. He loved to meet new people, and when there was one just standing at the end of the walkway, waiting for him, how was a Labrador to resist?

Remy was just glad that she wasn't holding a roast chicken, or even an apple or banana; then things could have gotten ugly.

He tried to gauge the woman's body language, her reaction to a seventy-pound dog bounding toward her.

She handled it like a pro—or at least a dog lover—bending down to meet his arrival, sticking her hand out for the animal to smell.

Marlowe licked her fingers furiously, and the woman started to laugh, squatting down to ruffle the dog's ears and talk to him, telling him how beautiful he was and asking his name.

"Sorry about that," Remy said, reaching the end of the walkway. He removed a leash from his pocket and attached it to the loop on Marlowe's chain collar. "His name is Marlowe, and as you can see, he doesn't care for people very much."

"I can see that," she said, rising from her squat to meet his gaze.

The first thing that passed through Remy's mind was that she was a very attractive woman, the next being that he knew her.

She continued to pet Marlowe, the black Labrador leaning into the woman's legs, his hunger for affection nearly pushing her back.

Remy must have stared too long, still shocked to be standing there, talking with Linda Somerset, the waitress from Piazza that had so captured Francis' attentions.

How weird is this? he thought.

"I know this is going to sound stupid, but have we met?" she asked, moving a lock of dark hair away from her pretty face with one hand, while continuing to pet an attention-starved Marlowe with the other.

He remembered how he'd been at the café with Francis, both of them willing themselves unseen.

"You work at the restaurant down the street, Piazza," he said. "A good friend of mine used to go there quite a bit."

She smiled, nodding. "I knew you looked familiar."

Remy smiled back, suddenly experiencing a bit of

what Francis must have felt with the woman. There was a warmth about her, an air that she was a good person.

He knew Marlowe would agree.

She looked to the brownstone.

"Do you live here?" she asked. There was a hint of awe in her voice.

"No," he said. "Marlowe and I live on the Hill. I'm just managing the property for a friend."

Linda continued to stare at the building. "I love this place," she told him. "I go by it every day on my way to work and I heard from an agent at the restaurant that there were apartments opening up. I couldn't resist stopping by to check it out. Don't know what it is, but there's something about it that just makes me feel safe."

She laughed again, returning her attention to the dog. "Bet that just makes me sound crazy," she said, rubbing Marlowe's ears, making his collar jingle like sleigh bells.

"Not at all," Remy said. "There's definitely something very special about this building."

He almost started to laugh, thinking how bullshit Francis would have been to see him now.

"It was very nice meeting you, Marlowe," she said, bending down to plant a kiss on top of his blockish head. "And it was very nice speaking with you," she said to Remy with a friendly smile. "I'm Linda."

She extended her hand, and he took it in his. He almost responded by saying that he already knew her name, but decided that it could come across as creepy.

"Remy," he said. "Remy Chandler."

"Marlowe!" the dog barked.

"And you already know Marlowe."

The handshake broke, and they continued to stand there in uncomfortable silence, each waiting for the other to speak.

"Linda go to park with Marlowe?" the dog asked in a series of whines and grumbles that only Remy, and other dogs, could decipher as language.

"No, I don't think Linda wants to go to the Common with you," he told the animal with a chuckle.

Linda laughed. "Is that what he asked you?"

"Yeah," Remy said. "We're going to the Common and he asked if you wanted to come along."

"So you speak dog?"

"Among other languages, yes."

She thought he was fooling around, of course.

"Tell him that I would love to go on a walk with him, but that I have to go to work," Linda Somerset said.

Remy looked down at Marlowe.

"Did you get that?" he asked the animal.

"Yes," Marlowe woofed.

"He got it," Remy said.

She looked at her watch, and quickly up Newbury, not sure how to end the conversation.

"Maybe I'll see you at Piazza sometime," he said, beginning to lead Marlowe away, toward where he'd parked his car.

"Maybe you will," she said, starting to walk backward. She waved, and then turned around to head up Newbury Street.

Nice girl, he thought, giving Marlowe's leash a tiny tug as they headed toward the car.

"I work Wednesday, Thursday, Friday, and every other weekend," he heard a voice call after him.

He turned to see that Linda was calling to him.

"You talking to me?" Remy asked jokingly.

She shook her head. "I was talking to the handsome one," she said. "I was talking to Marlowe."

"Linda say Marlowe handsome," the black dog said, his tail wagging excitedly.

He laughed at her joke and gave her a final wave.

"See you around, Remy Chandler," she said, heading on her way.

There was something in the way the words were said, like they had come from an old friend who hadn't been heard from in a very long time.

Something that he knew she believed.

"*Like*," Marlowe said walking alongside him.

And strangely enough, so did he.

"*See again?*" the dog asked, looking at him with dark, inquisitive eyes.

"Yeah," Remy finally answered as they reached the car, not sure exactly how he felt about it, "we probably will," at that moment understanding again how difficult it was to be human.

ABOUT THE AUTHOR

Thomas E. Sniegoski is the author of the groundbreaking quartet of teen fantasy novels titled *The Fallen*, which were transformed into an ABC Family miniseries, drawing stellar ratings for the cable network.

With Christopher Golden, he is the coauthor of the dark fantasy series *The Menagerie* as well as the young-readers' fantasy series *OutCast*. Golden and Sniegoski have also cocreated two comic book series, *Talent* and *The Sisterhood*, and wrote the graphic novel *BPRD: Hollow Earth*, a spin-off from the fan-favorite comic book series *Hellboy*.

Sniegoski's other novels include *Force Majeure*, *Hellboy: The God Machine*, and several projects involving the popular television franchises *Buffy the Vampire Slayer* and *Angel*, including both *Buffy* video games.

As a comic book writer, he was responsible for *Stupid, Stupid Rat Tails*, a prequel miniseries to the international hit *Bone*. Sniegoski collaborated with *Bone* creator Jeff Smith on the prequel, making him the only writer Smith has ever asked to work on those characters. He has also written tales featuring such characters as Batman, Daredevil, Wolverine, The Goon, and The Punisher.

His children's book series, *Billy Hooten: Owlboy*, is published by Random House.

Sniegoski was born and raised in Massachusetts, where he still lives with his wife, LeeAnne, and their Labrador retriever, Mulder.

Please read on for an excerpt
from the Remy Chandler novel

WHERE ANGELS FEAR TO TREAD

Available now from Roc

Boston, Now.

Remy Chandler watched the older woman as she sat across from him, sipping her Gin—*no*, her *Tanqueray* and tonic from a short brown straw.

She'd been quite specific with the waitress.

He was trying to figure out what it was exactly that he didn't like about her.

She leaned forward, placing her glass precisely in the center of the cardboard coaster in front of her. "My grandmother, God rest her soul, used to have two Tanqueray and tonics every day," Mrs. Grantmore said, straightening the coaster. "She said they helped her keep her wits about her. She was ninety-eight when she finally passed."

It was obvious that Remy was supposed to be impressed.

"Isn't ninety-eight the new eighty-five?" he joked, taking a sip of his soda water with lime.

Mrs. Grantmore's daughter, Olivia, sitting quietly beside her mother on the love seat in the lobby bar of the Copley Place Westin Hotel, chuckled before taking a drink of her Diet Coke.

Remy liked Olivia. She seemed like a sweet kid.

"I wouldn't know," Mrs. Grantmore said dismissively, reaching for her drink, bringing it to her mouth, careful not to drip any of the condensation from the glass onto her white silk blouse.

Remy crossed his ankle over his knee, pulling the cuff of his dark jeans over the tongue of his brown loafer.

This meeting was exactly what he had expected, and one he would have preferred to have had at his office. Having it at the Westin, out in the open, was uncomfortable, especially with Olivia present.

"So," Remy said, faking cheerfulness. He leaned forward in the overstuffed chair and placed his drink on the glass-topped table before him. "You're probably wondering about my findings." He grabbed the folder from the seat beside him and opened it.

Mrs. Grantmore turned to look at her daughter as she returned her glass to the coaster. "Of course, Mr. Chandler. I'm sure you're a very busy man. Go on. Tell us what you've found."

Olivia, who had been silently staring into the bubbles of her soft drink, looked up, making eye contact with him.

He tried to assuage her fears with a comforting smile.

"You asked me to look into the background of one James Wardley," he said, looking down at the file.

Mrs. Grantmore reached over and took her daughter's hand. The look Olivia flashed her made it clear the gesture was not appreciated.

"Go ahead, Mr. Chandler. What did you learn?"

Remy shrugged. "To be honest, not a whole lot."

He watched as the older woman's features momentarily tightened, her stare becoming more intense.

Olivia looked as though a huge weight had been lifted from her shoulders.

"You found nothing out of the ordinary?"

"Nothing," Remy said, continuing the litany of his findings. "James Wardley of Lynn, Massachusetts, born August 16, 1988, to Harriet and Robert Wardley. Attended Lynn Classical High School, graduated in 2006 at the top of his class. Enrolled at Northeastern University, currently majoring in electrical engineering and . . ."

"There was nothing . . . out of sorts. . . . Say, a criminal history?" Mrs. Grantmore interrupted.

Remy slowly shook his head. "Not really. There was something about a party and some underage drinking, but no charges were ever filed."

He closed the file and met the older woman's eyes. She was speechless. Obviously it wasn't the result she was looking for.

"See, Mother?" Olivia said, still clutching her mother's hand. "There's nothing for you to worry about. James is a good boy."

Silently Mrs. Grantmore removed her hand from her daughter's.

"I seem to be developing a rather bad headache," the older woman said. "Probably the humidity and this air-conditioning." Her handbag was on the floor at her feet and she bent forward, plucking out a wallet. Fishing inside for a moment, she found a twenty-dollar bill and handed it to Olivia.

"Would you be a dear and buy me a bottle of Tylenol from the gift shop?" she asked, a forced smile upon her strained features.

"Mother, you promised to let this go if I agreed to . . ."

"Please, Olivia," her mother snapped. "Go to the gift shop."

The pretty young woman rose from her seat, briefly glancing at Remy with pleading eyes before making her way across the hotel lobby toward the gift shop.

As soon as Olivia was out of earshot, Mrs. Grantmore turned back to Remy.

"A regular model citizen," she said sarcastically, picking up her drink and taking a gulp from the glass, this time forgoing the straw.

"Like your daughter said," Remy answered, "he's a good boy. You should be glad."

"Glad, Mr. Chandler?" she scoffed. "It's obvious that you don't have children."

Remy felt himself immediately rankle. Having children had always been a sensitive issue in his long, otherwise happy marriage to Madeline. No matter how much she had said that she understood they couldn't have a family, he had always believed a part of her resented him for it. Because she was human, and he . . . *wasn't*, he had deprived her . . . *them* . . . of something special.

But it didn't matter now, because she was gone. And, at that moment, he realized that was the first time he'd thought of her that afternoon.

And it bothered him.

"No, I don't have children," he replied tightly. "But I think if I did have a young, attractive, intelligent and respectful daughter like Olivia, I would be quite happy to see her dating someone with similar characteristics and not the local crack dealer."

Mrs. Grantmore used the stirrer in her drink to move the ice around.

"No, not the local crack dealer, but close enough."

Remy couldn't believe what he was hearing.

"What about the boy's father?" she asked. "One of the other investigators mentioned that his father might have had some trouble with the law."

"One of the other investigators?" Remy felt his pulse quicken.

"Well, you're certainly not the first I've hired since Olivia told me she was dating," the conniving woman scoffed. "Did you look into the father's background?"

It took all of Remy's strength to remain calm and professional.

But he could feel *it* stirring inside him.

The power of Seraphim had been much more active, and more difficult to silence of late. If he let his guard down, even just a bit, he could only imagine what the power of Heaven would do to the woman.

"His father did some time in a juvenile detention center for car theft over twenty years ago, but hasn't been in any kind of trouble since," Remy said. "But I don't see what that has to do with . . ."

"That's good," she said, ignoring him. "We can work with that, maybe make some connection to genetics."

"Genetics?" Remy started to laugh in disbelief. If he hadn't, he wasn't quite sure what he—what the angelic nature that he had squirreled away inside him—might have done.

For an instant he imagined the fires of Heaven leaping from the tips of his blackened fingers, consuming the woman's hateful flesh.

"This might seem funny to you, Mr. Chandler, but I assure you it is not," Mrs. Grantmore said with obvious annoyance. "My daughter is the most important thing in my life. Everything my husband and I have worked so hard to acquire will someday belong to her . . ."

"And someone that you deem worthy," Remy completed, not bothering to hide his disgust.

"The key word is worthy," Mrs. Grantmore agreed. She finished her Tanqueray and tonic, slamming the ice-filled glass down with enough force to rattle the tabletop. "I'm not about to allow some worthless piece of riffraff to use my daughter—"

"Mother."

Olivia had returned; neither of them noticing her approach, so wrapped up were they in their . . . *discussion*.

The older woman took a deep breath and composed herself. "Did you find the Tylenol?" she asked.

Her daughter let the bag containing the bottle of pills drop into her mother's lap.

"Thank you, dear."

Remy wasn't sure how much the young woman had heard, but the look on her face told him it was enough.

"I think we're finished here," Mrs. Grantmore stated, shoving the bag into her purse.

And Remy couldn't have agreed more. For a brief instant he imagined the woman on her knees, begging forgiveness from the frightening visage of what he truly was; golden armor glistening, powerful wings beating the air as they held his mighty form aloft.

A soldier of God.

Seraphim.

But no matter how his true nature fought him, that wasn't who he was anymore.

"Thank you for your time, Mr. Chandler," the woman said stiffly, offering her hand as they stood.

"You're welcome," Remy said, taking and quickly releasing her hand, yet again resisting the urge to end her hateful existence in a searing release of Heaven's fire. "I'll send you my final invoice before week's end."

Without comment, the woman bent to gather her things, and Remy turned to her daughter.

"It was very nice meeting you, Olivia," he said, holding out his own hand.

She took it with a small smile.

"I'm truly sorry about this," he told her, as his gaze drifted to a displeased Mrs. Grantmore.

"As am I, Mr. Chandler," Olivia said releasing his hand.

Remy left the two women then, feeling Mrs. Grantmore's eyes burning into his back as he walked toward the stairs, certain in the knowledge that it would take much more than Tylenol to kill the disease that grew inside her.

Outside the Westin it was hot and humid, but how else would Boston be in August?

A quick glance at his watch showed Remy that if he didn't hurry he would be late for his early dinner date with friend Steven Mulvehill. Not that it really mattered. The homicide detective was never on time anyway.

Remy walked up Dartmouth Street toward Beacon, not a little concerned about his reaction toward Mrs. Grantmore. It was taking less and less these days to rouse the angelic nature that he had worked so hard to contain. A sign of the times, most definitely, he mused as he stopped to let a cab pass—one that would most assuredly have run him down if he'd stepped in front of it.

And what then? he thought. *Would the Seraphim have emerged to smite the vehicle and its driver?*

A few years ago, a thought like that would have been just plain foolish. But now, since the death of his beloved wife, he couldn't be so sure. Everything had changed—in the earthly world, as well as in the unearthly one.

He looked around him. Things looked the same, but the difference was there, an undercurrent. Whether they knew it or not—the pretzel man, the student, the teller at the bank stepping out for a quick cigarette break— the world was different.

And not in a good way.

Remy's own world had begun to change dramatically when his wife first became ill. From there it was like a row of cosmic dominoes had begun to fall, with the disappearance of the Angel of Death and then narrowly averting the Apocalypse, the nearly unbearable pain of Madeline's death, the return of Lucifer Morningstar to Hell and the loss of Francis, the former Guardian Angel who had been Remy's friend and frequent comrade in arms.

And it was just the beginning—of this, Remy was sure.

He turned down Beacon Street, and the disturbing realization of how dramatically different things were became a reality when he caught sight of the bedraggled form of Steven Mulvehill waiting in front of the restaurant.

On time.

And the world became that much stranger a place.

The restaurant was pricey, even for an early dinner, but Mulvehill had a gift certificate that he'd gotten from another detective whose wife had developed a wheat allergy and, according to Mulvehill, couldn't go out to eat anymore.

Remy was pretty sure there was more to the story—there always was when it came to things surrounding Mulvehill—but he didn't feel the need to dig any further. A free dinner was a free dinner, and he would leave it at that.

"Working today?" Mulvehill asked, reaching for his glass of water, a fresh lemon slice floating amidst the ice.

Remy popped another french fry into his mouth, nodding while he chewed.

"More of the weird shit?" Mulvehill asked, leaning forward to pick up the second half of an amazingly swollen hot pastrami sandwich that he had slathered with dark mustard.

Remy was having the cheeseburger and, like the fries, it was excellent. He didn't have to eat—his sustenance came from the life energies around him—but it had become one of his biggest pleasures and he wouldn't give it up for anything.

"Nope, nothing weird this time," he said, picking up his burger. "Just a very wealthy woman looking to put the kibosh on her daughter's relationship."

"That bitch," Mulvehill snarled, wiping his mustard-covered hands on the cloth napkin. Remy noticed that some of the dark condiment had dribbled onto his friend's tie, but there were so many other stains there already, it wasn't worth mentioning. "Did you set her straight? No, wait. . . . Did you get paid, and then set her straight?"

"Final bill hasn't gone out yet, but it will," Remy said around a large bite of burger. He hesitated a moment, then continued. "She really pushed my buttons; I had to stifle the urge to fry her where she sat," he said, not looking at his friend. He pulled a slice of red onion from his sandwich and stuffed it in his mouth.

Mulvehill was strangely silent, and Remy looked up. The homicide detective knew all of Remy's secrets, and he was the only one Remy could share this with—now that Maddy was gone. He knew that Mulvehill often wished that he didn't know what he did, but that cat had been let out of the bag sometime ago.

And, besides, it always led to really interesting conversations.

"Seriously?" Mulvehill finally asked. "You really wanted to burn her alive with your angel superpowers?"

Remy halfheartedly nodded, shrugging his shoulders as he tried to explain. "It wasn't really me per se, but, y'know, the part of me that . . . you know."

Mulvehill slowly nodded. "Yeah, I know, but damn. Remind me never to piss you off unless we're near a fire extinguisher or a lake or something." He picked up a half-eaten pickle spear from his plate and took a bite.

"I'd never burn you alive," Remy said. He set what was left of his burger on his plate. "With all the booze you drink, you'd probably go off like some great big, fleshy Molotov cocktail."

"Oh, you're a fucking riot," Mulvehill said sarcastically. He reached for his water and held up the glass. "See, water." He took a drink.

"Only because you're on duty," Remy teased. "If you were off today, we'd probably need another three gift certificates to handle the bar bill."

"See if I invite you out on my dime again," the homicide cop said, going back to his mustard-drenched sandwich.

"It's a gift certificate," Remy reminded him.

"Yeah, that I could have used with any number of hot babes trying to become the next Mrs. Mulvehill."

Remy laughed, leaning back in his chair. "Any number of babes?" he repeated. He pulled a few more fries from his plate. "That's good."

"What, you don't think I'm desirable?" Mulvehill asked with a smile, a giant gob of brown mustard oozing down his chin.

"If we weren't in a public place, I'd take you now, you gorgeous hunk of man," Remy said.

They both laughed, then turned their attention toward finishing their meals.

"Did you really want to burn her?" Mulvehill asked suddenly, breaking their silence. "Seriously?"

Remy looked up into his friend's worried gaze. He couldn't lie to him. "Yeah, I did," he answered quietly. He took the napkin from his lap and wiped his mouth.

"I have to say that isn't such a good thing."

Remy agreed. "No, and it worries me. Since Madeline . . . I feel myself drifting . . . not all the time, but sometimes, when certain things push a button."

Mulvehill noisily chewed the last of his pastrami sandwich and wiped the grease and mustard from his face. "The next well-done corpse I find in the city, I'm looking for you, pal," he said.

Remy gripped his water glass, staring at the ice and lemon slice. "It scares me."

His friend remained quiet. No snarky comeback. It wasn't the time.

"I'm afraid of the day that I can't . . . that I don't want to keep it inside anymore."

"Is that a possibility?" Mulvehill asked.

"Could be." Remy shrugged. "Probably not right now, but there could come a time when I won't have the things around me that keep me anchored to this world."

"Like Maddie," Mulvehill said quietly.

Remy silently nodded. "She was the most amazing thing in my life here, but now there's just this giant void where she used to be." He could feel a darkened mood descending on him, as it had a tendency to do when he thought too hard about things connected to his fragile humanity.

"I know what your problem is," Mulvehill said, tossing his napkin onto the table top. "I should've given you the gift certificate."

Remy looked across the table at his friend. "Should've given me the gift certificate? What the hell are you talking about?"

"You could've used it for a date," Mulvehill said. "You could've taken somebody out for a nice dinner, and maybe found a new anchor ... not that anybody could ever replace Maddie. I'm just saying it might help."

Remy had to laugh. "You think I should date?" he asked incredulously.

"Yeah. Why not?" Mulvehill asked. "What was the name of that woman you told me about?" He snapped his fingers. "The waitress ... you know who I mean."

"Linda," Remy said, focusing on the water in his glass again.

"Yeah, Linda. Why not go out with her?"

It was all so very complicated. Remy had met Linda Somerset through Francis. During the Great War in Heaven, Francis had chosen the wrong side, but then he had seen the error of his ways and was desperate to make amends. The Almighty had given him the duty of watching over one of the passages to the Hell prison of Tartarus, which just so happened to be in the basement of the apartment building that the Guardian Angel owned on Newbury Street.

The last time Remy saw Francis, he had been badly wounded in the effort to prevent the Morningstar's catastrophic return to Hell. Remy still held out hope that somehow Francis had managed to survive.

Although, as time passed, it was becoming less and less likely.

Francis had been obsessed with Linda Somerset, even though she knew nothing of his interests. Remy had spoken to the attractive waitress at Newbury Street's Piazza Restaurant a few times since Francis's disappearance, and he could understand his friend's fixation.

There was definitely something about Linda Somerset.

"I'd rather not talk about it," Remy said, hoping, but doubting, that comment would be the end of the discussion.

Their waiter approached the table then. "Are you gentlemen finished?" he asked, reaching for their plates.

"Could you wrap that last piece of burger in some foil for me?" Remy asked the well-groomed Hispanic man who had introduced himself as Harry.

Harry smiled. "You must have a dog?" he asked, lifting the plate from the table.

"No, he's gonna have that as a snack later," Mulvehill offered. "He's really cheap."

"Will you shut up?" Remy snarled. "Yes, I do, and if I don't bring him something, I'm going to be in trouble."

"No problem," Harry said. "Any coffee or dessert?"

They both declined, Mulvehill sticking out his belly and patting it as a sign that he was sated.

The waiter said that he'd be back with Remy's food, and the check, excusing himself as he left with their dirty plates.

"So why not?" Mulvehill started up again

"I said I don't want to talk about it," Remy said, trying not to become upset with his friend. He did not want to even think about burning his best friend alive. "It's far too early for me to even be thinking about things like this; Madeline hasn't even been gone six months."

"Stop right there," Mulvehill said. "I don't mean to be cold or heartless, but you just said the magic words."

Remy tilted his head inquisitively to one side, as he'd so often seen Marlowe, his four-year-old Labrador retriever, do.

"Madeline's gone, Remy," the detective said. "I know how you felt about her. I loved her too, but if her being gone and you being lonely means that you're going to start losing your shit and frying people every time you get annoyed, maybe you should think about the benefits of some female companionship."

Mulvehill's words were like a kick to the teeth, and Remy really didn't know how to react.

"You're not pissed that I said that, right?" Mulvehill asked cautiously, as Harry returned to the table with their check and Remy's leftovers wrapped in foil.

"No," Remy lied.

"You're not gonna cook my ass?" he asked, pulling the wrinkled gift certificate from the inside pocket of his sports jacket and placing it inside the leather folder with the check and an equally wrinkled twenty-dollar bill.

At first Remy didn't answer.

"You heard what I said about the dangerous levels of alcohol in your body."

"Screw you. Are you mad at me or not?"

"I'm not mad. I just don't want to talk about this anymore," Remy said, slowly getting up from his seat.

"You said Maddie's been gone for less than six months, and I bet it's been the longest near six months of your life, hasn't it?" the normally unemotional man said, as he gripped Remy's elbow. "I hate to see you like this, and then to hear you say things about losing control, it just gets me thinking that . . ."

"I'm all right, Steven," Remy said, forcing a smile. "Really, I'm all right. I think this case just brought out my bad side, but it's done now, and I can get back to my naturally cheerful self."

He felt his friend studying him, searching for a sign, a crack in the armor. Remy started for the door so Mulvehill couldn't look closer.

"Hey, Chandler," his friend called.

Remy turned slowly.

The homicide detective was holding the piece of foil-wrapped hamburger. "You taking this, or do you want to be on your dog's shit list?"

Remy returned to take the package from Mulvehill. If there was one shit list he couldn't bear to be on, it was Marlowe's.

Marlowe paced excitedly in the backseat of Remy's Corolla.

"*Rabbits,*" Remy heard the dog mutter beneath his breath in the guttural language of his breed. "*Rabbits, rabbits, rabbits.*"

"And maybe squirrels," Remy contributed, looking at the dog's reaction in his rearview mirror.

"Maybe squirrels," Marlowe repeated. *"Rabbits, maybe squirrels."*

Remy had returned to his Pinckney Street home strangely agitated after his dinner with Steven Mulvehill. His friend had definitely touched on a particularly sensitive nerve.

Putting his signal on, Remy took a right into the parking lot of Mount Auburn Cemetery. He had the pick of the lot, and eased into a space in a nice patch of shade thrown by an oak tree.

His wife had been gone for almost six months and he still felt the magnitude of her passing each and every day. The idea that he could push her memory, and the love that he still felt for her, aside was unthinkable.

So why was it that deep down he knew his friend was probably right?

Marlowe was panting like a runaway freight train as Remy turned off the car's engine and opened the door to a blast of August heat.

"All right, all right," Remy said, opening the back passenger door.

Marlowe leapt out, immediately placing his nose to the ground and beginning to track his prey.

"Anything?" Remy asked.

"Rabbits, maybe squirrels," Marlowe reported quite seriously.

"Thought so," Remy answered.

There was no one in sight, so he let Marlowe roam. He followed his dog through the metal gateway onto the winding path that led through one of the prettiest cemeteries in the greater Boston area. Marlowe continued the hunt, nose moving along the ground, and off the path to the grassy areas around the trees and grave markers.

"Hey!" Remy called.

The Labrador stopped and lifted his head.

"No peeing on the headstones," Remy reminded him.

"No pee," Marlowe grumbled.

It was certainly hot, but there was a hint of cooling breeze from the North, a harbinger of less stifling weather, and perhaps even some much-needed rain, the angel thought.

The vast lawns surrounding the grave sites were dappled with dried brown patches of grass, and even the trees had that parched, withered look with branches hanging low.

But things couldn't have been more different at Madeline's plot.

The green around her grave site was lush, dark and healthy; wildflowers more vibrant than all the colors of the rainbow surrounded her concrete marker as if in celebration. This was how it was year-round, a special gift to her memory—a thank-you from the Angel of Death, Israfil, to Remy, for his help in preventing the angel from triggering the Apocalypse.

Remy approached the grave as he normally did, feeling the same pangs of sadness then that he'd had from his very first visit.

"Hey, beautiful," he said, reading her name from the stone, while admiring some of the more unusual blooms that flourished there. He was pretty sure that a large majority of the flowers flourishing there weren't even native to this hemisphere, but here they were, growing just for her.

"How's things?" he asked, kneeling upon the grave. There were some weeds growing up amongst the flowers, and he reached down, plucking them from the always fertile ground.

Remy knew that his wife wasn't actually there anymore.

He knew full well that when she had passed, her remaining life energies had immediately left her body and returned to the source of power in the universe that

made all things. The stuff of creation. Madeline was in
the sun and the stars, the trees and the grass—a part of
everything that flew, crawled, swam, slithered, ran and
walked upon the surface of the Earth.

Yes, Madeline as he remembered her wasn't there
anymore, but he liked to come to this place of beauty to
honor her memory. It was a monument to the amazing
person that she was, and the special love that they had
shared.

Remy found himself pondering Mulvehill's words.
They'd struck a deep chord within him.

It wasn't as though he'd never had the thought himself. Remy knew that he was lonely, and in moments
of weakness, he had briefly considered the what-ifs of
seeking companionship. But his thoughts would always
return to Madeline, and how it all felt like some sort of
horrible betrayal to her memory.

That was why he had come today, just the thought
that Steven Mulvehill might be right sending him to his
wife's grave site for penance.

"There could never be another you," he used to tell
her, and he remembered the smile that would appear on
her face. It still had the same effect on him, even if it was
only from memory.

His stomach sort of dropped, like when an elevator
first starts down to the next floor, and then he smiled,
recalling how lucky he had been to have had her in his
life.

But now she was gone, leaving behind a sucking void
of loneliness that seemed impossible to fill.

And did he truly want to?

That was the question, and why Mulvehill's observation that maybe it was time to let go of the past and look
to the future disturbed him so.

"If I can't have you, do I want anybody else?" he
asked the grave, not expecting an answer.

He rose to his feet, brushing some stray blades of
grass and dirt from the front of his jeans, and looked

to see where Marlowe had gotten to. He could see the dog off in the distance, circling the base of an oak tree, and called to him. The dog glanced threateningly up the tree, and gave a single bark—a warning to the squirrel that next time it wouldn't be so lucky—before bounding across the cemetery toward Remy.

"Did you give that squirrel the business?" Remy asked the Labrador as he lovingly patted his head.

The dog panted furiously, lapping up the affection. *"Gave business,"* Marlowe agreed, thick pink tongue lolling with the heat.

"I think it's time to go," Remy told him, and the dog agreed, turning toward the trail back to the parking lot and the air-conditioned car.

"Aren't you going to say good-bye to Madeline?" Remy asked the back of the animal.

"Not there," Marlowe said without even turning around. *"Madeline gone."*

Madeline gone.

They returned to Beacon Hill only a little late for Marlowe's supper, and the dog wasted no time in letting Remy know that.

"I don't remember you ever being this demanding," Remy said. He picked up Marlowe's water bowl and rinsed it, before refilling it with fresh water. "Is this some new teenage phase you're going through?"

"Hungry," the dog said, tail wagging.

"You're always hungry," Remy said, pulling a plastic container filled with food out of a lower cabinet. Using a metal measuring cup, he dumped a full scoop of the nugget-sized food into another metal dish.

"This stuff looks delicious," Remy said jokingly, giving the bowl a shake. The contents rattled enticingly.

Marlowe's eyes were locked on the bowl as Remy crossed the kitchen to set it down beside the water.

"Go to it," he said, stepping back as the hungry Labrador charged the bowl and immediately began to eat.

"Don't forget to chew," Remy warned. They'd had some problems with this in the past, usually on the living room carpet or in Remy's bed.

"Is it all right if I have a moment to myself now?" he asked the animal.

The dog ignored him, chowing down on the tasty morsels that filled his bowl.

"I guess that's a yes," Remy said. He reached down and thumped the dog's side with his hand, before turning toward the kitchen doorway.

And noticed the flashing red light of his answering machine on the counter.

"Huh," he said, having a hard time remembering the last time he'd had a message on his landline, never mind received a call. Most of his calls these days came over his cell or the office phone.

He stopped and pushed the PLAY button.

You have one new message, the machine told him in a clipped mechanical voice, over the sound of Marlowe slurping at his water bowl.

At first there was the hiss of silence, and for a second Remy thought it might be a hang-up, but then a woman began to speak.

"Um, hi . . ." There was another pause, the woman grumbling something beneath her breath that Remy couldn't make out.

He leaned closer to the machine.

"Yeah, ummm, this message is for Remy Chandler. . . . I'm calling because . . ."

Again she paused and he listened as she whispered to herself, "How do I say this without you thinking I'm crazy."

Marlowe had joined him, wiping his face, still wet from his drink, on the side of Remy's leg.

Thank you very much, Marlowe, he wanted to tell the dog, but he was still listening to the message.

"I'm calling to ask . . . Why am I calling?" She sounded frustrated, and perhaps a little confused.

"I was calling to ask… I was calling to ask if you had a big black dog," she finally said.

Remy quickly glanced at Marlowe, who was looking up at him with that patented Labrador smile and tail wag.

"Oh, my God, I can't believe I did this," she finally said and, without another word, ended the call.

End of message, his machine then told him with a high-pitched beep.

"Okay," he said himself, and then to the dog standing beside him, "What the hell was that all about?"

But Marlowe didn't have any answers either.

Remy knew it was going to be one of those days.

"It's hot as Hell in there," the man from McNulty Heating and Cooling warned, as he held open the front door to Remy's office building.

He was short and a little fat. The front of his light blue shirt was stained with grease, his dark navy work pants powdered with dust.

"Let me guess," Remy said, passing through the foyer. "The air-conditioning is broken."

The repairman laughed. "You must be the detective." He pointed at the building registry hanging on the wall in the lobby.

"Bingo! Any idea when it'll be fixed?" Remy asked, more out of curiosity than anything. He really wasn't affected by temperature, be it hot or cold.

The McNulty guy smiled, shaking his head. "Haven't a clue. We're gonna have to order some parts. Could take a few days."

Another McNulty employee came up from the building's basement with a disgruntled look on his face.

"What's the verdict?" the first asked.

"Put a fuckin' bullet in it," he grunted. "Gonna need a whole new unit." He kept right on walking through the doorway and out to a van parked in front of the building.

"There you have it." Remy's new friend shrugged.

"Guess so," Remy said turning toward the stairs.

"What, you're still going up?" the repairman asked from the doorway.

"Yeah, probably push some papers around and take an early lunch."

"Better you than me," the man said, letting the door close as he left to join his partner. "It's gonna be hot as Hell up there."

Remy continued up the stairs to his office, letting the man's words bounce around inside his skull. He was tempted to explain that Hell was actually a place of extremes—of both intense heat and numbing cold—but he doubted the repairman would have really much cared, and then of course, he would want to know how Remy knew so much about the infernal realm.

Why I was just there on business, he imagined saying.

He chuckled out loud and unlocked his office door. But still he couldn't help wondering what was happening in Hell. After usurping Heaven's power there, the Son of the Morning had begun to reshape the realm. What had once been prison to those who had followed him in his rebellion against Heaven was slowly becoming Lucifer's twisted version of the Eternal Realm. And how exactly did Heaven plan on dealing with that?

Remy shook his head. Matters of the damned and the divine, with humanity caught square in the middle.

He stepped into his office and realized the air-conditioning repairman had been right. It was stifling in the room. He closed the door and went directly to the window, opening it wide in the hope of catching a breeze to air out the stale, musty smell.

Then he checked his phone for messages and, finding none, decided to spend the morning working on invoices and paying some bills. But first there was a mighty need for coffee.

He had just filled the machine, and set the carafe to

collect the elixir of life, when there came a knock at the door and a woman cautiously entered the office.

"Hi," Remy said cheerfully, moving toward her in greeting. "Can I help you?"

The woman was wearing a dungaree jacket and skirt and a bright red T-shirt. She was about five-six, with bleached blond hair, and looked at first to be in her late thirties. Although, as Remy drew closer, he realized her eyes didn't seem as old as she appeared.

The woman closed the door behind her, nervously moving her bag from one shoulder to the other.

"Umm," she said, uncertainty in her tone. "You're Remy Chandler, right? The private investigator?"

"Yes, I am," Remy said, smiling kindly. This woman looked as though she was about to snap. "Is there something I can do for you, Mrs. . . . ?"

"York," the woman replied, her sandaled feet scuffing across the hardwood floor as she stepped farther into the room and extended her hand toward him. "Deryn York." Remy shook the woman's warm and clammy hand.

"Why don't you have a seat, Mrs. York?" He directed her toward the chair in front of his desk, then headed back for the coffeepot.

"Coffee?" he asked her. "I've just made it."

"Yes, thank you," she said, pulling at the front of her skirt so it just about touched her knees.

Remy realized that he had only one clean mug, the other sort of dusty.

"Let me just rinse this out," he said, going to the tiny bathroom across the room. "Really warm out there today," he said, raising his voice over the water in the sink.

"Yeah," he heard her answer. "Hot as Hell."

Y'know, Hell is a place of extremes. . . .

"It certainly is," he said instead as he left the bathroom. "How do you like your coffee?"

"Oh, just sugar, please."

"How many?" he asked, pouring her a cup, and placing it on the edge of the desk in front of her. He went around his desk and opened the center drawer, where he'd recently seen a few packs of sugar.

"Do you have six?" she asked.

"Six?"

She smiled self-consciously and shrugged. "I like it really sweet."

Remy counted the packs in his drawer. "I've only got five," he told her.

"That's fine," she said. "Five should be good."

He set the packs of sugar down. "Here you go," he said.

"Thank you." She immediately ripped open the packs one after another, pouring their contents into the dark brown liquid.

"So, Mrs. York," Remy said as he sat down in his chair, taking a sip from his mug with the picture of a black Labrador retriever, "what can I do for you?"

She sipped her own coffee and made a face. Obviously it wasn't sweet enough.

"I called your home last night," she said, setting the mug carefully down on the edge of his desk. "But I didn't leave a name...or much of a message, really." She laughed nervously.

"I thought that might have been you," Remy said.

"Yeah, I'm sorry. I really didn't know what to say, and I had no intention of coming here even but..."

"But here you are," Remy finished for her.

"Exactly," she responded. "You're all I have left...my last resort."

"Okay then." Remy grabbed a pad of paper and a pen. "What's brought you here, Deryn York?"

She had another sip of coffee, perhaps to fortify herself, before starting to speak.

"My daughter," she said, her eyes becoming misty. "My daughter, Zoe."

"All right," Remy encouraged her. "Take your time, and tell me what happened." He was trying to make her feel comfortable; the tension was spilling off of her in waves. "Are you from this area?"

Deryn shook her head. "Originally I'm from South Carolina, but we moved to Florida about five years ago."

"You and your daughter?" he probed.

"And my husband," she added, reaching for the coffee again. "We've since separated, but I can't seem to get rid of him. He insisted on coming here with Zoe and me, even though I didn't want him to."

"So you've moved here from Florida?"

"Not permanently," she quickly corrected. "I hate the cold, but I heard the best doctors are here, so I didn't really have a choice. As soon as they figure out what's wrong with Zoe, we'll go right back home."

Remy nodded, taking a drink of his coffee. "Your daughter is sick then?"

Deryn stared down into the contents of her mug. "The doctors in Florida say she's probably autistic," she explained quietly, then looked up at Remy. "But Carl wanted to be sure, and he said the best doctors are here. He's from here originally."

"Where were you taking her?"

"Franciscan Children's Hospital." She stopped, reaching down to her bag and removing a pack of cigarettes. Without even asking Remy if it was okay, she popped one in her mouth and lit it with a disposable lighter.

"I can't believe how fucking stupid I was," she said, dropping the lighter and package of smokes back into bag. "Oh, is this all right?" she asked suddenly conscious of what she was doing.

"It's fine," Remy said, not wanting to upset her. They were finally getting someplace, and he didn't want to cancel the momentum. "Why do you say you were stupid?"

"Because I trusted him," she said angrily. "I let my guard down." Deryn feverishly puffed on the cigarette, forming a toxic cloud around her head in the too-warm office. "I wasn't feeling good, so I stayed at the hotel and let Carl take Zoe to an appointment. And that's the last time I saw them. It's been six days." Deryn choked back a sob, bringing a hand to her mouth.

"There hasn't been any contact with Carl since he took Zoe?" Remy asked.

"No," she said miserably, finishing the smoke and dropping the butt into her coffee mug with a faint hiss.

"Have you contacted the police?"

"Yes, once I realized what the son of a bitch had done. There's a warrant out for his arrest."

"And you have no idea where he might have taken your daughter?"

"I don't have a clue."

Remy stood and grabbed his mug. "Would you like another cup? I can rinse yours out."

"No. No, thanks," she said with a nervous shake of her head. "I'm good."

Remy refilled his cup and returned to his desk. "So tell me about your relationship with Carl," he began. "Was it an amicable split or—"

"We only stayed together as long as we did because of Zoe," Deryn explained. "We thought a baby would help us, but with her being different and all. . . . " Her voice trailed off, and she looked as though she had the weight of the world upon her shoulders.

"Does Carl have any history of violence?" Remy asked. "He wouldn't want to cause Zoe any harm, would he?"

"Oh, no," she said quickly. "Carl really is basically a good guy. We both had kind of screwed-up childhoods, but we managed to get beyond that. We were good parents, Mr. Chandler."

"Except that Carl has taken your daughter."

"Yeah," she said, her voice cracking with emotion. "But maybe if I had paid better attention this could all have been avoided."

"Mrs. York, you can't beat yourself up about—"

"I need to show you something, Mr. Chandler," Deryn interrupted, pulling her bag up onto her lap.

Remy leaned forward, curious, as she withdrew a handful of folded pieces of construction of paper from inside the bag. Carefully she unfolded them, looking at each, before she handed them to Remy.

He looked at the first. It was obviously a child's drawing, done in crayon, crudely depicting a little girl and a man leaving what appeared to be a hospital. The next picture was of the same girl and man, only they were in a car. The man was in the front seat driving while the child stared out the back window, yellow circles beneath her eyes, which Remy guessed were probably falling tears.

"Zoe did these?" he asked, looking up at Deryn.

She nodded. "About three weeks ago."

He was looking at the drawing again when the woman's words permeated his brain. "Three weeks ago?" he repeated. "So your husband must have been preparing her for this?" He waited as Deryn shook her head no.

"She drew those pictures without any knowledge of what her father was going to do," the woman explained. "But she knew he was going to take her, Mr. Chandler, just like she knew that I would be coming to see you."

Deryn leaned forward and handed him one last drawing.

Remy's eyed widened in surprise as he studied it. Zoe had drawn a childlike depiction of the front entrance to his brownstone, a person, that he was certain was himself—*the feathered wings were a dead giveaway*—standing in front with a black dog on a leash. And floating in the air, written in a small child's handwriting, were his address and telephone number.

KINSMAN FREE PUBLIC LIBRARY
6420 CHURCH STREET
P.O. BOX 166
KINSMAN, OHIO 44428

NEW IN TRADE PAPERBACK

WHERE ANGELS FEAR TO TREAD

A REMY CHANDLER NOVEL

by Thomas E. Sniegoski

Six year-old Zoe York has been taken and her
mother has come to Remy for help. She shows
him crude, childlike drawings that she claims are
Zoe's visions of the future, everything leading up
to her abduction, and some beyond. Like the
picture of a man with wings who would come
and save her—a man who is an angel.

Zoe's preternatural gifts have made her a target for
those who wish to exploit her power to their own
destructive ends. The search will take Remy to
dark places he would rather avoid. But to save an
innocent, Remy will ally himself with a variety of
lesser evils—and his soul may pay the price.

**Available wherever books are sold or at
penguin.com**

R0013

ALSO AVAILABLE FROM

Thomas E. Sniegoski

A KISS BEFORE THE APOCALYPSE

A REMY CHANDLER NOVEL

Generations ago, the angel Remiel chose to renounce heaven and live on Earth. He found a place among ordinary humans by converting himself into Boston P.I. Remy Chandler, but he can never tell anyone who he was or that he still has angelic powers. Remy can will himself invisible, speak and understand any foreign language (including any animal language), and hear the thoughts of others. All these secret powers come in handy for a private investigator, especially when the Angel of Death goes missing and he's assigned to find him. As he gets deeper into the investigation, he realizes this is not a missing persons case but a conspiracy to destroy the human race—and only Remy has the powers to stop the forces of evil.

Available wherever books are sold or at penguin.com

R0014

AVAILABLE NOW

An anthology of all-new novellas of dark
nights, cruel cities, and paranormal P.I.s—
from four of today's hottest authors.

MEAN STREETS

Includes brand-new stories by

JIM BUTCHER
FEATURING HARRY DRESDEN

KAT RICHARDSON
FEATURING HARPER BLAINE

SIMON R. GREEN
FEATURING JOHN TAYLOR

THOMAS E. SNIEGOSKI
FEATURING REMY CHANDLER

The best paranormal private investigators have
been brought together in a single volume—
and cases don't come any harder than this.

**Available wherever books are sold or
at penguin.com**